THE
SHUDDERING

THE
SHUDDERING

ANIA AHLBORN

47N⬥RTH

Published by 47North
PO Box 400818
Las Vegas, NV 89140

ISBN-13: 9781611099676
ISBN-10: 1611099676
Library of Congress Control Number: 2012954822

CHAPTER ONE

Don slapped the trunks of the trees with his left hand as he ran past them, a small ax held tight in his right. He struggled for breath as steam rose from his lungs. As he twisted midrun, casting a wild-eyed look over a shoulder, he was sure he'd see them snapping at his heels, their hard black eyes glinting in the grayness of the morning. He saw nothing—only thin swaying pines bending in the breeze, cutting into the cold blue of the sky, drowning him in their shadow—but Don knew they were there. The drips of blood that trailed him like scarlet breadcrumbs assured him that this wasn't a dream. They were watching him as his legs burned with each footfall, waiting as his boots kicked up snow. The trees shuddered all around him, shaken by an invisible hand. No matter how fast he ran, they were one step ahead of him, obscured by branches and tree trunks and snow, keeping themselves concealed despite their conspicuous movements. It was a game, and Don was their target.

His heart thudded in his chest as he skidded to a stop, his mind reeling as he stared at the blood dripping from the fingers of his ungloved right hand. The throbbing of his arm reminded him that his heart was still beating, that he was still alive; that ax gave him a glimmer of hope. Maybe, by some miracle, he still had a chance. Maybe he could still make it home; he could survive. He launched himself forward despite the pain, stumbling headlong into what he hoped would be escape, unable to wrap his mind around the simple fact that the monsters his father had told him about—terrible stories whispered by the pale yellow glow of a lamp, quiet so that his mother wouldn't scold them both—had been far more than childhood fiction. The monsters of his youth were chasing him. They were hungry. They were real.

It was unbelievable to think that just an hour before he had been sitting at his kitchen table, listening to his wife hum as she washed the breakfast dishes. The only thing out of the ordinary that morning was the bitterness of the cold. Don felt the oncoming storm in his bones long before it hit the news, long before those so-called meteorologists fumbled the prediction. His right knee ached, and that meant more snow—snow on top of the four-inch base that already blanketed the mountains of southwestern Colorado.

It was the perfect reason to pile firewood high against the side of the house. Don had been lazy for the past few days, spending more time in his recliner watching *Antiques Roadshow* than keeping the place in order. The unseasonable chill meant that the firewood was almost gone, and the throb in his joints assured him that if he didn't get out there now, the impending blizzard would see to it that he paid for his idleness later.

But free firewood was one of the perks of living out in the middle of nowhere. There wasn't anyone to stop a man from grabbing his ax and doing it the old-fashioned way. So he finished his eggs and toast, buttoned up his North Face jacket, tied a hand-knitted scarf around his neck, and pulled a fur-lined hat over his slept-in hair. When Jenny turned to him, she couldn't help but smile. It was coming up on their thirtieth wedding anniversary, twenty-three years of which he'd spent half-hidden by an unruly beard that had turned white with age. It made him look like an off-season Santa, and Christmas was her favorite time of year.

"You be careful," she told him, tightening the scarf around his neck before kissing the tip of his nose. "Don't go chopping off any fingers."

He gave a sideways grin at her warning. Jenny still treated him like he'd never held an ax before, though Don had worked as a logger his entire life. It had been a tough way to make a living, but it had afforded them a nice little house and a full ten acres of unspoiled land. Grabbing his hatchet from next to the front door, he ducked into the cold morning without a good-bye.

His boot caught a buried tree branch and Don skidded onto his front, the snow momentarily blinding him as it blew into his face, stinging his eyes and catching in his beard. Had he known it would have ended up this way, he would have told Jenny he loved her; he would have reminded her she was still the woman of his dreams, always and forever, even today. And Jenny would have rolled her eyes at him and dismissed his boyish proclamations with a giggle and a wave of her hand.

Fumbling back onto his feet, he winced against the burning of his fingers as he swept them through the snow, grabbing hold of his weapon. The tips of his digits were beyond red, a bright magenta Don had never imagined flesh could turn. He'd lost his gloves when he had first spotted those shadows, obscured by branches but undeniably standing in a pack. Reeling with fright, he had run in the wrong direction—away from the cabin rather than toward it…because they had blocked his path.

The tree in front of him shuddered, and before he could react, one of the things that was tracking him leaped at him from the high branches of a pine. Don instinctively swung the ax over his head as the creature bolted for him, lodging the blade in its monstrous skull. The thing fell at Don's feet, convulsing, teeth clacking together as it bucked in the snow, giving Don his first look at what these creatures truly were. The twitching savage looked just like his father had described: all awkward angles, nothing but skin and teeth. He didn't think to pull the ax free from its skull when he stumbled away, desperate to put distance between himself and his childhood nightmare, the snow beneath the beast soaking up red so dark it nearly looked like oil. He reeled around, ready to run. And that was when he saw them, lined up like undead soldiers just beyond the trees, still hidden by branches as if afraid to come into full view. Don couldn't see them outright, but he could make out their shapes: skinny, sinuous, terrifyingly tall.

They only come when it snows, his dad had told him, repeating the stories his own father had whispered into his ear in the dead of winter. As a kid, Don assumed it was why he and his family packed up their stuff and left the cabin when the weather got bad. But as he grew older, he reasoned the stories away. Myth. Legend. Whatever he called them in the past made no difference.

The snow buffered all sound save for the haggard shudder of his lungs. His pulse whooshed in his ears as he tried to take in everything around him, every possible angle from which he could be attacked. Steam crept past his lips, coiling upward like smoke, making it harder to see. When the convulsing beast finally went still, something in the air shifted. Perhaps that was why the creatures had been keeping their distance. They had been watching, waiting to see the outcome of Don's attack on their comrade. But when that monster's movements went static, Don's blood ran cold. A low, unified growl sounded from the trees. It rattled deep in their throats, an eerie, almost human quality to its tone.

It may have been smarter to stand motionless, to play dead. But Don didn't think.

He turned and ran.

Twisting against the bulky padding of his coat, he was shocked at how difficult it was to move, having completely forgotten how tough it was to trudge through the waist-deep snow. He tried to slog through it as quickly as he could, his breaths coming in panicked gasps, the growling behind him rising in volume, becoming more aggressive, like the grunts of wild boar, the snarling moans of chattering hyena.

He was still running the wrong way, away from home rather than toward it, but they had left him no choice. He'd circle around, get back to the house, save both himself and Jenny—

Oh god, my Jenny.

She was alone.

She'd be afraid.

She'd be waiting for him, chewing her fingernails, wondering where he was.

He had to get back to her, had to keep her from stepping outside to search for him. He had to survive to save her, had to get back…had to—

Something hit his right shoulder.

He spun around like a top, lost his footing, and fell into the deep powder that covered the ground. Scrambling back to his feet, Don instinctively grabbed at his right arm—fire seizing his biceps, snaking up to his shoulder—while he searched the trees for the creature that had buzzed him, that had clawed him so fast he hadn't even caught its approach. The winter chill bit through the slash in his sleeve, down puffing out of the tear like a tiny cloud, almost immediately turning red from the blood that was sheeting down his arm. *Oh god. Oh Jesus.* He pulled his hand away from his arm, his fingers slick, sticky with red.

The damn thing could have taken him down, but it hadn't. They were toying with him, playing a game of cat and mouse. He was still alive, left to fend for himself.

Inside his head, his daddy leaned in and whispered, *They never let anyone get away, Donnie.* Inside his head, Jenny screamed, *Run!*

Balling his hands up into fists, his left hand sticky with gore, he released a primal yell and ran. The trees whizzed by him. For a moment he felt incredible—as though he could outsprint anyone, any*thing*. His adrenaline numbed the pain, the fear. It numbed the terror and pushed him forward, away from home but inexorably toward it. If he could outrun these bastards, he'd eventually get there.

His feet flew behind him as he leaned forward, leading with his head, a constant stumble as his legs failed to keep up with his body. Catching a shoulder on a tree, he grunted in pain but kept on, knowing that stopping would seal his fate, knowing that those things—those savages—were waiting for him to give up.

Fuck them, he thought. *Fuck them, whatever they are.*

But after a minute of his running flat out, that sense of invincibility began to fade. His pace slowed. His legs grew heavy. His heart thudded in his ears. He could hardly breathe, the glacial air burning the lining of his lungs. *No*, he thought. *Get back to her. Get back home.* But his legs stopped working. His knees went rubbery. His mind screamed, *Keep going*, but his body was spent. He ducked behind a tree as the snapping of branches echoed all around him. Jamming his shoulder blades against the trunk, he tried to make himself as small as he could, his bottom lip trembling, his vision going wavy with defeat. The longer he stood there, the more silent the woods became. That horrible, unified, groaning growl had faded. The trees failed to shake, and eventually the crack of branches ceased. The forest went ghostly quiet.

Opening his eyes, he dared to peek around the side of the pine at his back.

Nothing.

Could they really be gone?

He blinked, his arm burning with pain. It was impossible. He knew he hadn't outrun them. The one that had darted toward him was faster than anything he'd ever seen, running so fast it seemed to glide over the snow. *Maybe they found something else,* he thought. Something else to devour. Something else to kill. Because that was what they were doing out here—hunting. At least that was the story. That was what his father had said.

He was afraid to move, sure it was a trap, but he couldn't stay there long. His arm felt as if it were on fire. The blood that had overtaken the inside of his sleeve was seeping out from around his cuff, rolling down the inside of his palm, dripping onto the colorless ground cover next to his boot. If he didn't bleed to death, they'd smell him and come back. He had to move.

So he moved.

And crashed into the chest of a beast.

It had been waiting for him, utterly silent in its stance, its lips pulled back into a sneer, exposing a collection of jagged teeth in a maw that opened impossibly wide. He didn't have time to take in the horrifying view, hardly had half a second to take a backward step as it flared its nostrils, ready to strike.

It leaped.

Don screamed as he fell backward, the beast's teeth sinking into the side of his neck. Pain bloomed beneath his jaw, simultaneously hot and cold. He struggled, beating the creature above him with his fists, kicking his legs, bucking to free himself. The thing growled, a foul gurgle rasping from the back of its throat. And then it shook its head like a dog, tearing flesh, snapping tendons. It pulled away, mouth full of soft tissue oozing blood onto the snow.

Don gasped for air, his eyes wide as he watched the demon chew a piece of him, throwing its head back and swallowing the meat that was missing from his neck. Letting his head fall backward, he closed his eyes, squeezed them shut, and imagined himself back in his kitchen, back in front of Jenny as she kissed the tip of his nose. He pictured her hands, soft despite their years. He sucked in a breath of cold air and smelled vanilla. She was always baking something, her cakes and cookies making their tiny two-bedroom cottage forever smell of a five-star bakery. She loved music, always humming Bob Dylan and the Beatles beneath her breath. Don could hear her singing in the startling quiet that surrounded him now, humming just beneath the weakening rattle of his lungs.

"You think I haven't seen worse than you?" he croaked, the sound of his own voice sending a shock wave up his spine. He sounded rough, inhuman. "You ugly son of a bitch." Attempting to stand, he had to pause. Vertigo rocked him back and forth. Something warm filled his throat. He coughed, and blood bubbled from between his lips. When he finally managed to look up, he was alone again, the shadows of those creatures watching him from the safety of the pines. "You fucking cowards," he hissed. "Come out and fight!" Crashing to his knees, he pressed a cold hand to his neck, then pulled it back as though he'd just scalded himself. Half of his neck was missing, nothing but a void. He coughed again, a thick slew of blood dribbling down his chin into his beard, his gored hands leaving prints in the snow.

"You ugly sons of bitches," he repeated, choking, feeling himself start to slip. With his final wind, he forced himself to look up at the growling shadows of the hidden demons. "Take me, then," he hissed, extending his arms to his side like Jesus on the cross. Because if he sacrificed himself, perhaps they'd be satiated enough to move on, to distance themselves from his home, from his wife.

They fell on him, but Don didn't feel a thing. He was too busy picturing Jenny in her wedding dress, twirling in the sunlight that filtered through the stained-glass windows of a tiny church. He was too busy listening to her hum, her singing blocking out the silence of winter, distracting him from the tearing of his own flesh.

Ryan Adler squinted at the road and exhaled through his nose, his breath silenced by the music that coiled through the Nissan's interior. He loved the way fresh snowmelt made the road look black, like a stretch of satin ribbon glistening in the sun. The cabin wasn't near a damn thing, and that was why Ryan loved it. Out here, there was nothing but mountains, trees, and an endless expanse of sky—pale blue with brushstrokes of wispy white.

He'd seen more of the world than he had ever expected to see, jetting off to places like Switzerland and Austria in the name of fresh powder, excusing the expense because business was business. He'd been born lucky; he was smart and handsome, thankful that he'd managed to escape most of his father's traits save for a few. Ryan was an entrepreneur, just like his dad; his charm and disarming smile had gotten him far. But to his father's chagrin, Ryan had no interest in "real" business; no passion for stocks and investments—the very things that had built Michael Adler's empire. Ryan's passion was tangled in the swaying pines that dotted every black diamond run of every ski resort on earth. But his heart was forever present in the San Juan Mountains; his passion had been born in those hills.

Ryan slowed the Nissan and hung a left onto a rough road. The potholes were treacherous but still visible, most of the snow that had fallen onto the pavement having melted in the afternoon sun. The change of pace pulled Ryan's blue-eyed husky, Oona, out of her nap; he watched her move around in the rearview mirror, pressing her sleep-dried nose against the back window, her dog breath stinking up the place. The farther they drove, the rougher the road and thicker the snow became. Aspens and ponderosa pines flanked both sides of the drive, tall and swaying despite the air around them seeming calm. Stopping the car completely, Ryan lowered his window with an electrical buzz.

"What is it?" Jane asked her brother, stretching in the passenger seat with a road-tired moan. She peered through a dirty windshield up at the trees that towered ahead of them.

The space between them was filled a moment later when Lauren leaned forward between the driver and passenger seat, hiding a yawn behind the palm of her hand. She hadn't made a peep for a good few hours, and Ryan had nearly forgotten that his sister's best friend was back there at all. He reached down and twisted a knob close to the bottom of the dash, engaging four-wheel drive.

"Are we going to make it?" Jane asked, a little worried. She had always hated the road that led up to the cabin, especially in the winter. Its steep pitch made it treacherous, and they had had a close call on their previous visit, the Nissan catching some black ice and nearly careening into the ravine that ran along both sides of the road.

"Of course we're going to make it," he told her, slow-rolling into a couple of inches of hard-packed snow.

Jane tried to relax as they progressed forward, but her muscles refused. It was Ryan's idea to come up here during the winter. He was the one who got snow-crazy at the mere suggestion of winter precipitation. Jane was more of a summer girl—bikinis and floppy-brimmed hats and suntan oil.

Her eyes widened as the Nissan started to slide sideways.

"Oh god." The exclamation came from their backseat passenger, and Ryan couldn't help but grin. Jane rolled her eyes at his glee. He loved freaking her out with his driving, and she'd learned that keeping her mouth shut made him less prone to try stupid maneuvers. But this was Lauren's first time as a passenger, and her little outburst was enough to have him stomping on the gas a little too hard, the Nissan spitting gravel out from beneath the back tires like a rock geyser.

"Almost to the driveway," he assured them, only to have Jane groan in reply at the reminder.

"What's with the driveway?" Lauren asked.

"It's not a driveway," Jane said. "It's a nightmare."

"It's a driveway."

"It's a nightmare, and it's more of a road than a driveway. It's like a quarter of a mile long, and it's all uphill."

"Well," Lauren said, casually crossing her legs as she leaned back in the center of the bench seat. "That sounds promising."

The Nissan spit dirty snow onto the road behind it as Ryan stepped on the gas, pushing it up a precarious incline—a slope that was scary to drive up when it was dry, let alone when it wasn't. The Adlers had had many a mishap on that hill, the worst of which had happened during their final winter break as a family—her and Ryan, Mom and Dad. The road thick with snow, Michael Adler had insisted that he and his two kids get out and push the car that refused to make it up the slick incline while their mother jammed her foot onto the gas. Mary Adler had nearly burst into tears as her husband yelled for her to get behind the wheel. They never made it up that hill. The car caught traction and lurched forward just enough to have Ryan stumbling onto his knees while Jane fell onto her chest, hitting her chin on the frozen ground, nearly biting her bottom lip clean through.

Jane covered her eyes as the Nissan rambled upward, holding steadfast to her silence, and after a few tense minutes, the car crested the drive and Chateau Adler came into view. Lauren blinked at the house.

"The hostess didn't mention the size of this place, I gather," Ryan murmured.

A massive stone-and-log home stood before them, tucked into the trees so thoroughly that it was invisible until, suddenly, it wasn't, its grandiose two-story front entrance dominating its facade.

"Holy shit," Lauren said. "*This* is the cabin?" She made eyes at Jane, then looked back to the house ahead of them. "This is a goddamn mansion."

It was a trophy home—the kind of houses the rich built for themselves as an occasional getaway. The landscape had been dotted with these estates for the last ten miles, no two less than miles apart, thousands of acres of heavily wooded hills separating one from the next. They were regal, inevitably decorated with the finest furniture, with expensive paintings that were far more status symbols than declarations of the owners' discriminating taste. The same could be said of the Adlers' chateau. Michael Adler had decorated the place in the style of a hunting lodge, but the man had hunted all of a handful of times in his life. The walls were decorated with mounted heads of deer and elk, of beasts that Ryan assumed his father considered a "catch," but they had been bought and paid for. It was all for show—as was everything in Michael Adler's life.

"Wait until you see it all lit up," Jane mused. She loved this place as much as Ryan did, though she liked it more when she could lie out on the deck and bask in the high mountain sun. There was something magical about sitting out on the porch, listening to the trees sway in the wind. But she could see why Ryan loved the snow. It gave the place a mystical feel; paradise in the middle of nowhere.

Lauren stood in the doorway—a side entrance that led from the porch into a massive stone-walled kitchen. She watched Jane disappear down a hall directly ahead of her, apparently on some sort of mission—probably headed for the thermostat. It was cold inside, no more than fifty degrees. Ryan took a seat on the edge of a heavy table to the right of the door, bags at his feet, his phone already glowing as he checked his reception, not seeming the least bit interested in the grandeur laid out before him. But Lauren was stunned.

"This place is incredible," she confessed, almost afraid to step farther inside. The island at the heart of the kitchen was bigger than her apartment's bathroom. The cabinet doors were rich cherry gleaming with varnish. There were two ovens, one on top of the other, next to a stove that looked like it had come straight out of one of those fancy Food Network cooking shows. She paused, furrowing her eyebrows at a pair of massive doors, both of them paneled to match the cabinets.

"Is that the fridge?" she asked.

Ryan nodded, still fiddling with his phone. "Probably empty," he admitted. "Jane's going to drag you into town for groceries. I guarantee it."

Lauren twisted a piece of blonde hair around her finger, looking through the kitchen to the centerpiece of the living room, visible through a large stone arch that connected the rooms. The fireplace was ostentatious, big enough for her to lie down in and not have her head or feet touch either end. Imposing stones crawled up the wall above the hearth, and she couldn't help but wonder how on earth anyone had managed to get them inside the house, let alone up on the wall like that. An elk's head stared at her from across the room, challenging her to recall a more impressive creature, dead or alive. The challenge was a futile one. Growing up in a two-room trailer in Winnfield, Louisiana, the only elk she'd seen before this one were the ones her dad skinned in the backyard.

Oona padded past her, crossed the expanse of the kitchen, and jumped onto the leather sofa. Lauren opened her mouth to protest but stalled when amusement danced across Ryan's face.

"That's okay?" she asked, nodding to the dog, who was dancing a circle on top of an expensive-looking couch cushion, her paws wet from the snow.

"It's fine," Ryan replied.

"Huh." She hadn't expected him to be so obliging. "I wouldn't have guessed." Her face flushed before the words had completely escaped her throat, her heart fluttering at the shadow of a beguiling smile lingering at the corners of his mouth.

There was something about Ryan that held her attention—the way he carried himself, graceful and self-assured; the way he leaned against the table, his feet crossed at the ankles. He was one of those people who seemed always ready to be photographed even while doing the most everyday things; annoying, when she always looked awkward in pictures even when she tried to look good.

She had heard things about him over the years, like the fact that he was an adrenaline junkie, and how he'd turned his passion for snowboarding into a winning business venture. From what Jane had told her, what was once little more than a hobby now pulled in a hefty salary by way of advertising. Big companies paid to have their ads on Ryan's website—snowboards and winter gear—and all Ryan had to do was pay for bandwidth and travel to exotic destinations all in the name of photographs and reviews. And judging from the size of the place, if Ryan was anywhere near as successful as his father, he was as loaded as he was attractive.

"Are you going to come?" she asked, turning to face Ryan fully for the first time. "To the store," she clarified. "With us."

Ryan lifted his shoulders in a shrug, haphazardly tossing his phone onto the table, assuring her that cell phone service out here was a bust. "I guess I should," he said. "She doesn't drink, so, you know, asking her to buy booze... You haven't been brainwashed into her wino ways, have you?"

"Wino ways?"

"Sure," he said, sliding off the table. "You don't believe that whole 'oh, I hate the taste of anything but Bordeaux' argument she gives, do you?"

Lauren stood silent, not sure whether to play along or defend Jane's honor.

"I'm convinced this is just the beginning. Today, only red wine; tomorrow, she'll be converting to Mormonism."

"I'll go find her." She hooked a thumb toward the hallway, waiting for Ryan to tell her it was okay to breach the perimeter of the kitchen and explore further.

"Sweet," he said, failing to look up.

Lauren ducked into the hallway, feeling awkward.

Jane paused at the top of the stairs and glanced down the hallway, which was gloomy despite the bay window at its center. The only door on the right side of the wall led to the master bedroom. She was sure Ryan wouldn't want it—too many bad memories, too much resentment—and she wasn't about to give it up to Sawyer and his girl once they arrived.

Her heart twisted against the splinter that had been lodged there since high school. She'd nearly bailed on the entire outing when Ryan had broken the news, but had stopped just shy of telling him to forget it. The place was on the market, ready to sell to the highest bidder, furniture and all. And to pile one heartache on top of another, Ryan had just sold half his company to a guy out in Switzerland. It was a huge step forward for Powder 360, but her brother would be spending six months out of the year traveling Europe, living in an adorable Swiss bungalow at the foot of the Matterhorn and calling her on Skype. She was sick over it, not sure how she'd be able to handle life without her twin brother at her elbow, always there when she needed him—sometimes there when she didn't. This was their last chance to visit their childhood haunt: Ryan's favorite place in all the world. She refused to screw it up, no matter how hard her heart thudded in her chest at the mere thought of seeing Sawyer with another girl.

Veering right, she pushed the door open into the master bedroom—her favorite room in the house despite its history. There had been many a fight within those walls during family getaways that had been intended to be fun but always turned sour, and the master bedroom was where all of that bitterness was born. But the window that swallowed the majority of the far wall pushed the sadness of her father's yelling and her mother's tears out of her mind. Spectacular in its size and view, that window overlooked tree-dotted hills and a stone-topped mountain distant against the sky. She'd spent many an afternoon sitting in front of that very window as a girl, gazing out onto the wilderness. The view, and the fact that the room had its own fireplace, was irresistible.

Lauren stepped inside the room, gaping at its size.

"Please tell me we're bunking together," she said. "I know there are plenty of rooms to go around, but, *Janey...*"

"I know," Jane mused, still appreciative of its grandeur after all these years.

Lauren immediately went for the bathroom, and Jane couldn't help but laugh when a gasp sounded from the open door. The master bathroom was just as extravagant as the bedroom, fit for a queen, with its oversize tub and vanity. For the next four days Jane planned on forgetting her students, the fact that Ryan was going to leave her soon, and that Alex was still back in Phoenix, waiting to make her life a living hell; she'd soak in that amazing bathtub every night. If she was lucky, their father's Italian girlfriend had left expensive toiletries that could be exploited. It was the least that bombshell of a runway model could do.

"Oh my god." Lauren's voice echoed from inside the bathroom. Jane crossed the length of the room and cocked a hip against the doorjamb, her arms pretzeling over her chest as she chuckled at her best friend's astonishment. "You don't get it," Lauren protested, plucking a delicate perfume atomizer off the vanity and lifting it to her nose. "I grew up in a trailer."

"I know."

"In the *back* country."

"With the alligators, right?" Jane smiled.

"Why didn't you tell me?" Lauren asked, and Jane shrugged a single shoulder in reply.

"It makes me feel weird, I guess."

"What does?" Lauren asked, uncapping a tube of lipstick, twisting it to reveal fire engine red. "This house?"

"The money," Jane confessed. Her father's piles of cash had always been a source of discomfort for her. Ryan had embraced it, investing it wherever he could, taking advantage of the fact they had an absent father who liked to buy their love with hundred-dollar bills. But Jane had always turned away.

"Yeah?" Lauren cast a sidelong glance her way. "At least you don't let it show."

Jane gave the bathroom tile a sad sort of smile, unsure whether that was good or just plain stupid. She'd settled into an almost mundane lifestyle of teaching second graders how to glue together collages and how to play the recorder because it made her happy, but she struggled.

"Sometimes I wonder whether my dignity outweighs my brain." Jane shifted her weight from one foot to the other, watching Lauren lean into the oval gilded mirror. She pulled the lipstick across her bottom lip, running her pinkie along the rim of her mouth a second later.

"That's what makes you who you are, Jane," Lauren reminded her, hypnotized by her own bright red mouth.

"Yeah, except that I borrowed money from Ryan last month for rent." Jane rolled her eyes at herself. "I won't take the money from my father, but I'll take it from my brother. It's completely idiotic."

"Maybe it's because you love your brother but hate your dad." Lauren turned to face Jane, puckering her lips, revealing the new her. "Slutty," she said, raising an eyebrow at her friend. "Speaking of daddy, does this stuff belong to that chick he's banging?"

Jane pushed away from the door, taking a seat on the edge of the tub while Lauren snooped around, completely unabashed in her curiosity.

"Alessandra," Jane said. "From Milan."

"I bet it's easy to look amazing when your lipstick costs fifty bucks a tube," Lauren said, then struck a pose. "What do you think? Am I runway ready? Think Mr. Adler would approve?"

Jane furrowed her eyebrows. "Your brother, not your cheating ass of a dad." She puckered again before capping the lipstick and tossing it onto the vanity. "Or is this too brazen for him?" She mussed her long blonde hair, piling it on top of her head before glancing over her shoulder at Jane.

"I thought you didn't like guys with money." Jane smiled to herself. She was glad Lauren found her brother so intriguing—God knew he needed a good woman in his life. There had been so many girls—athletic types, clubbing types, the kind who wore nothing but sneakers following the type who grocery shopped in heels. After a few dates, Ryan had dismissed them all.

And then there was Summer.

He had met his dream girl in a business management course at ASU. Summer was smart and funny and drop-dead gorgeous, and she knew how to ride as well as he did. She had been tenacious, challenging him like nobody else ever had, pushing him further than he thought he could go, and Jane had loved her for it. Summer had been the one who had believed in him when he had come up with the crazy idea of starting a website dedicated to the sport they both adored—she had been the one to convince Jane it was a fantastic plan, that it didn't matter that they had to drive hours for a mediocre mountain at best. It was the passion that mattered, and Ryan had enough of it for the whole world. And yet, despite the love Jane was sure Ryan had for Summer, their relationship crumbled. Jane hoped that infidelity—the very thing that had destroyed their family—hadn't been what had done them in. She didn't want to think of her brother like that, didn't want to think that he could be as callous as the man he insisted he didn't want to become.

"I don't know," Lauren said. "He's starting to grow on me."

"What, after spending six hours with him?"

Lauren made a face, let her hair sweep across her shoulders, and plucked a tissue from its holder before rubbing the lipstick from her mouth.

"And what about Sawyer; you're sure you're okay with this?"

"I'm here, aren't I?" Jane shrugged. "Ryan already asked me that like a hundred thousand times, anyway."

"I'm sure he has, but did you tell him the truth?"

Jane offered her friend a tight-lipped smile. That was the million-dollar question, and the answer was no. She'd spared Ryan the truth and told him what he wanted to hear—it was fine, she was over it. Because what kind of a girl pined over a guy for a decade? If she wanted to grieve the loss of a relationship, it should have been the one she'd lost less than three months ago, not one that ended in her senior year of high school.

"There's probably nothing to eat downstairs," Jane concluded, changing the subject. It would have been nice to have stopped at the store along the way, but Ryan had taken a shortcut to save them nearly an hour, and they had bypassed the nearest town by a good twenty miles.

Lauren gave her a strange smile in response, like she'd just remembered a joke.

"What?"

Lauren shook her head and tossed the red-smeared tissue into the trash can next to her sneakered feet. "Nothing," she said. "Let's go."

Pulling the wood-paneled door open, Jane stared into an empty refrigerator. There were a couple of bottles of Evian lined up in a row along the right side of the unit. A half-empty bottle of merlot sat in the door, along with a collection of condiments. She grabbed the wine bottle by its neck and uncorked it, breathing it in, immediately recoiling at the smell. As far as alcohol went, wine was the only thing Jane could stand, but this had turned to vinegar. She let the fridge door swing shut as she stepped away from it, abandoning the spoiled bottle of wine on the counter. She pivoted on the soles of her sneakers and stepped into the walk-in pantry, flipping on the light. When they were kids, their mother kept the pantry lined with a barrage of various dried goods—boxes of whole-grain pasta and rice; enough to keep them fed in case someone dropped an atom bomb. But Michael Adler, while amazing at mergers and acquisitions, wasn't much of a planner; for the two years they had known her, Alessandra hadn't exactly proven herself to be "domestic." The pantry was nearly empty. Jane and Ryan hadn't visited the cabin in over a year, and from the look of it, if Alessandra and her father had ventured to southwestern Colorado, they certainly hadn't shopped. Next to the obligatory boxes of stale saltines and graham crackers nobody ate, a bag of gluten-free chocolate chip cookies roused a smirk. Their father had a serious sweet tooth, one that had been passed on to both his children, but since he'd gotten together with his Italian girlfriend, it was sugar-free this and gluten-free that. Jane considered it karma.

She plucked a can of tomato soup off the shelf and checked the expiration date: still good, but most certainly not enough.

"I already looked," Ryan said, startling her. She pressed a hand to her chest and gave him a look. He responded with a sheepish grin. "But we knew we'd have to swing into town, regardless."

"You should have thought of that earlier," she told him. "Your shortcut is actually going to waste time, not save it, and I don't think I can make it up the driveway myself."

"I don't want you to make it up the driveway yourself." Ryan unclipped the bag of cookies and stuck his nose inside. "I need the Nissan for another few months. After that, you can destroy it all you want." Fishing one of the cookies out, he took an overly cautious bite. She watched him as he chewed, his face twisting in confused disgust. "Sawdust flavor?" He coughed, checking the bag to see what in the world he was eating, and, despite his protest, stuck the rest of the cookie in his mouth before rolling up the bag and tossing it back onto the shelf. "I'll just leave those right there. Sweet Jesus."

"There's water in the fridge."

"Is it gluten-free?"

"Pretty sure."

"That's good," he said, turning to walk into the kitchen. "Because I wouldn't want to break my diet."

Jane and Lauren shopped while Ryan wandered the produce department, plucking grapes off the vine one at a time, covertly popping them into his mouth as he continued to mess with his phone. Jane had nearly talked him into piling Oona back into the car for the twenty-five-mile trip it took to get into town, but Ryan refused. He wasn't about to drag the dog back into the car and put up with the hassle of keeping her on a leash while the girls bought groceries. It wasn't like it mattered what Oona did to the house anyway. If they returned to a steaming pile of crap on the couch, he'd congratulate the husky on a job well done.

"I think we're ready," Jane announced, rolling a grocery cart alongside a pyramid of oranges. Ryan eyed her selections, raising an eyebrow at the amount of stuff.

"You think that's enough?" he asked.

"It's four days."

Leaning forward, he plucked a box of oatmeal out of the mix, giving her a look.

"For breakfast," she said.

"This isn't even flavored."

"You put fruit in it."

Lauren stepped up behind Jane, tossing a box of Lucky Charms into the cart.

"See, that," Ryan said, motioning to the cereal. "That's good taste... This?" He shook the box he was holding.

"I hate oatmeal," Lauren confessed. "There's just something about it."

"Baby vomit," Ryan told them. "The look, the texture."

"Am I to assume you've eaten baby vomit in the past?" Jane asked, snatching the box away from him.

"You're in big trouble, pal," Ryan said. Jane rolled her eyes at the *Happy Gilmore* quote before he finished it, having heard it a million times. "I eat pieces of shit like you for breakfast."

Lauren didn't miss a beat. "You eat pieces of shit for breakfast?"

Ryan blinked at her, impressed, surprised at the shared joke, both of them trying not to laugh. Ryan finally spit out an offended "no" and they cracked up, catching the attention of the lady working the only available checkout lane.

"By the way..." He lifted his phone. "If anyone needs to make a call, now is the time. No reception at home."

"The Wi-Fi isn't working?"

"Disconnected. I checked."

"What about the house phone?"

"Disconnected too."

"Makes sense." She shrugged.

"Maybe," Ryan countered. "But I'd rather blame it on pockets so tight they squeak when he walks."

"Your dad's a miser?" Lauren asked, doubtful.

"Oh, he's not a miser when it comes to buying stuff for himself," Ryan assured her. "But if it comes to leaving the Wi-Fi connected, he's going to cancel it and save himself fifty bucks a month."

"You think it's abnormal to disconnect the phone if the place is up for sale?" Jane countered. "Especially if he's not going to come back?"

"If he's not going to come back, then he should have taken all his crap with him."

"So we could sleep on the floor?"

"Why are you defending him?" Ryan asked, suddenly annoyed. It was just like her, sticking up for that prick for no reason at all.

"I'm not *defending* him," Jane countered. "You're just being overly critical and a little ridiculous."

"Ridiculous," Ryan muttered with a scoff.

Jane shot Lauren a wry look. "Let's go. Dinner is going to take a while, and I want to make a cake."

With a trunk full of groceries, Ryan guided the car back up the mountain, squinting at the glare of the snow through his sunglasses while Jane tapped her fingers against her thigh and Lauren bobbed her head to Huey Lewis and the News.

Turning off the main highway, the Xterra bounced along the snowy road that would eventually lead them to the cabin's steep driveway. Jane held her chin in her hand, watching the scenery glide by—the skinny pines that swayed in the breeze, the roll of phantom mist as the sun baked the top of the snow into a fine, brittle crust. She always watched for animals, hoping to see a family of deer with their noses buried in the snow or a squirrel bounding up the trunk of a tree.

As her eyes scanned the beautiful scenery, her heart lurched into her throat. There, upon a blanket of virgin snow, was a large swath of red. She opened her mouth to speak, but no words came. She mutely tapped her finger on the window instead, the urgency of her motion catching Ryan's attention.

"What is that?" She finally managed to spit out the question, her finger still pressed to the window. "Do you see it?"

Ryan slid his shades down his nose.

"Stop," she told him, reaching over to the stereo and turning Huey down to a whisper. When the Nissan continued to amble along at the same pace, she turned to look at Ryan with wide eyes. "Stop!" she repeated, this time with more intensity.

"What? *What?*" he asked, slamming his foot on the brake. The SUV skidded to a stop, the three of them lurching forward, only to be shoved back into their seats.

"What is it?" she asked, pointing to the blotch of red. It looked like something had been killed and dragged into the trees.

"I don't know." Ryan shrugged. "Roadkill or something."

"Roadkill is usually on a road," Jane corrected.

"Are there wolves out here?" Lauren asked from the backseat, wrinkling her nose.

"Werewolves," Ryan said flatly. "That or serial killers."

"It's a forest," Jane cut in, incredulous.

"Woodland serial killers, then," Ryan corrected, amused with himself. "They're the worst kind. They've all got cabin fever. And axes. And a dozen kids to feed."

"God, totally creepy," Lauren said. "Wolves like in that one movie, the one with Liam Neeson."

"Like *Texas Chainsaw Massacre*," Ryan added. "But, you know, with snow instead of Texas."

"Don't start," Jane warned. She had never been a fan of gore and Ryan knew it. He also knew she was terrified of the forest at night. As a child, he had convinced her little girls were bears' favorite food.

"That movie where the plane crashed," Lauren continued, sounding oddly worried, "and they had to walk through all that snow. Did you see that?"

"Oh yeah, we saw it," Ryan told her. "Planes crash here all the time."

Despite Jane's own trepidation, she bit back a pang of amusement. It was a nice change of pace, Ryan teasing Lauren rather than her.

"There aren't really any wolves out here, are there, Janey?"

"Sure there are," Ryan cut in, not allowing his sister to answer. "Giant mutant wolves that stalk the forest at night, looking for fresh meat."

"Stop." Lauren chuckled, but her tone was laced with apprehension.

"And what's safe, anyway; a car, a cabin? What if they have a key?"

Jane covered her mouth, trying not to laugh.

"I'm just saying"—he shrugged—"we think we're safe until we're dead."

Lauren leaned forward and punched him in the arm, and he beamed at her childishly.

"You're a true gentleman," she told him. "Prick."

"Don't listen to him," Jane told her. "He's an idiot."

Ryan opened his mouth to protest, feigning a look of offense.

"Drive," Jane told him.

"Driving," he replied, turning his attention back to the road, leaving the tract of bloody snow behind them. "The hapless trio, driving back to the cabin..."

Jane leaned forward, shooting Lauren a look.

"You never mentioned you have an *evil* twin," Lauren told her.

"But I did tell you he's an idiot." She smirked, then twisted the volume knob on the stereo, a saxophone solo drowning out her brother's laughter.

CHAPTER TWO

It wasn't like Don to stay out so long. It was well past lunchtime, and he had left the house hours before. It never took him this long to collect the wood. The little sled he used to pull it behind him could only hold so much. Jenny stood at the window, her fingers dancing against her mouth. Maybe he had gotten winded, injured… She turned away from the glass, shaking her head. Of course he was fine. They'd lived out here for three decades. Don knew how to handle himself. He was just running late.

It was only after she pulled her cinnamon raisin bread out of the oven that she realized just how long it had been. Crossing her arms over a waist that had expanded over the years, she stared at the ham sandwich she'd prepared for him nearly two hours before and frowned. Don hadn't eaten since breakfast. No doubt he was starving. Reaching behind her, she grabbed hold of her apron strings and pulled, tossing the plaid pinafore onto the counter before marching out of the kitchen.

She stopped in the door of their bedroom and stared at the photograph on the dresser—the two of them smiling in front of that very cabin thirty years before, she in a pretty summer dress, he with his fluffy beard and ridiculous Bermuda shorts. Grabbing her coat and scarf, she pulled a hat tightly over her ears, wrapped his ham sandwich in a square of wax paper, tucked it into her coat pocket, and stuffed her hands into a pair of gloves. If he was going to insist on staying out and catching his death, he may as well eat first.

She grabbed Don's gun from beside the front door. They'd noticed the wolves early this year, the beasts stalking through the trees in search of prey; yet another reason why Don should have known better. He had his ax, but he wasn't young anymore. If a pack fell on him...Jenny put it out of her mind as she stepped outside, the snow crunching beneath her boots.

She looked to the west, squinting against the sun. The snow-capped summit of the nearest peak was clear, but clouds loomed in the not-so-far-off distance. He had complained about his knee the night before, so they knew a storm was closing in. She had been the one to remind him about the wood. The nights had been unseasonably cold, and they had burned through their supply in half the expected time. Had she not mentioned it, there was the possibility that they would have been snowed in without a fire, but at least she would have known where he was; home in his recliner, chuckling beneath his breath at disillusioned antique collectors. She turned away from the mountain, putting the clouds to her back, and began to follow his tracks—footprints flanked by two straight lines left by the rails of his firewood sled.

It was his usual route. Don hardly ever trekked more than a mile before sinking the blade of his ax into the trunk of a tree. He had learned his lesson the hard way. Thirty years before, when the newlyweds had settled into their mountain home, he had stepped into the first snowfall of the season and chopped down a pine not three yards from their front door. Jenny had screamed at him for weeks after and brought up his indiscretion for years, unable to help herself whenever that ugly stump came into view. Ten acres of land and a thousand miles of timber to either side of them, and he had to chop down trees in their front yard. She had made her demand: if he insisted on chopping down trees rather than buying wood in town, he'd have to walk himself out far enough so she'd never see another stump again. She smiled at the memory. That man, just like her father had been, lacking foresight but quick to learn.

A half mile into her search, she stumbled across the first splintered trunk. But the cuts were old, and his tracks trailed past it farther east. She continued forward, one hand squeezing the cold barrel of the gun while the other stole half of Don's sandwich. It was his own fault. He knew she never ate without him.

Idly chewing and humming beneath her breath, she slowed her footsteps when she caught a blip of fire-engine red. It was his sled, half-obscured by the trees. And while that meant he had to be close, there wasn't a sound to be heard in that forest; nothing but the quiet whisper of wind and the shiver of pine needles.

"Donnie?" she called out, but the snow deadened her yell. Holding her breath, she listened for a response, but none came. She stopped next to his sled, her eyebrows knitted together. It didn't make sense. He'd never leave his sled behind, half-piled with wood. Jenny veered around, trying to look in every direction at once. "Don?!" Panic slithered into her tone. What if he'd thrown out his back, collapsed in the snow? She'd warned him not to overexert himself, but he was a stubborn old fool, convinced he was in his thirties instead of sixty-five.

She left the sled behind, jogging along the footprints Don had left in the snow. Her breath hitched in her throat when his path shifted from straight to erratic, and dread coiled itself around her belly, threatening to cut off her air. She could see it in the way his footprints were deeper toward the toe, the way snow had been kicked out behind each footfall: he had been running, weaving through the trees. And he hadn't been alone. There were prints all around his, but she couldn't make out exactly what type of animal they could have belonged to. They were too big to be wolves', too lean and long to be bears'. They looked almost human, despite their wide, lurking gait. An animal with that wide a step must have been huge.

She fell into a run as well, following her husband's footprints no matter how scared she was of the tracks that surrounded them. His name fell from her lips in a gasp. And then she stopped, her eyes wide as she was assaulted by a fetid stink. There was something lying in the snow. An animal. Don's ax handle jutted out from its skull like a crooked flagpole.

Jenny crept toward the carcass, her grip tightening around the barrel of the gun as she pressed it against her chest, her heart thudding in her ears. It wasn't an animal as much as it was a monster, a thin and hairless *monster* so bony its arms looked like twigs in proportion to its wide, skeletal chest. She couldn't make out its face, Don's ax having cut it in two. But she was glad she couldn't tell exactly what it looked like. Wide at the temples, its head looked almost alien, like a creature that had fallen out of the sky or had crawled out of hell itself. Its stomach was deflated, little more than a hollow cavity covered by thin gray skin. Her breath puffed out from her lungs in short, staggered bursts as she slowly approached, terrified but unable to help herself. It was like nothing she'd ever seen, its long, angular body spread out on the snow. It was its teeth that snapped her out of her daze, reminding her that Don was missing, that there were far too many tracks to belong to this one creature alone. Its teeth were thick and jagged, like the fangs of a massive dog.

She twisted away, breaking into as fast a run as her sixty-year-old legs would allow.

That thing was dead, which meant Don was out there somewhere, alive. Alive. He had to be alive.

But those long, thin, alien tracks followed Don's footsteps away from the kill. He had fought one of them off, but there had been far more than one. She readied the gun as she ran, determined to blast every last one of those freaks off the face of God's green earth.

Skidding to a stop, she sucked in a breath and yelled as loud as she could. "Don, where are you?!"

This time there was a response.

This time a communal moan rose in the distance.

A jolt of terror shot through her torso, radiating out to her arms and legs, because it didn't sound like any animal she'd ever heard. It sounded almost human, like a battlefield of dying soldiers wailing as they waited for death. Her breath hitched in her throat as she staggered backward. That haunting cry surrounded her on all sides, at first distant, but slowly growing louder until it transformed completely. The last thing she heard was a rattling growl. The last thing she saw was a shadow sprint across the snow.

———

Ryan stood on the deck overlooking the pines, his coffee cup on the railing, steam wafting out of it like a witch's brew. The silence of the outdoors was staggering—not a sound save for the whisper of wind through the conifers, those green giants swaying gently in the mounting wind, ebbing and flowing like a waterless tide. The occasional gust made it colder than it already was, carrying the distant groan of what must have been a gang of elk upon the wind. The chill bit at his cheeks and fingertips, at the back of his neck where the air slithered beneath his coat. Jane and Lauren were inside. He could hear them laughing over Wang Chung's "Dance Hall Days."

Ryan didn't need music out here. He liked the silence, the soft creak of tree trunks bending in the wind. He snowboarded without headphones, loving the sound of his board carving into the snow as he zigzagged down a steep grade. But if Jane needed Duran Duran to be one with nature, he wasn't about to deny her. With the possibility of this being their final visit, it was all the more important to make this trip count.

Plucking his coffee mug off the deck's railing, he lifted it to his lips and let the steam drift across his face. The fur lining of his trooper hat shivered in the breeze, the pelage snagging on the bristles of his day-old beard. Fresh laughter spilled from inside the house. He smiled against the edge of his mug, watching his sister through the window as she twirled in the kitchen, a spatula covered in frosting held above her head. She looked just like their mother: fair skin, dark easy curls cut short—the kind of girl who didn't try too hard. The kind of girl Summer had been.

Jane lowered the spatula, singing into it before slapping it against the top of a chocolate cake while Lauren stood next to the kitchen island, trying not to choke on her coffee. Ryan had offered to pay for retail space for Janey to open a bakery, knowing that she hated taking cash from their dad; offered to buy all the equipment and even a neon sign in girly pink font—*Janey Cakes*—but she refused every time. Her students at Powell Elementary were more important to her. She insisted that she was happier supplying sprinkle-covered cupcakes to her kids than to stuffy housewives who couldn't be bothered to bake for themselves. She loved watching second graders smear sweet frosting across their faces, giggling in sugar-induced ecstasy.

Lauren spotted Ryan watching them and gave him a ghost of a smile. A second later the music swelled when the kitchen door swung open and his sister's friend stepped onto the deck with a chuckle, closing the door behind her. She tossed her blonde hair over a shoulder before shrugging against the cold.

"Jesus," she said, jerking up on the zipper of her hooded sweatshirt. "It's freezing out here."

Ryan cracked a sideways smile and extended his free hand, swooping it outward as if presenting the snow-covered trees to Miss Lauren Harvey for the taking.

"Yeah, yeah." She ducked beneath the thin veil of her cotton hood.

"You realize it's, like, twenty degrees out here?" he asked. "Think that hood is going to help?"

"I'm just waiting for chocolate cake," she admitted, blowing into her hands before fishing a pack of cigarettes out of her front pocket. "I wouldn't be catching pneumonia if Jane would let me smoke inside."

Had it been Ryan's call, he would have let her smoke in every single room, if not just to stink up his father's place, then to oblige his twin sister's quite attractive best friend.

Lauren tapped the hard pack against an open palm, her teeth clacking as she shivered. She noticed him looking and offered up a sheepish grin. "Bad habit, I know."

"You should quit. Three days."

"What's three days?" she asked, lighting up a smoke and offering the pack to Ryan. He waved it away.

"It's how long it takes your body to get used to something. You know how diet soda tastes funny if you've never drunk it before?"

"Tastes like a chemical dump," Lauren brooded.

"Drink it for three days and you won't remember the difference. Same goes for quitting smoking."

"No shit?"

"That's what they say."

Lauren took a long drag. She gave him a wry grin, raising a shoulder in a shrug. "This is my last one," she said. "I swear."

Ryan breathed a quiet laugh and looked away from her, surveying the endless wave of trees before them to keep himself from staring. He liked her. She was witty, charming, not afraid to crack a joke.

The report of a gunshot echoed through the hills.

"What the hell was that?" Lauren asked, startled.

"Someone shooting their neighbor," Ryan said. "Land dispute."

She gave him a look and he bit back a grin.

"Probably just hunters," he told her. "I think it's turkey season or something."

Satisfied with his answer, Lauren sucked in a lungful of smoke. "So, we're waiting for Sawyer?"

"Sawyer and April."

Exhaling, she squinted at the burning tip of her cigarette, smoke and steam rising upward like a soul escaping a body. "You don't think that's going to be a little awkward?" she asked, plucking a bit of tobacco off the tip of her tongue, canting her head toward the kitchen. "Janey and him and some chick in the same house?"

He drained his mug, coffee warming him from the inside out. "I asked her," he said. "Like a million times."

"And she said she's cool with it," Lauren cut in, ashing her cigarette onto a patch of snow next to her feet. "But you know as well as I do that she's lying."

"Yeah," he said, looking Lauren over thoughtfully. "She is."

"But you still decided to roll with it."

"Last chance," Ryan said. "It was either roll with it or never see this place again."

"Couldn't come out here alone, just you and her?"

"What is this," he asked, "the Spanish Inquisition?"

Lauren gave him an apologetic smile. "Sorry," she murmured.

Ryan frowned at the mountaintop in the distance, coiling his arms around himself for warmth as Lauren smoked next to him. "It wasn't the original plan," he offered after a long pause. "Sawyer bringing this girl."

Lauren quirked an eyebrow. "No?"

Ryan shook his head. "I've never even met her."

"So, this was supposed to be some kind of, I don't know, reunion or something?" Lauren pressed.

"Is that stupid?"

He watched Lauren's face soften as he waited for her response. "Yes," she said after a beat, "stupidly sentimental."

"I guess I just don't want her to be alone, you know?" He shifted his weight from one boot to the other, his gaze fixed on the porch's banister.

Lauren leaned against the railing. "Ooh," she said, a spark of realization crossing her face. "This is all because of Switzerland, isn't it?"

Ryan shrugged almost helplessly. It was an amazing opportunity, but leaving his sister behind wasn't exactly easy.

Sawyer had grown up with them. Sawyer and Jane had been together for more than three years in high school. It had been weird at first—his best friend dating his twin sister—but he'd learned to like it. Now, with Zurich in his not-so-distant future, it would make him feel better to know that his two closest friends were together again, taking care of each other. Without that assurance, Ryan would be stuck picturing Jane alone in her apartment grading badly colored drawings and fighting with her louse of a future ex-husband.

"You know she'll be fine," Lauren told him. "Jane is always the brave one. Besides, what about me?"

"What about you?"

Lauren scoffed teasingly. "Well, am I good for nothing?"

"I don't know. I don't know you that well."

"Lucky for you, you have four uninterrupted days."

"I only need three," he joked, and she blushed and turned away.

A snap of branches pulled both Ryan and Lauren's attention to the trees. Lauren opened her mouth to speak, her expression startled, when a family of deer stepped out of the trees and dashed across the steep driveway. She laughed as she pressed a hand to her chest, shaking her head at herself, only to jump at the scratching behind her a second later. Oona was standing behind the kitchen door, her nose smearing the glass as she waited to be let out.

"Jumpy?" Ryan asked as he stepped away from the railing and cracked the door open to let the husky onto the porch. Oona bounded through the door, nearly skidded on the slick planks of wood beneath her paws, and launched herself off the steps like a furry missile.

"I wouldn't be if you hadn't purposefully freaked me out earlier," she complained.

"Me?" Ryan looked flabbergasted at the accusation as Oona's bark echoed off the trees. She did wild doughnuts in front of the house, her feet punching holes in the hard crust of snow, before looking up at her owner, wagging her flag-like tail, ready to play. Ryan didn't hesitate. He excused himself with a smile, fishing his gloves out of the pockets of his coat as he descended the stairs. Oona bolted away from the cabin before Ryan's boots hit the ground, barking up a storm as she sprinted through the trees. She leaped like a gazelle, then threw herself down to roll in the powder before storming back toward her owner. Scooping up a gloveful of snow, Ryan packed it into a loose snowball and launched it at Oona's feet. She barked, burying her nose in the ground where it exploded, searching for the ball that must have been hiding there. Lauren laughed from atop the deck as Ryan packed another, letting it zip by the dog's nose. Oona snapped at it with her teeth, baffled yet again when it vanished into thin air as soon as it hit the ground.

Just as he leaned down to make a third, a low rumble cut through Jane's muffled music. Oona perked, standing at attention, her big ears pointing straight up, her tail stark still. Ryan narrowed his eyes as he listened, realizing that it was the sound of an engine the closer it approached. But rather than facing the driveway, Oona was still facing the woods, a repressed growl roiling in her throat. Ryan clucked his tongue at her.

"It's just a car, genius," he told her, but Oona refused to let up. "Oona, come," he commanded, and eventually the husky turned and padded toward him, distracted by the black Jeep that rambled up the steep drive. Ryan crouched down, hooking a pair of fingers beneath her collar. Despite her unfailing obedience, he never risked it when it came to cars.

The dog slipped away from Ryan's hold as soon as the metallic zip of a parking brake accompanied Siouxsie Sioux's melancholy vocals from inside Sawyer's Jeep. Oona dashed across the snow, stopping a foot from the driver's-side door. Plopping her butt down on the frozen ground, she waited to greet the occupants of the vehicle while they gathered their belongings. A second later she was excitedly jumping against a pair of black jeans, miring them with white powder.

Sawyer bent down, gathering Oona in his arms as she decorated him with kisses, her tail whipping back and forth, little squeals of canine joy rumbling deep from her throat. Ryan's gaze drifted to the girl still inside the car as she buttoned her coat and gathered her things. She was a beautiful waif, her short black hair bobbed in a style that reminded him of 1920s starlets—a striking contrast against her fair skin and eyes as blue as the winter sky. She was just the kind of girl Ryan pictured Sawyer ending up with. Dark. Mysterious. Also a fan of funeral attire. She looked glamorous in her military-inspired coat, a black scarf that matched Sawyer's hat wrapped around her neck. But she was also the girl who was about to completely derail Sawyer's life.

Sawyer eventually straightened when Ryan closed the distance between them as he extended his right hand. Ryan caught it in a firm grip, pulling Sawyer forward into an embrace, both men patting each other on the back with their free hands.

"You're late," Ryan complained with a grin, squeezing Sawyer by the shoulder before taking a backward step, Oona excitedly sniffing at Sawyer's shoes. "Still forever attending funerals, I see." Ryan raised an eyebrow at Sawyer's all-black ensemble—a style Sawyer hadn't been able to shake since high school.

"They don't start with 'fun' for nothing," Sawyer said. "And we took a wrong turn." He rolled his eyes at his own admission. "Ended up fifteen miles in the wrong direction before I realized I'm an idiot."

"At the lake?" Ryan asked as Sawyer ruffled the fur on top of Oona's head.

"That entire thing is frozen through. Have you seen it?"

Ryan peered at Oona as she snorted. She was picking up a scent, exhaling a loud blast of air against Sawyer's shoe.

"Elvis," Sawyer concluded. "April's ferret."

Ryan wrinkled his nose at the news. "Please tell me you didn't bring rodents."

"God no," Sawyer muttered beneath his breath. "I'm not a fan either."

"They're creepy as hell."

"Hey," Sawyer lifted his hands up in front of his chest. "You don't have to tell *me*. Try waking up next to one of those long-bodied fuckers at three in the morning; one wrong move and you get a face full of tiny fangs." He moved a hand in front of his mouth, wiggling his fingers to imply teeth. Ryan shuddered.

"You *sleep* with it? Sweet Christ."

Sawyer looked toward the house, its glittering facade blocking the view of the side porch. "Jane?" he asked, lowering his voice.

"Kitchen," Ryan told him.

When the passenger door swung open, Sawyer gave Ryan a look, motioning to the girl who was making her way around the front of the Jeep. She kept one hand against the hood of the car, careful not to slip on the ice that had formed there. "Ryan, April," Sawyer introduced them.

Ryan found himself face-to-face with the girl Sawyer had told him about. She extended a delicate hand toward him in greeting, a reserved smile pulling at the corners of a cotton-candy mouth.

"Nice to meet you," she said, dipping her chin downward shyly as she shook Ryan's hand. "I've heard a lot about you. Thanks for letting me tag along."

"The more the merrier," he told her, smiling through a pang of annoyance. Their group minus April would have been perfect— he and Lauren could get to know each other while Sawyer and Jane reacquainted themselves on the opposite side of the house.

Smiling at Oona, April crouched down to offer the dog a hand to sniff, ice fracturing beneath the soles of her combat boots. "Aren't you beautiful?" she said, glancing up to Ryan after burying her fingers in the dog's fur. "Is she yours?"

Ryan nodded. "The only woman in my life," he teased, and Sawyer choked back a laugh.

"Here we go." Sawyer waited for the punch line.

And she's a real bitch.

Ryan cracked a stupid smile at his childhood friend and resisted the urge to finish the joke, motioning to the house. "Come on," he told them. "The girls are inside."

Jane was sick with nerves. Standing over her half-frosted choco-late cake, a sugar-coated finger stuck in her mouth, she listened for footsteps while her stomach churned. She hadn't seen Sawyer in more than five years, and their last encounter had been quick. He'd passed through Phoenix on the way to Los Angeles this past fall, and they had spent ten minutes of an early morning together in a sticky Denny's booth before she excused herself; it had been a school day; she had kids to teach—and first loves to forget. The two of them hadn't had an honest conversation in nearly ten years, their last one emotional enough to remain a vivid memory. But that had been high school. Nobody should be held account-able for the bad choices they made between freshman and senior years.

And yet the sound of footsteps on the porch woke a flurry of sleeping butterflies, her pulse fluttering in her throat. She swal-lowed her anxiety, trying not to look nervous as she watched her brother and a pair of dark-clad figures drift past the window. Sawyer had fallen into an all-black phase the year he had dis-covered Depeche Mode, and had never grown out of it, but it suited his features well: sharp, Norse, desperately pretty even as he toed the line of thirty. Jane squared her shoulders when Ryan appeared at the side door, cleared her throat, and put on her best smile.

A cold blast of air cut through the warmth of the room as the door swung inward and Oona padded inside, her tongue hang-ing out of her mouth, her tail whapping the air. Ryan stepped in after her, holding the door for Sawyer and his girl.

Had Sawyer given her the chance, she would have immedi-ately felt intimidated by the woman who stepped inside behind him. She was stunning—the kind of girl who demanded atten-tion without saying a word. But before Jane could wrap her mind around the beautiful creature that tailed him, Sawyer closed the distance and Jane found herself in his embrace. Like a long-lost lover, she reflexively pulled in a deep breath to catch his scent: soap and clove smoke, the subtle spice of well-worn leather. She wanted to shut out the world, to hold on to that moment for longer than she cared to admit.

"Hi, Janey," Sawyer murmured against her hair.

"Hi, Tom," she said softly. Sawyer Thomas had a predictable nickname. He declared that if he was to be named after anybody, Tom Sawyer wasn't a bad kid to have as a namesake.

Jane was the one to step out of their embrace when Lauren came into view. She could feel Ryan's gaze on the pair of them, sure that Sawyer's girl was staring a hole into her spine. Jane flashed a smile at the pretty stranger standing next to her brother, sidestepping Sawyer to greet the girl she truly had no desire to know.

"April?" she asked. Jane wrapped her arms around the girl in a casual hug, surprised at how small April was. Ryan and Lauren cast raised eyebrows at each other over April's shoulder as they watched the exchange. Their shared glance made Jane feel awkward, but she was determined to be as welcoming as possible.

"So good to meet you," Jane told her, sounding a little too excited. She took a backward step, feeling as plastic as possible. "I like your coat," she said, unsure how to continue. *How's it like to be with the guy I still think about?* "God, sorry, this is Lauren." She motioned for Lauren to come over.

"And this?" Sawyer asked, standing threateningly close to Jane's half-frosted chocolate cake.

"That," Jane said, stepping over to the island to save the cake from an early fate, "is not finished, so don't even think about it." She swept it up and moved it out of the way, placing it on the counter beside the sink.

Jane was quick to notice the way April was looking around the place, sure she had expected some tiny two-bedroom shack in the middle of the woods.

"Sorry," Jane said, offering April an apologetic smile. "It's... not really a cabin, I guess."

"Why are you apologizing?" Sawyer asked.

"Because it's embarrassing," Ryan cut in. "This whole trip would be far more comfortable if we had rented a tar-paper shack." He glanced at Lauren. "Complete with outhouse, so you have to go outside in the middle of the night."

Lauren rolled her eyes at him.

"Don't you think they should make a movie like that?" he asked her.

"Like what?" Lauren asked. "A movie about an outhouse?"

"Exactly. And every time one of the characters goes outside to use it, they end up being killed by a werewolf."

"A werewolf?" Sawyer bit back a laugh. "What the hell, why a werewolf?"

"Lauren loves werewolves," Ryan told him.

"I'll give you the grand tour," Jane told April, too nervous to enjoy the back-and-forth banter.

"Sawyer doesn't need a grand tour," Ryan told her. "Sawyer needs to come outside and unload his crap." He nodded toward the door they had entered through. Jane watched the boys shuffle back out onto the deck. Looking back to April and then Lauren, she lifted her shoulders up to her ears with a smile. *Boys.*

"So, Jane looks good," Sawyer confessed, leaning against the back bumper of his Jeep as he lit up a smoke. "For being married, I mean." He knew it wouldn't come as a surprise to Ryan that Sawyer had checked his sister out; Ryan was, after all, the person who'd supplied him with updates about Jane for the past ten years, something Sawyer was sure would creep Jane the hell out if she ever found out. Sawyer had tried not to ask about how Jane was doing for a while, and he actually held out for a good few years, but not asking had stilted conversations with Ryan to the point of embarrassment. Ryan was the one who eventually caved, giving Sawyer the occasional scoop without being asked: Jane was getting married; Jane was getting divorced.

"Yeah, well…" Ryan joined Sawyer against the Jeep's bumper, his hands buried in the pockets of his coat. "April's more attractive than I imagined." A droll grin spread across his mouth, and Sawyer laughed with a shake of his head.

"Yeah?" he asked, smoke curling past his lips. "You thought she was going to look like Oona?"

"Hey, Oona's majestic."

Sawyer pushed away from the bumper and walked a few steps ahead before turning to face the cabin, taking a long drag off his cigarette. "So the old man is really selling this place?" he asked. "Why don't you just buy it? You've got the money."

Ryan snorted at that.

"Spent it all jet-setting?" Sawyer asked. "Let me guess, you're already a quarter mil in debt?"

"I wouldn't buy this place if it was free," Ryan confessed.

"You know that's bullshit."

Ryan shifted his weight from one foot to the other, his arms coiling across his chest.

"What?" Sawyer asked. "Like I don't know this is a sore subject?" Growing up as practically the third twin, Sawyer knew Michael Adler well. "He still running around with that Italian chick?"

"*Oh* yeah," Ryan scoffed.

"Buzzing around on one of those tiny scooters. Circling the Leaning Tower of Pizza."

Ryan cracked a cynical smile.

Sawyer straddled the air, riding an imaginary Vespa, his cigarette clinging to the swell of his bottom lip as he lifted his right hand, pageant-waving to an invisible crowd of tourists. "*Ciao, bellas,*" he said, bringing his fingertips to his lips and releasing the kiss into the air.

"I'm sure that's totally accurate," Ryan said. "Totally."

Sawyer shrugged. "Is there anything *else* to do in Italy? Or in Switzerland, you asshole?"

Ryan ignored the dig. "What, other than look like a day-tripper? You'd fit right in," he said. "Constantly smoking that shit like some hipster."

Sawyer rolled his eyes. "Europeans are known for their love of nicotine. Just wait until you move into your fancy loft in Zurich, traitor. I'm a lightweight compared to their carton-a-day habit." Sawyer freely admitted that a pack a day was extreme, but it was a vice he couldn't seem to shake. "I didn't smoke on the way up here," he confessed. "It was glorious. You would have been proud."

"April making you quit?" Ryan asked as Sawyer took his final drag, grinding the butt against the sole of his boot.

"Please, she can take my life, but she can't take my smokes." Reaching into the trunk, Sawyer slung a Timbuk2 backpack over his shoulder. "She's pretty low maintenance."

"For now."

"At least she's hot."

"There is that."

"What's with Janey's blonde friend, what's her name…"

"Lauren."

"You and her?" Sawyer asked. "You know…" He curled up the fingers of his right hand, thrusting the heel of his palm outward, knocking it against the chill in the air.

"Maybe, you never know…" Ryan smirked.

"She's cute."

"So are a lot of other girls."

"You'll have to settle down eventually," he warned. "Scared shitless or not."

"Yeah?" Ryan asked, hefting a duffel bag full of boarding gear out of the back. "Because that ended well for Jane, right? It's the fucking Adler curse."

"Yeah, well, nobody likes a forty-year-old bachelor."

"You're right. It's better to get married and run around behind her back."

"Now you're talking." Sawyer slapped Ryan on the shoulder. "Carry on the family tradition."

Ryan gave him a look.

"Jesus." Sawyer laughed. "I'm kidding, man. Come on."

"I'm not carrying on any tradition unless I get a Vespa."

"Dude, I'll buy you a fucking Vespa if only to see the wind in your hair."

They looked at each other, both of them deadpan.

"If it wasn't for that stupid earflap hat," Sawyer continued, "I'd run my fingers through your locks right now."

"Tonight," Ryan promised. "After the girls have gone to bed."

"By the fire?"

"With Jane's chocolate cake between us. I'll whip us up a bearskin rug."

Sawyer let his head loll back, the steam of his breath rising from his throat as he laughed. "Perfect," he said. "Just don't complain if I smoke afterward. That, my friend, I cannot help."

Ryan tossed the bag over a shoulder. "It's fucking cold out here," he said. "Let's go."

Sawyer reached up to close the Jeep's hatch when he paused, narrowing his eyes at the trees closest to the driveway. Something had shifted in the corner of his eye, a shadow drifting behind the trunk of a tree. Glancing up, he watched an army of clouds speed across the sky, the breeze making the trees creak and sway. The sun blinked on and off like a strobe, throwing the pines into shadow one second, brilliant light the next.

"Did you see that?" he asked, motioning to where he'd seen the shift.

"What?" Ryan asked.

"Something was moving around back there."

"Deer," Ryan announced. "Lauren and I saw a family wandering around just before you guys pulled up."

"Just like old times. You sure you can let this beauty go?" Sawyer asked, nodding toward the cabin. "Good memories, great location..."

"I couldn't buy the house even if I wanted to."

"Don't screw with me."

"It's already sold," Ryan confessed. "I checked the listing on a whim, called up the Realtor because I was feeling nostalgic. Someone's already bought it."

Sawyer stopped where he was, blinking at his best friend. "So, what, is it empty inside?"

"Everything's still there. They're waiting to close the deal—but once they do..."

"So, wait a minute...we're, like, staying in somebody's house right now?"

"Technically, no."

"*Technically?* Dude."

"Don't say anything," Ryan warned. "If Jane finds out..."

"If Jane finds out she'll fucking flip. Maybe this isn't a good idea. What if someone shows up to look at the place? Maybe we should get a hotel or something, play it safe."

"A hotel? You mean a *motel*—one of those roach-infested ones. You don't think Jane will flip out *there*?"

"Maybe, but imagine her in a jail cell."

"Nobody's going to jail," Ryan assured him. "Besides, it's an honest misunderstanding. The dick didn't bother to tell me, and I still have a set of keys. How was I supposed to know?"

Sawyer considered the plausibility of Ryan's story, then raised his shoulders in a shrug. "It's your ass, not mine."

"We're a million miles from anywhere," Ryan said. "It's just us and the trees. Nobody will know, because nobody knows we're here."

CHAPTER THREE

T he guy working the ski lift held up his hands.

"Sorry, folks." He tried on his best look of sympathy. "No more going up today."

"Oh, come on!" Jake shoved the sleeve of his jacket up his forearm, checking the time. "It's two minutes till four, man. We've got sixty seconds until the cutoff."

Tara stood uncomfortably next to Jake, rubbing the back of her neck with a gloved hand, her eyes fixed on the board strapped to one of her feet. They were coming up on their two-year anniversary, but she still hadn't gathered the nerve to tell him she hated snowboarding—hated everything about it, from the bitter cold to getting off and on the lift. Every minute spent standing in line to get on that confounded thing gave her an anxiety attack, because getting on the lift meant getting off, and getting off meant eating it at the top of the hill. This was only her second season, and she already knew boarding wasn't for her. But there was something to be said for keeping up appearances, especially for a guy who was as fanatical about winter sports as Jake.

"Hey, let's just go to the lodge," she suggested. "Get something to drink; I want cocoa."

But he wasn't satisfied with her suggestion. They'd paid good money for their lift tickets and he was determined. "I have a better idea," he said, pulling the glove off his right hand and shoving it into the pocket of his waterproof pants. "Here." He held out a crumpled twenty-dollar bill. "Get yourself a beer, huh? Let us on."

The operator frowned at the money, hesitating, and eventually gave in with a sigh. "Fine," he said. "But up and down, all right?"

Jake held up his hands, as if to say the operator had his word. Tara shut her eyes, trying not to groan. She'd have done anything to get that snowboard off her feet. Her pinkie toes had gone numb inside her boots hours ago. Jake grabbed her by the elbow and slid into place, both of them craning their necks backward, waiting for the chairlift to scoop them up.

Tara winced as the chair slammed against the backs of her thighs. The safety bar came down across their laps and she ducked into the scarf wrapped around her neck. It was cold, the sun having dipped just beyond the crest of the mountain, leaving the entire ski area in frigid shadow. And to make things worse, the slush of the day was starting to freeze into a slick of ice. She could hardly maneuver on fresh powder, let alone on hard-packed permafrost. The idea of catching the edge of her board and flying headfirst down the hill twisted her stomach into knots—but an injury wouldn't have been so bad. It would have put her out for the rest of the season. A broken wrist almost seemed worth it.

Jake was the first to launch off the lift. Tara always hesitated, calculating the least terrifying, least treacherous trajectory to take. But no matter how much she steeled her nerves or planned her dismount, she always ended up on her back, and this time was no different. She crashed a few seconds after shoving herself off the chairlift, clenching her teeth behind the woven wool of her scarf. At least there wasn't another group of boarders behind them to see her fall; at least the hill was completely devoid of people, all of those right-minded skiers at the base of the mountain, packing up their gear and getting out of the cold. Jake came to a stop a few yards away, snapping his left foot into his board as he waited for her to get up and join him. She sighed, shoving her boot into her binding.

"It's too icy," she called out to him. He lifted his hand to his ear, shaking his head at her. Pushing her scarf away from her mouth, she made a face at him. "It's slick. I'm going to kill myself."

Jake looked away, and she hoped he was considering the steep downgrade ahead of him. The hill was an intermediate blue, interspersed with a handful of well-camouflaged moguls—ones that were virtually invisible in the shade. If it had been a green trail it wouldn't have been so bad, but naturally he had to make their last run count.

"We'll take a detour," he told her, motioning to a line of pines. "There's a side trail just beyond those trees. It'll be less hard-packed there."

"*Off* the trail?" She shook her head. There was no way she was going off the trail, not when the slope was empty like this, not when there weren't any people to help them if they got into trouble. Jake looked away again, and she could feel him rolling his eyes at her. If worse came to worst, she'd unstrap her board and use it like a sled, sliding all the way down the hill until she was safe and sound in front of the lodge. Hell, that might actually be *fun*.

"It's a trail," he told her. "It's on the map."

"Are you sure?"

"Babe, come on. I'm sure."

"Goddamnit," she whispered, securing the strap of her binding before rocking onto her feet.

The trail wasn't a trail.

Tara nearly screamed when she found herself knee-deep in a snowdrift. Jake was hopping in front of her, trying to dislodge his board from an impossible depth of powder while she silently raged behind him. After a few minutes of fruitless effort, she was the first to throw in the towel.

"*This* was on the map? I swear, sometimes you just..." *drive me fucking nuts.* She bit her tongue, trying to keep herself from boiling over. This wasn't his fault. He hadn't *purposely* led them into a snowdrift. She continued to echo his innocence inside her head, trying to keep her anger in check, but the cold was making it difficult to stay quiet. The snow, which had found its way into her boots and was now melting against her socks, was making it hard not to launch into a tirade that would end in a statement she'd been wanting to make since last season: *I'm never going snowboarding again.* She reached into the snow and unsnapped her bindings, struggling to step off her board without toppling over. "I'm walking," she announced through clenched teeth, hefting her board up by its leash and tossing it onto her back.

"Are you serious?" He looked surprised, but his little laugh of disbelief only made her angrier.

"I'm serious," she snapped, shoving one foot into the snow ahead of her, the knee-deep powder sucking her leg down like quicksand. Less than ten steps forward and she was already gasping for breath. She held back her tears, pressing on, determined to get off that damned mountain so she could never return.

"Look, we'll just get back to the main trail, okay? It's not far." Jake unstrapped his own board, but rather than following her downhill, he turned toward the trees. She stopped, watching him waddle toward a thick grouping of pines, their branches bent low with snow.

"And if it's deeper in there?" she asked. "People die in snowdrifts, you know."

"Well, what do you want to do? Freeze up here?"

"Yeah," she said. "That's exactly what I want to do." Sighing, she relented, begrudgingly turning to follow him into the thicket. "This is…your fault…you know," she said between gasps for air. "We…should have just…gone…to…the…lodge." Each word punctuated another exhausting step, but Jake continued forward, not saying anything. After a few minutes she had to stop; bending at the waist, she tried to catch her breath. "Wait," she said, lifting a hand to signal she needed a break. "I can't." Her lungs were on fire. Every inhale of icy air felt as if she were swallowing fire. Her feet ached with numbness. Her fingers prickled with pain. For a second she teetered on the brink of panic. What if they didn't get out of here? What if they did get swallowed by a snowdrift as soon as they set foot in those trees? There were signs posted along the mountain to stay on designated trails— there had to be a reason for those. What if people *died* doing this? "Hey," she said, wincing against the pain in her chest. "Hey, maybe we should go back the way we came."

"What?" He shook his head at her. "I thought you wanted to get out of here." He hovered just beyond the trees, extending an arm outward to push a snow-laden branch to the side.

"I do," she insisted. "I just…I don't know. I have a bad feeling."

"It's called first-degree frostbite," he told her, ducking his head to peer into the wooded area.

"Great," she said as she continued forward. "That makes me feel so much better."

"It looks fine," he assured her. "Totally cool. We'll be back on the trail in a few minutes."

She looked up just in time to see him duck into the trees. And then he quite literally disappeared. Her eyes went wide as his snowboard stuck in the snow. "Jake?!" Her heart launched itself into her throat. She tried to run forward, terrified that her worst fears were being realized. It looked like he had fallen straight down, like the snow had swallowed him whole as soon as he breached the perimeter of those pines.

"Oh my god, Jake? Can you hear me?" No reply. Tears sprang into her eyes, hot against the bitter cold. Her board slid out of her grasp, sliding down the slope of the hill as she ambled forward, panic choking her every breath. But when she reached his snowboard, that panic bloomed into terrified confusion. His tracks ended abruptly. He was nowhere to be found.

She stumbled headlong into the woods, turning around in an attempt to face every direction at once. "Jake?!" His name was little more than a hysterical shriek. "If this is a joke, it isn't funny!" But something about the situation assured her that this wasn't a prank. It was too cold. She was too freaked out for him to pull a stunt like this. Catching the toe of her boot on something beneath the snow, she pitched forward and crumbled to her knees, her tears coming freely now. "I just want to go home," she wept. "Jake, I'm cold and I want to go home."

Nothing.

"I hate snowboarding!" she screamed into the pale blue silence. "I've never liked it! I've only been coming along because you expected me to." Her words faded into a whisper. She blinked, swiping a gloved hand across her cheek. "Jake?"

Still nothing.

She swallowed against the lump in her throat, getting back to her feet. "I'm going down the mountain now," she told the forest. "I…" Hesitating, she looked around herself again. "I can't stay here. I'll send somebody, okay?"

Silence.

Then a phlegmy, guttural groan.

Fear speared her heart as she spun around, looking for the source. It sounded more like a wounded animal than a human, but it had to be Jake.

The moaning continued, now sounding as if it came from above her, as though daring her to turn her gaze skyward. When she did, her breath caught in her throat.

A creature loomed overhead, one long, angular arm clinging to a tree a good dozen feet up, while the other wrapped around a body wearing a familiar jacket and pants, the garments spattered with blood. She stumbled backward as its groan shifted from what almost sounded like pain to a full-on growl. The sound vibrated deep within the thing's throat, its canine teeth glistening with red. And then it looked like its gaping maw almost leered when the creature dropped what it was holding, Jake's body landing at her feet in a gruesome offering.

She opened her mouth to scream, her eyes wide as he turned his head to look at her. His face was virtually gone, eaten away, leaving little more than a skull wrapped in tattered, bleeding flesh. She reeled back, her cries stifled by air that simply wouldn't come. She was suffocating, stumbling backward. Blood bubbled from where his lips used to be, and that was when she caught enough of a breath to scream. He was still *alive*; his gaze silently pleading for her to save him. But she couldn't; she *couldn't*. That creature was perched in the branches above him, voyeuristic, waiting to see what Tara would do.

Her hands flew to her mouth as she backed up, the world spinning the wrong way around, vertigo threatening to lay her out. She turned, trying her damnedest to run despite the depth of the snow. But her steps slowed when Jake tried to cry out behind her—a different sound from the one she had heard before, a wet, smacking gurgle like a kid blowing bubbles through a straw. When she looked over her shoulder she couldn't see him anymore. Two gaunt figures were perched above him. Their bodies were covered in scars, either from their prey or from each other. One of them shook its head back and forth like a dog, blood spraying from its mouth to either side. The other shoved the first creature away with its...its *hands*, like an annoyed little kid. Tara watched them snap their jaws at each other, her eyes wide, horrified. Jake was convulsing beneath them as if overtaken by a violent case of shivers. He was dying, but she was too terrified, too hopped up on adrenaline to stand there.

She felt like she was going to vomit, gasping for air as she clambered up a tree-dotted slope. The mountain went wavy behind her panicked tears, but she was sure if she kept going she'd find the main ski trail. Those things were distracted, fighting over their kill, and if she could just make it out into the open she'd be okay.

Her heart thudded in her ears as she threw herself forward, clawing at the embankment, scrambling up the incline as fast as she could. Panic having squelched her sobs, the icy slope of the blue run came into view, offering the hope of safety with its groomed, wide-open expanse. She struggled, trying to pull herself up to its surface from the snowbank, her legs stuck in the soft snow four feet below. Sucking in a steadying breath, she coiled the muscles of her legs and sprang forward, the front of her jacket kissing the iced-over surface of her escape route. Her gloved fingers curled into the ground as she crawled, kicking her legs in desperation, trying to find some leverage to get the rest of her body onto the same level as her torso and arms. Finally managing to get one knee up, she shoved herself forward. Overwhelmed with a rush of relief, she crawled out of the snow. She was going to make it.

But her heart stopped when her foot caught on something behind her. She shot a look over her shoulder, as one of those things coiled a huge hand around her ankle—almost human save for the wide flat of its palm, three crooked fingers and a thumb clamping around her foot so viciously that she could feel the pressure from inside her boot. She thrashed against its grip as she screamed, desperate to get away, but the more she fought it, the more it exposed those predatory teeth, the more she was convinced it was *smiling* as she fought. She pulled in a breath for another scream, but it soundlessly escaped her lungs when the creature yanked her backward, so quickly that the world became a pale blue blur. It pulled her back into the snowdrift.

Back into the snow.

———

Sneaking up behind her, Lauren rested her chin on Jane's shoulder. Jane was standing at the step that separated the kitchen from the living room, holding a steaming mug of tea between her palms, pretending to watch *The Thing* while the dual ovens worked away beside her. The scent of roasted meat that coiled through the house only reminded Lauren how hungry she was, not having eaten since breakfast. But Jane's seemingly steadfast interest in the TV didn't fool Lauren for a second; Jane hated horror movies. April and Sawyer were sitting on the couch together, Sawyer's arm looped around that dark-haired pixie's shoulders.

"Is watching movies about monsters stalking through an icy tundra while *in* an icy tundra kind of masochistic, or is it just me?" Lauren asked. Jane's mouth quirked up in a halfhearted smirk, as though she had been wondering the same thing. "When's dinner?" Lauren asked, turning toward the top oven. She cupped her hands against the oven's glass door and peered inside.

"About an hour," Jane told her, her gaze still focused on the living room, hypnotized by the couple that sat less than ten yards away, seemingly happy as could be.

"Is it weird?" Lauren asked, her words quiet enough to remain between only them.

Jane finally turned away from the living room and stepped to the kitchen island.

"A little, but it's good." She nodded as if affirming her own hushed words. "It clears things up, you know?"

"How's that?"

Jane lifted her shoulders, letting them fall a moment later. "You stop thinking about it," she said quietly, casting a glance over her shoulder to make sure the others weren't eavesdropping. "About the possibilities, you know? I guess it's kind of nice to know that the cards are off the table."

Lauren nodded faintly. She admired Jane for her ability to stay positive, sure that if she were in Jane's position, she'd avoid even looking at April, let alone occupying the same house with her. But that was Jane's nature. She took the good and discarded the bad; she was nice to everybody, even if they didn't deserve it, even if she secretly loathed their existence—though Jane would say that everyone deserved kindness and that she didn't really *hate* anybody. Lauren supposed that sort of compassionate patience came with spending five days a week with a gaggle of kids. Once you could handle that, you could handle just about anything—even a waif of a girl who, in Lauren's opinion, was trying to look way too French with her glossy jet-black hair and her flawless skin.

"Well, you're a stronger man than I," Lauren told her, grabbing an apple from a basket that sat on the island, biting into it before Jane seized it a second later.

"Don't," she said. "You'll ruin your appetite."

"Okay, *Mom*," Lauren teased, then turned to the kitchen door when what sounded like something between a growl and a bark echoed from outside.

Jane padded across the kitchen to peer through the glass embedded in the door. "Is Ryan out there?"

"I think he's in the garage. I saw him dragging the boards through the hall a few minutes ago."

A snarl tore through the air before one of the trees just beyond the porch shuddered. Lauren blinked, shooting Jane a startled look, a jolt of anxiety lodging itself in her throat. But she laughed quietly when a young doe bounded into view. It looked panicked, terrorized by the husky that was nowhere to be seen.

Jane took a sip of her tea before abandoning the mug next to the kitchen sink with a frown. "She shouldn't be out there by herself," she said, marching across the kitchen and down the hall before hanging a right past the laundry room. Lauren followed.

Jane pushed the door to the garage open, the smell of hot paraffin wafting up from five feet below. Down a set of cheap wooden stairs that didn't match the cabin's character, Ryan had set up shop; four snowboards lay suspended between two pairs of sawhorses, their colorful undersides exposed. The workbench at his elbow was littered with wax blocks and tuning tools. He didn't look up, the melodic buzz of his headphones predictably blocking out the rest of the world. Lauren couldn't help but wonder what he was listening to, whether they had the same taste. They had listened to Jane's eighties stuff all the way up from Phoenix. He hadn't complained even once.

It was by her own avoidance that she hadn't met Ryan before this trip. She had evaded every get-together when she knew he was in town, sidestepped every invite she knew would put them in the same room. His accomplishments intimidated her. His ability to travel the world while she was stuck in 160 square feet of cubicle space made her hate him a little. He was *that* guy: the one everyone secretly detested not because he was loaded, but because he was free. But the more time she spent around him, the more she wanted to know him.

Lauren bit her bottom lip as she watched him work on her board, the muscles of his arms rippling with each graceful pull of wax.

"Ryan." Jane tried to get his attention, but Ryan was dead to the world, intently focused on his task. Lauren pushed her hair behind her ears, wondering whether Ryan was thinking about her, wondering if there was a reason he had started with her board rather than his own.

Jane sighed and tried again. "Hello? Damnit."

"I'll get him," Lauren offered, descending the stairs, trying to give Ryan a wide berth so as not to startle him. She stepped around the other side of the sawhorses and waved. Ryan blinked at her before pulling his headphones from his ears.

"Hey," Lauren said.

"Hey," he replied. "What the hell did you do?" He drew his fingers across the gash she'd acquired two seasons ago when she just about Sonny Bono'd it into a tree. Lauren blushed as she considered another "accident" if only to have him tend to her wounds.

"Nearly died," Lauren said lightly, a little embarrassed.

"Oona's outside," Jane said from atop the stairs. Ryan glanced up at her, then shook his head as if to ask what the big deal was. "You think that's a good idea, letting her be outside on her own? What if she gets lost?"

"She's not going to get lost."

"Right, until she gets lost," Jane said. "Besides, it's annoying." She motioned toward the door, the barking not only continuing, but growing more incessant by the second.

"Then why didn't you let her in?" Ryan asked, dropping the block of wax onto his worktable with a frown. "Too difficult? You'd rather come bother me about it?"

"She's not near the house," Jane told him. "She's out there chasing deer."

"So?"

"Seriously?" Jane's tone went edgy, and Lauren blinked up at her from the garage in surprise. It was rare to see Jane annoyed, but Lauren supposed that if anyone could push her, it was her brother.

"I'll go find her," Lauren announced, trying to alleviate some of the tension. "Janey's making a five-course meal up there. I just need to grab my coat."

"Don't be a jerk," Jane said from atop the stairs, her gaze still dead set on Ryan.

"What?" He looked perplexed, unsure of what she wanted from him.

"Do *not* make Ren go out there on her own."

"It's okay," Lauren insisted. "I don't mind."

Lauren slid a finger across the bottom of her board thoughtfully, fresh wax warming her fingertip. She tried to make out the whispered melody from the buds hanging around Ryan's neck. It sounded twangy, Jack White or the White Stripes or the Raconteurs. She looked up when the tone of Oona's bark shifted into something more serious. Ryan straightened, his attention wavering from his sister.

"Would you go get her?" Jane asked, irritation dancing around the edge of her words. "It's driving me crazy."

Ryan's face twisted in concern as the bark grew more frantic. "What the hell?" Stepping over to the cheap pine staircase, he pressed a button on the wall. The garage door whined as it rolled up, cold air unspooling across the bare floor, instantly turning the room into a freezer. Lauren coiled her arms around herself and followed Ryan outside, wincing against the wind. Ryan stood in the chill, seemingly unfazed by the cold as Oona went crazy somewhere. "Oona!" He yelled the name into the trees, and for a moment the barking ceased. But the silence wasn't reassuring. When Oona didn't appear a few seconds later, Ryan marched past the driveway toward the steep slope of the road. Lauren shot back a look to a now obviously concerned Jane.

"Goddamnit," Jane snapped, then pivoted on her socked feet and rushed through the door behind her back into the house.

"Oona!" Ryan's voice was carried in the wrong direction by the wind. Lauren pulled the hood of her sweatshirt over her hair and braced herself and walked farther into the bitter cold, her bare fingers clamping the hood closed beneath her chin as storm clouds swirled overhead. She wondered whether the dog could even hear him—Oona could be a mile away and they would still be able to hear her, but Ryan's call would never make it far enough to reach her ears, carried upon the cutting gale. Lauren's stomach twisted at the idea of it—their first official day at the cabin and Oona was missing.

Ryan was a quarter of the way down the road when Lauren saw a streak of black and white bound from the trees. She sighed with relief as Oona bolted up the road toward her owner, Ryan crouching down to greet her. But she'd spooked him, and instead of welcoming her home with a ruffle of fur, he grabbed her collar and gave her a stern "no." Releasing her a second later, he pointed toward the cabin, barking an order as Oona ran past Lauren and skidded into the garage, her tail between her legs.

Lauren had grown up surrounded by dogs; a lazy yellow Lab was waiting for her back in Phoenix. But it didn't take an expert to see that Oona was scared, and it wasn't because she'd just been scolded. When Lauren crouched down and took one of the husky's ears between her finger and thumb, a whine rumbled deep within Oona's throat, those stunning blue eyes searching for understanding.

"What is it, girl?" Lauren whispered, soothing the animal by pushing her fingers through Oona's fur.

There was something out there. Oona had seen it.

Jane clasped her hands together as she looked at the table. There were five place settings: two on each side and one at the head, each setting identical to the one beside it—square white plates, their father's best silverware, delicate crystal wineglasses glinting beneath the glow of an antler chandelier. It was one of the things she missed the most about married life—she loved being domestic, making fancy meals for no particular occasion at all. Now, after four years together, she was left alone in an apartment big enough for two.

Their father had bought her a three-thousand-dollar wedding dress—one made out of silk organza that made her think of forest nymphs and fairy tales. Their parents had spent the entire day avoiding each other—Michael Adler doting on the girlfriend he had brazenly brought with him to the ceremony, their mother keeping her eyes averted and her emotions in check. After a dozen years apart, they still couldn't sit at the same table without trying to tear each other's throats out.

Ryan had sat with Jane in the back room of the church while the quartet played, quiet as a mouse, a hand pressed over his mouth as he stared at the ground like the Thinker. Jane knew he was scared for her. He didn't trust Alex, afraid that history would repeat itself, that Jane would become their mother, torn apart by a cheating husband. And she was scared too, but she loved Alex; she couldn't allow herself to be controlled by fear—a face that Ryan couldn't seem to accept for himself. He had that same pensive look the day she told him Alex was gone, choking on her tears as she described the texts she'd found on his phone. Ryan listened in silence, his anger dulled by a glint of vindication. She knew what he was thinking without him saying the words: he had predicted the worst four years before, but she hadn't listened because that was Ryan's thing—when it came to relationships, he was nothing but doom and gloom. And for nearly four years, everything had been perfect. For four years, Ryan had been wrong.

Until he had been right.

In a way she was glad for the pain. It brought her closer to understanding her brother's fear, and she supposed Ryan was right: relationships were complicated, volatile things. They were riddled with lies, with hidden secrets, ones you only found out about when it was too late. She had loved Alex, convinced that they were destined to have a beautiful life together. And then it all fell apart—just as she and Sawyer had ten years before. With Sawyer, there hadn't been another woman, but another city. Boston was a world away, and it was either her or an education that would lead to the career of Sawyer's dreams. That was why she had forgiven him. A future was just that: the rest of your life. A relationship could crumble at any opportunity.

Taking a step away from the table, Jane wiped the palms of her hands down the front of her apron, smoothed the fabric across her thighs, and smiled at the perfection that was the dinner table. It was a fancy dinner party in a life that had become nothing but stillness: silence at work after her eight-year-olds went home to their mothers, quiet at home as silence rang in her ears.

Ryan slid up beside her, a green glass beer bottle held between his fingers. He took a swig, assessing the table before him. Jane sighed, motioning to his drink.

"Really?"

"I'm thirsty."

"Isn't there a rule about mixing beer and wine?" she asked. "You do realize I bought a bottle of Bordeaux."

"One bottle for five people isn't going to cut it, Janey," Ryan told her. "Unless you're feeding midgets."

"It goes with the meal." Jane turned back toward the kitchen. Despite the cabin's size, there wasn't a proper space for the table, just a large nook jutting out of the kitchen's north side. The table their mother had bought hardly fit within it— Mary Adler had assumed it would go in the dining room, but their dad had already ordered a pool table and refused to send it back.

"Whatever. You want to drink beer with boeuf bourguignon, suit yourself." The Talking Heads drifted in melodic waves from the living room. She could hear the shuffling of cards, which meant a new game of poker was about to start. "Can you call everyone in?"

"Only if I can sit at the head of the table." Ryan pointed the beer bottle at his sister, waiting for her to answer in the affirmative.

"What're you going to do, give a speech?"

Ryan raised an eyebrow as if considering it, but simply bobbed his head to the music, the bottle's neck still pointing at her like a distant microphone, waiting for her reply.

"Would you go get them already?"

He took another swig and wandered away while Jane pulled out drawer after kitchen drawer, searching for a wine opener among a menagerie of kitchen utensils. She smiled as her friends started to filter into the kitchen. Sawyer touched her elbow as he followed April in, and Jane closed her eyes after they had passed.

Opening her eyes, Jane shot Ryan a pleading look, but he was already on top of it, jiggling the bottle opener at her from across the room.

Jane held up her wineglass with a smile. Ryan sat in his requested seat at the head of the table, his wineglass full of lager instead of Bordeaux.

"To the next three days," she said.

"To the mountain," Ryan interjected. "Good powder."

"To new friends," Jane added, a faint smile directed at April. "And old." Her gaze wavered, pausing on Sawyer a moment later.

"And an incredible host," Lauren said, nudging Jane in the ribs.

"But most important, to my brother, who will be sending us obligatory boxes of Swiss chocolate from the foot of the Matterhorn for the next who knows how many years." Jane's smile wavered as she met Ryan's gaze. "I miss you already," she said softly, then lifted her glass higher to keep herself from tearing up.

Dinner was relatively quiet save for the music that filtered in from the living room, a hush that Jane was satisfied with as she watched everyone eat. There was an occasional quip between the boys, a random joke and easy laughter to accompany the quiet jingle of forks against porcelain plates. Afterward, Lauren helped clear the table while Jane replaced the dinner plates with smaller ones, the three-layer chocolate cake making its appearance on a footed glass stand. Sawyer rubbed his hands together childishly when Jane placed the cake between both boys. She caught April rolling her eyes at her boyfriend's antics, but only smiled when she caught April's gaze.

They drank coffee and stuffed themselves with sugar, talking about old times—about how the boys used to sled down the driveway when they were kids, nearly knocking their teeth out because the slope was too steep and Jane and Ryan's dad would leave the Land Rover parked at the base of the hill.

"I'm just glad the road was clear," Sawyer mused, a bite of cake balanced on the tines of his fork. "Walking up that slope, especially when it's covered in snow…"

"It's a killer," Ryan agreed.

"You should install a lift," Lauren suggested. Ryan leaned back in his chair and raised his hands, his eyes on his sister.

"Have I not been saying that for years?"

"He has," Jane confessed with a laugh. "But it's too late now, I guess."

"Now you'll be installing a lift in front of your Swiss chateau?" Lauren asked.

"If there isn't already one there."

"There won't be one in Zurich," Jane told him.

"But there will be in Zermatt. Nothing but snow and cheese fondue."

"You're going to gain a thousand pounds."

"I think he'll be okay," Sawyer cut in, lifting another bite of cake. "If he hasn't gained a thousand pounds living with you for the past thirty years, a little cheese isn't going to hurt."

"What's it like?" Lauren asked, leaning in on her elbows. "Switzerland, I mean."

"You've seen *The Sound of Music*?" Ryan asked, and Lauren nodded. "It's like that, but multiplied by ten."

"Raindrops on roses?" Sawyer asked.

"And whiskers on kittens…" Jane jumped in.

"Bright copper kettles?" Lauren singsonged.

"And warm woolen mittens," they all finished together, laughing as April watched in silence, a smile pulled tight across her mouth.

"Don't tell me you haven't seen it," Ryan said, his comment directed at the quiet one of the group. "'Sixteen going on seventeen'?" he asked. "'How do you solve a problem like Maria'?"

"Who's Maria?" April asked, countering Ryan's faux shock with a confession. "I don't like musicals. They give me the creeps."

"She won't even watch *Rocky Horror*," Sawyer told them.

"You know, we used to call Sawyer Frank N. Furter back in high school," Ryan told her. "He had a fishnet and lipstick phase."

Jane couldn't help the laugh that burst from her throat, covering her mouth a second later. Sawyer slouched in his seat, looking a little embarrassed but far from annoyed.

"You caught so much hell." Ryan chuckled, shaking his head at his best friend. "You remember Coach Miller?"

"Oh *god*," Sawyer muttered. "I haven't thought of that guy since we graduated."

"What was with Coach Miller?" April asked, finally deciding to join the conversation.

"Coach Miller was our biology teacher, but he wasn't qualified," Jane explained. "They just stuck him there because there wasn't anyone else to teach it."

"So Sawyer walks into bio one on the first day of freshman year," Ryan began, "his face full of makeup, his hair pulled up into a six-inch Mohawk—"

"That I had to iron to get to stand up straight, might I add—" Sawyer noted.

"And Coach Miller looks up from his desk like he's just seen a goddamn nightmare. He looks straight at Sawyer and he goes…" Ryan squared his shoulders and squinted his eyes, scrunching up his face in an attempt to look seriously perturbed. "'Son, what in the Sam Hill is wrong with your face?' And Sawyer says…"

"'I'm ugly, sir?'" Sawyer replied, a nostalgic grin pulled across his face.

"And *that* is why you should watch *Rocky Horror*," Ryan concluded. "Because Sawyer used to be a sweet transvestite."

April forced a smile, then covered her mouth, hiding a yawn. Jane looked down to her plate, a pang of irritation scratching at her heart. April wasn't even *trying*. She wanted to ask her why she had even bothered to come at all. But she swallowed her annoyance and offered the table a conclusive nod.

"That's our cue," she said. "We should get to bed if we're getting up early tomorrow."

"Six o'clock sharp," Ryan clarified, only to be met with a communal groan. "What?" he asked. "It takes an hour to get up there, not to mention packing up, eating breakfast..."

"Chocolate cake," Lauren mused, sliding her finger across the bottom of the cake plate to scoop up a bit of frosting. "The breakfast of champions."

Jane plucked the cake off the table, more than half of it still up for grabs, and Lauren picked up their dirty plates and icing-smeared forks, walking them over to the sink as the rest of the group stretched and rose from their seats.

"I should take a shower," Lauren said. "Or I'll have to get up even earlier, and you know me and mornings."

Jane nodded. "Go ahead," she said. "I'll finish up here."

"Are you sure?" Lauren asked, making a face at the stack of dishes on the counter.

"I'm just going to run the dishwasher. I'll meet you up there."

Lauren was the first to disappear down the hall, followed a moment later by April and Sawyer. Jane watched them for a long while, her heart twisting around a seed of jealousy.

"Hey," Ryan said, snapping her out of her daze. "You okay?"

She turned to the sink and nodded sternly. "Fine," she said. "Just tired."

He leaned in, pressing a kiss to her temple. "Thanks for dinner," he said. "You're tops, Janey. Just swell!"

Jane smirked and smacked him with a dish towel as he turned to join the others upstairs. "Idiot," she murmured, turning on the tap.

After running the dishes beneath a stream of hot water, Jane arranged them in the dishwasher, occasionally glancing up at her own reflection in the window above the sink. She wondered what Sawyer saw in that girl. Maybe Jane was just being harsh—maybe April was great; she was just uncomfortable around so many new people. But the way she had sat at the table while they all laughed, stone-faced, like she couldn't have been bothered to even try to be part of their group…it made Jane angry. It was as though April had come up to the cabin with Sawyer only to ruin his good time—their *last* time at their childhood haunt, at a place they'd never see again.

Jane squeezed her eyes shut, feeling the burn of tears at the backs of her eyes. Everything was different. Ryan was leaving. She and Sawyer felt like strangers. The house already felt like a memory. And then there was that girl, screwing it all up.

With a dinner plate in hand, she paused at what sounded like thumping on the deck. She knitted her eyebrows together, listening for it again, and there it was—a muffled shuffling against the wooden planks, like Oona wandering around just beyond the kitchen door.

"I swear to god," she said beneath her breath, sliding the plate into the machine before snatching the dish towel off the counter and wiping her hands. She had warned Ryan over a dozen times that bringing Oona with them was more trouble than it was worth. Lots of guests meant lots of distractions, and this was the proof: Ryan had let her out, only to forget her again. Lucky for Oona that Jane was still downstairs, or that dog would have been frozen through come morning.

Squinting against her own reflection, she tried to see through the glare of the window. Sidestepping the sink, she cupped her hands against the glass of the door and peered outside, looking for the husky. She flipped on the outdoor light, spotting a shadow just beyond the corner of the house. Unlocking the kitchen door, Jane stuck her head out into the cold.

"Oona?"

She puckered her lips to whistle, but all that came out was a squeaky breath of air. She couldn't snap her fingers either. These were talents that hadn't been bestowed upon her, no matter how hard Ryan had tried to teach her when they were kids, and up until now Jane couldn't have cared less. Exhaling a sigh, she hissed the words into the cold.

"Oona, come!"

But she received no reply. The shadow loomed, seemingly alert but not responding. Shaking her head, she shut the door and went back to the sink. If Oona wanted to come back inside, she'd show her furry face before Jane was done with the dishes. If not, she'd have to tell Ryan to go outside in his pajamas and catch pneumonia, which she supposed served him right. She ran the water again, not wanting to do dishes at dawn. But as soon as she started clanging plates together the scuttling out on the deck returned.

"Not this time," she said to herself, choosing to ignore it, scraping a bit of leftover food off a plate before hitting a switch next to the sink. The garbage disposal roared to life, chewing up bits of meat and vegetables. She killed it and looked back up to the window, only to have her heart launch into her throat.

Sawyer stood behind her, having sneaked up on her without knowing it.

"Shit, sorry." He winced at his own reflection in the glass.

Jane closed her eyes, trying to regain her composure. The jolt of surprise sizzled in her blood before subsiding, immediately replaced with an unidentifiable warmth when Sawyer reached for a dirty plate, nudging her out of the way.

She kept her hips flush with the counter, not daring to face him, her bottom lip between her teeth.

"What're you doing?" she finally asked, casting a sidelong glance at him.

He glanced at her through a veil of wavy hair a few inches shy of his shoulders.

"Dishes," he told her, sticking a plate beneath the stream of the faucet.

A flare of hope ignited deep within Jane's chest. Was Sawyer choosing *dishes* over going to bed with the nymph upstairs?

The water caught the plate's beveled edge and sprayed sideways, soaking the hem of Sawyer's Stabbing Westward T-shirt—washed-out black cotton immediately turning as dark as the sky beyond the window. He grumbled and slid the plate into the machine before pressing a dish towel to his shirt.

Jane's heart thumped in her ears. She stepped away from the sink and moved to the table, gathering up used napkins and place mats, desperate to keep her hands busy and her eyes averted. She didn't want to be alone with him. It made her want to say things, to ask questions, to slide back into his arms and forget the last ten years.

The hiss of the sink eventually gave way to the sound of the bottom rack sliding into place. The dishwasher door snapped closed and she cringed at the sudden silence, afraid to turn around. She stood at the head of the table, her eyes downcast, her fingers nervously folding napkins that needed washing.

"I heard about what happened," Sawyer said from the sink. "With you and Alex."

She squeezed her eyes shut, forced a reply. "Yeah?"

A moment of silence, then: "He's an idiot."

She clenched her jaw, not sure what the hell he expected her to say.

"Either way, I'm sorry. I was going to call, but, you know…"

"Yeah," she said, pulling at the edge of a napkin. "I know."

"At least it happened when it did, right?"

Jane said nothing.

"Shit, that came out wrong. I'm just saying that—"

"Yeah," Jane cut in. "I get it. No kids, no big deal." She frowned at the edge in her voice. "Thanks, Tom," she said, trying to soften her tone.

She heard Sawyer pull in a breath behind her, imagined him standing there with the sink to his back, the heels of his hands resting against the edge of the counter, studying the tips of his combat boots. "Listen," he said after a long pause. "I feel like an asshole. Losing touch…" He hesitated. "It's my fault, I know that. I should have fixed it."

"Why didn't you?"

"Come on, Janey."

She sighed, crumpling the napkin up in her hand, slowly turning so that she could see him. He stood just the way she had imagined, his head bowed, his legs crossed at the ankles.

"I was out in Boston; you started teaching; then you got married." He looked up at her. "Still are, right? What was I supposed to do?"

She felt numb.

"You could have at least come to the wedding," she said softly.

"So you could have had a severely uncomfortable guy sitting alone at a table during the reception?"

He was right. Inviting Sawyer to the wedding had been a strange thing to do. She'd never admit that after dropping his invitation in the mail, she'd hoped he'd show up, if only to answer the pastor's call: "Speak now or forever hold your peace."

"Well, you could have at least RSVP'd," she whispered.

"I know. I'm sorry."

"I kept wondering if you had just forgotten."

He held his silence.

"I left a spare seat open at the head table." It was a secret she had sworn she'd never confess. "I was worried that you'd come and you wouldn't have anywhere to sit."

"Jesus." The word came out upon a breath. "Ryan didn't tell me..."

"I asked him not to."

"It was your day," he said. "I didn't want to screw things up."

She dared to look up at him then, chewing her bottom lip before diverting her eyes again. "Your hair's gotten long," she told him, her gaze focused on the floor. "It looks good; like a proper musician."

It was the reason he had left for Boston: to become a sound engineer, to rub elbows with his favorite artists and make them sound more amazing than they really did. She couldn't imagine what was going through April's mind, Sawyer's closest friend looking like he'd stepped out of an Abercrombie & Fitch catalog rather than a rock club. She wondered how weird it was for April to realize her edgy boyfriend hung out with a bunch of trendy yuppies who—

Without warning, Sawyer pushed away from the counter and breached the distance between them. He reached out, took Jane's head in his hands, his palms pressing against her cheeks. Her heart stopped as she felt his breath drift across the curve of her bottom lip. She let her eyes flutter shut, not wanting to see what was coming. When he pressed a kiss to the top of her head, a tiny voice inside her head cried out, screaming that he wasn't fooling anyone, that they both knew what they wanted. Maybe if they just gave in...

"Good night," he whispered. He turned away from her and grabbed a can of Coke out of the fridge. She opened her mouth to speak as he lingered there, the cold refrigerator light casting a halo around his frame, but couldn't find the words. He glanced back at her as if about to say something more, but he silently left the kitchen instead.

The moment he was out of sight, Jane slid into Ryan's chair, the drumming of her heart threatening to choke her. Maybe she was wrong. Maybe Sawyer didn't want more. He had April, and April was beautiful. He had moved on, while she continued to cling to the past.

"Shit," she whispered, pressing her fingertips against her eyelids, fighting the sting of tears. She was pathetic. Weak. She had sworn up and down that she was ready for this, but she wasn't. She had insisted that everything would be fine, but nothing was.

Oona padded across the kitchen and nudged Jane's elbow with her nose. Instinctively, Jane scratched behind the dog's ears before getting up, flipping off the kitchen lights, and moving down the hall, the husky at her heels.

It was only after she was halfway up the stairs that she realized it hadn't been Oona she'd heard outside.

"I'm in love." Despite her wet hair, Lauren was already in bed when Jane came into the master bedroom, the covers tucked beneath her arms, a *Vogue* magazine she'd found in the bathroom opened to a Chanel ad. "I just thought it fair to tell you now rather than springing it on you later, when I'm knee-deep in wedding planning and packing my bags for Switzerland."

Jane shook her head as she closed the door behind her, and Lauren's smile faded when she saw Jane's shoulders slump.

"What?" she asked. "Why were you down there so long? What happened?" She sat up, tossing the magazine aside. "Did that chick go back downstairs, looking all frou-frou French even though she's totally not? Did you see her all quiet and demure at dinner, like she was too good to participate in the conversation? What the hell was that all about?"

Jane pushed her fingers through her hair.

"So?" Lauren pressed. "What happened?"

"Nothing. I'm just tired."

Lauren frowned. "Why do you do that?"

"Do what?"

"Pretend like nothing's wrong? It's okay, Janey; the world won't crumble if you show some weakness."

Jane sighed and moved across the room to her bag, crouching beside it before fishing through her things.

"Do you want to go home?" It was the right thing to ask—the best-friend thing to ask. Lauren was sure Ryan would understand, confident that if he knew Jane was having a hard time he'd pack them up and drive back to Phoenix at first light. She saw the way they were with each other, amazed that a pair of siblings could be as in sync as they were. It made her jealous. She could never be like that with Kevin. She'd hardly spoken to her older brother, or any of her crazy family, in over a year. They were all two-faced, dramatic, needy. But Jane and Ryan both had this one perfect person they could tell everything to. They probably didn't even have to speak for one to know what the other was thinking.

"No," Jane said from the floor, tossing a pair of pajama pants onto the carpet beside her. Lauren said nothing as she watched her friend slip into thoughtfulness, Jane's eyes fixed upon the floor, her short hair framing her face. Feeling the sadness waft off her friend like waves of heat, Lauren crawled across the bed to get closer. She hadn't seen Jane like this before.

"Janey..."

"I could stay here forever," Jane confessed. "Isn't that sad?" When she looked up, Lauren offered her a faint smile.

"Sawyer isn't what I expected," Lauren said.

"He isn't what anyone ever expects."

"There's definitely something about him," Lauren agreed. "Mystery."

"Grace," Jane said softly. "He doesn't walk; he floats. His feet don't touch the ground."

"Well, he's obviously human," Lauren assured her. "Look at the girl he picked to be with. There's something wrong with him for sure."

"Maybe." Jane shrugged.

"Oh, come on, Jane. Stop being so fair all the time. She sucks. You can hate her."

"I don't want to hate her. I want him to be happy."

"And what about you?" Lauren asked. "Don't *you* count?"

Jane frowned at that and Lauren sighed. She pushed the blankets away from herself, crawled across the bed, and slid onto the floor next to her friend.

"Why don't you just tell him?"

"I can't," Jane said. "It wouldn't be right."

"Except that you invited him to your wedding because you wanted him to crash it," Lauren reminded her. "You probably shouldn't have ever married Alex at all."

Jane opened her mouth to protest, but Lauren shook her head, refusing to let her talk her way out of it.

"Who does that, Janey? Who invites a guy to her wedding with the sole hope of that guy sweeping her away from the altar? It's insane. It's always *been* insane, and maybe that's why it didn't work with Alex. I know you loved him, and he's a bastard for cheating on you—I hope that asshole burns in hell—but have you ever stopped to think that maybe all of this fell apart because it wasn't meant to be in the first place? Have you ever stopped to think that maybe you should screw all this fairness and finally tell Sawyer how you feel?"

Jane shook her head, her bottom lip trembling.

"Why?" Lauren demanded. "Because it'll put him in an awkward position?"

Jane covered her face with her hands.

"And what if he's in the same boat?" Lauren asked. "What if he's just as tortured as you? What if all he wants is to be with you again?"

"Then why would he come here with his stupid girlfriend?" Jane spit out.

"Because he's a guy," Lauren said flatly. "And guys are morons."

They both went silent for a moment, and eventually Jane pulled in a steadying breath and looked up at Lauren. "You really like him?" she asked softly.

"Sure," Lauren said. "I mean, I don't really know him very well, but—"

"No," Jane cut in. "I mean Ryan."

Lauren diverted her eyes to the carpet as she tucked a strand of damp hair behind an ear, a bashful smile coiling across her mouth.

"He likes you too," Jane said softly. "I can tell."

"Really?"

She nodded. "You're not afraid of him. Most girls are."

"What's there to be afraid of?"

"He's aggressive, determined," Jane listed off. "He stole my share of ambition; that's what our dad used to say."

"How sweet of him."

"It's true." Jane shrugged. "You can't argue with facts."

"You also can't argue that your dad has a way with words," Lauren scoffed.

Crumpling her pajamas in her hand, Jane got to her feet and moved to the bathroom.

Lauren listened to the sound of an electric toothbrush. "You still haven't answered my question," she said after the water shut off, staring down at her hands, wondering how much aspiration was too much to bear. She knew about Ryan's inability to keep a relationship, and maybe that was his problem—his inextinguishable drive, his determination to be something bigger than himself. Maybe that resolve eclipsed everyone around him, dooming him to a life of solitude despite his smile, despite his undeniable appeal. "You were down there a lot longer than it takes to stick dishes in the washer, and I know that look."

Jane stepped out of the bathroom, tossing her clothes onto the floor next to her bag before crawling into bed. Lauren slid back onto the mattress as well, fluffing her pillow before sticking her legs beneath the sheets.

"If you know that look, then you shouldn't be asking," Jane told her.

"Did he stay down there with you?"

Pressing her lips together in a tight line, Jane offered Lauren a hesitant smile.

"Seriously?" Lauren asked. Jane slid beneath the comforter and grabbed the *Vogue* from the center of the bed. "What did he say?"

"Nothing."

Lauren snatched the magazine from her grasp, and Jane chuckled at her insistence.

"Don't be an ass," Lauren told her. "Spill it."

Jane lifted her shoulders in a faint shrug. "How about this; I won't ask you what Ryan said when you both end up behind a tree."

Lauren rolled her eyes, but Jane didn't give in. She pulled the sheets up to her chin and shut her eyes against the light. Lauren tossed the magazine onto the floor and followed suit after clicking off the lamp next to the bed.

They lay in the darkness together for a long while, the wood crackling in the fireplace, the flames casting weird shadows across the walls. Eventually, Jane's voice whispered through the shadows.

"We have the same problem."

And for a while Lauren couldn't put together what Jane meant—not until she remembered what she had said the second Jane had stepped into the room.

I'm in love.

Except that Lauren had mostly been joking, and Jane was heartbreakingly sincere.

"It's interesting," April said, pulling one of Sawyer's old T-shirts over her head. "I expected them to be...I don't know, more..." She hesitated, searching for the right words.

"Like us?" Sawyer asked, sliding the can of Coke onto a side table.

April shrugged her shoulders. Stepping over to the window, she parted the slats of the blinds to look outside—nothing but night.

"I guess," she said after a moment, tossing a look at him over her shoulder. He was throwing cushions onto the floor, their bed a foldout couch that would have her hunchbacked and sore by morning. She had been irked when Ryan had led them to the farthest room down the hall, away from everyone else, parking them in a room that was more a makeshift library than it was meant for guests, but she'd held her tongue. She hadn't mentioned that it seemed like they were being quarantined from the rest of the group, doubting that if Sawyer had come alone he'd have been stationed so far from everyone else. Sawyer hadn't mentioned their room assignment either, and April wondered if he simply hadn't noticed or was keeping quiet like she was.

"It just seems like something you would have told me," she said, stepping across the room to grab the can of soda while Sawyer unfolded the bed, the stiff metal springs creaking in the quiet of the room. She cracked the can open and turned away from him, her gaze scanning the spines of hardback books squeezed tight onto a shelf. They were all classics—Austen and Brontë and Sir Walter Scott. Her fingers drifted across Stoker's *Dracula*, one of the few she'd read. All those books made her feel small, uneducated, but they also made her inwardly grimace at how ostentatious they were. Not a trace of King and Koontz, of books people actually read and enjoyed.

"Does it?" Sawyer asked, stepping away from the couch as if to assess his morning back pain. April frowned as she tugged down on the hem of her shirt, her bare legs growing cold.

"Don't get mad about it," she said. "I'm just making an observation."

"Did I say I was mad about it?" he asked, tossing a folded sheet onto the bed. April took a sip of soda before grabbing the end closest to her, sliding an elastic hem over one of the mattress corners.

"You don't have to say it," she told him. "It's kind of obvious."

"What?" Sawyer straightened, pushing his fingers through his hair. "That I'm upset they aren't like *us*?"

She didn't like the emphasis he put onto that last word. It made it sound like there was no *us* at all.

"Why are you so touchy?" she asked. Jane had left a folded comforter on the chair in the corner of the room. April grabbed it, tossing it at Sawyer with a scowl. "You're acting completely weird."

Sawyer shook his head. "Sorry, it just bothers me."

"What does?"

"The whole 'they aren't like us' thing. I hate it."

April stepped around the bed as he straightened the comforter, stopping when she was chest to chest with him. She gave him an apologetic smile before sweeping a strand of his hair behind an ear.

"I'm sorry," she mewed, tugging on the neckline of his shirt. "I like your friends."

It was a bald-faced lie. These were the kind of people who made going to school a living hell for her. Ryan all but made her skin crawl with how much he reminded her of the jocks, the preps, the guys who twisted their faces up in judgment as the girl in the combat boots and ankle-length duster tried to make her way to class. Lauren had most certainly been on the volleyball team; probably dated the quarterback and wore the homecoming crown. And Jane...she was the one who piqued April's curiosity. There was something about her—a shadow of something that April was picking up on but couldn't place.

"Let's just go to bed," Sawyer suggested.

April nodded, allowing her hand to trail down his chest before grabbing the soda he'd brought upstairs for her and turning away. She frowned as soon as he couldn't see her face. She'd always been a bad liar. If she had been better at it she would have laughed it up at the dinner table with the rest of them, convinced them all that, oh *yeah*, *The Sound of Music* was her favorite, that she'd grown up watching *Mary Poppins* and *Oklahoma!* and whatever other ridiculous musicals she could think of on the spot. She would have convinced Sawyer that she *did* like his friends when, in fact, she would have been happy driving back to Denver in the dead of night.

"Ape."

She crawled onto the bed, waiting for him to say what he was going to say. But Sawyer shook his head after a while, dismissing whatever had been on the tip of his tongue.

"I still say you're acting weird," she said.

This time Sawyer didn't dissuade her uneasiness. He held fast to his silence instead.

Exhaling a sigh, she pulled the covers over herself and closed her eyes. He had been right to discourage her; she shouldn't have come, but she didn't like being alone and had figured, hell, if she had already met his parents she might as well meet his friends too.

Sawyer fell asleep almost immediately while April tossed and turned. At first she blamed it on the mattress, but after half an hour of lying in the dark, she realized that it wasn't the bed; it was the noise outside. She was a light sleeper, and even the faintest of sounds could keep her awake all night or rouse her from sleep. This was an odd moaning noise; a deep, throaty, repetitive groan accompanied by scratching, like something skittering across the porch one story below. Nearly convincing herself to get up to peer out the window, she decided against it. She was warm under the covers, and she wouldn't be able to see anything anyway. If Ryan wanted to leave his dog outside in the cold, that was his problem. It would have been nice if the guy had an ounce of courtesy and realized the husky was probably keeping people up, but what was she supposed to do, march down the hall and demand Ryan let Oona in? Rolling over, she pulled the comforter over her head with a rough sigh and squeezed her eyes shut, one ear against the pillow, her palm pressed over the other to block out the sound.

CHAPTER FOUR

The sun rose over the hills to reveal new beauty. It had snowed overnight—the lightest dusting, like powdered sugar. The trees sparkled, flocked with a fresh blanket of white, glittering as the sun burned away the early morning haze.

Despite Ryan's best efforts to keep the group on track, they were late piling into the car, but they were cheerful and warm, bundled up in their gear while the Nissan rolled down the slope of the drive. Jane gazed out the passenger window, oddly quiet; Sawyer sat in the middle of the backseat like a sultan, a girl on each arm. After half an hour of highway, the Nissan coiled up a series of twists and turns, ascending a mountain that only got more gorgeous—leafless aspens shining in the crisp morning air, as though their branches had been dipped in silver. The clouds that had been thousands of feet overhead were suddenly nothing but a fog slithering around the bases of tree trunks, whispering across a glistening onyx tarmac. The ebb of downtempo music offered the perfect sound track, lulling Ryan into Zen-like contentment. By the time they reached the ski resort's parking area he felt renewed, ready to embrace the day despite the early hour.

Ryan climbed onto the Nissan's running board and unstrapped the boards from the roof rack while Jane and Lauren shoved thickly socked feet into their boots, awkwardly waddling around the car after their ankles had been secured. Sawyer concentrated on his iPod, shuffling through playlists, making sure he was ready to go—because when it came to Sawyer, music was key; everything else came second. April sat in the backseat, her legs sticking out of the Xterra, her shoulders pulled up to her ears against the chill. She looked uncomfortable as she watched everyone busy themselves around her.

When Sawyer had admitted that April hadn't boarded before, Ryan had been pessimistic. It was hard to tell with novices—they either took to it like a duck to water or had a miserable time. Jane had been in the latter group, having spent two days on her ass, overcome by a few fits of frustration that had reduced her to tears. Ryan had stuck with her, spending days on the bunny hill with his sister. He eventually got her on her feet, but it had taken a lot of time, a lot of patience, and, on Jane's part, a lot of pain. He wasn't sure how it was going to work with April: whether she was the type of girl who would stick it out because it was something she really wanted to do, or whether she'd throw her hands up and admit defeat after a handful of falls. After a few minutes the group left the car, the four of them stiffly marching toward the lift ticket windows while April trailed behind.

The closer they got to the ticket counter, the less April wanted to go through with it. There was a ski lift to the right of them—a four-at-a-time monster that whipped around the curve at a speed that seemed impossible; yet people were falling into the chairs, unscathed, laughing as though they were having the times of their lives. Up ahead, a girl in a pink jacket caught the edge of her board on the snow. April winced as the girl flew onto her stomach with a squeal, her hat popping off her head and landing a good three feet ahead of her. For a second April was sure the girl wasn't going to get up, but she did, giggling madly as a couple of skiers helped her to her feet.

She tugged at one of Sawyer's many jacket zippers, chewing her bottom lip as they continued to walk forward. Ryan was leading the pack, a good ten paces ahead of everyone, probably trying to make up for lost time.

"I don't know if this is such a good idea," she whispered.

Sawyer shook his head and pulled the bud out of his ear.

"This," she said, waving a hand at the lift. "Me."

"What?"

"I don't know if this is such a good idea," she repeated. "You know..." She gave him a look, willing him to understand without making her explain.

Sawyer slowed his steps, allowing distance to grow between them and the rest of the group.

"Really?" he asked, jabbing a finger under his thickly woven hat, scratching an itch. It matched the scarf that April had noosed around her own neck—a set she had knitted when they had first gotten together. He looked like a rock star with those giant sunglasses glued to his face, sure to turn heads all day. She looked away from him, tired of staring at her own reflection in the black lenses of his shades.

"I'll just sit in the lodge." She gazed toward a massive A-frame, outdoor tables dotting its redwood deck, multicolored umbrellas decorating the majesty of an otherwise white and green landscape.

"All day?" Sawyer asked. "Ape, you're going to be bored out of your mind."

"I don't care," she told him, growing more insistent by the second. "I don't want to do this. I know I said I did..."

"You said you did."

"I *know*."

Sawyer slid his glasses down his nose enough to look at her. She caught a glimpse of his chocolate-colored eyes, immediately knowing that look. He was trying not to be annoyed, but she was cramping his style.

"Don't worry about me," she insisted. "I'm sure they have magazines or something." She nodded, reassuring him that her decision was firm. There was no way in hell she was getting on that lift, especially with some slippery board strapped to her feet. There was no way she was going up to the top of that mountain—a mountain that, she was sure, would be the death of her. She hated sports, having no idea what had possessed her to think this was a good idea in the first place, that snowboarding would be any different. A couple of kids on skis buzzed past them. April squeezed her eyes shut, unnerved.

"It probably isn't safe anyway," she said, but it wasn't what she had told him earlier. It had been the first argument Sawyer had made. But she had lied, had told him that she had checked with her doctor, that she'd be okay. Sawyer had wanted to come up here on his own, had offered to drop her off in Colorado Springs to see her grandparents—she had complained that she hadn't seen them in so long—and yet, for some reason, she couldn't bring herself to let him take this trip alone. And upon seeing Jane, she was glad that she'd fought him, because there was something there, something she didn't trust. But despite her wariness, she couldn't strap her feet onto a board in the name of espionage. "Just go," she said. "Have a good time."

Sawyer sighed, pulling the glove off his right hand before unzipping his jacket pocket and fishing out his wallet. "Here." He pulled out a couple of twenties, folded them in half, and tucked them into the palm of her hand. "We'll come back for lunch."

"I'm sorry," she murmured.

"It's okay," he said softly, hiding behind his glasses. He was trying to be understanding, but she could tell he was upset. "The rental line is probably massive anyway." April didn't have gear of her own. She gave him a guilty smile.

"Hey!" Ryan waved at them from yards away. "What's the holdup?"

She and Sawyer exchanged a glance before he smiled in return.

"See you later," he said, then readjusted his board against his shoulder. She took a step toward him to give him a parting kiss, but he didn't notice, too distracted by his friends.

April looked down at the money in her hand, chewed her bottom lip, then tucked the bills into her jacket pocket. When she looked up, Jane and Lauren were looking her way. Feeling her face grow hot, she looked away from them and turned toward the lodge.

They fell backward as the chair swept them off the ground and into the air, three boards pointing right while one pointed left. Ryan shifted his weight, an arm wound around the pole on the far left side of the lift, the weight of his board pulling heavy on his boot.

"I feel bad," Jane admitted, her shoulder flush with Ryan's as they continued to ascend.

"Don't," Sawyer told her. "It's her choice."

"Maybe she'll change her mind," Lauren countered. "After lunch or something."

"Yeah, maybe," Sawyer mused.

"It's better," Ryan confessed. It had been the one thing that had bothered him since Sawyer had mentioned April tagging along—the one thing beyond April tagging along at all. Someone was going to have to spend an entire day on the bunny hill with her if she did change her mind, and that hadn't been the point of this trip. With the beginner's hill directly beneath them now, they bore witness to dozens of people lying in the snow like the dead, boards strapped to their feet, unmoving, probably wondering what bone they'd just broken during their most recent fall. "You'd be down there, otherwise," he said.

Jane nudged him to shut him up, but Sawyer was smirking at the bodies fifty feet beneath them.

"What, you don't like the bunny hill?" he asked.

"No, man, I *love* it," Ryan said, "especially at thirty-five miles per hour."

"I'm not going on any black diamonds," Jane said. "So just forget it."

"You can stay on the greens with your pal," Ryan teased.

Lauren laughed dryly at the far end of the lift.

"What?" He leaned forward against the rail, shooting a look across the chair to the blonde at the far end. "Is that a challenge I hear?"

Lauren grinned, shrugging beneath the thick padding of her coat.

Ryan leaned back, peering at his sister.

"What'd you do?" he asked, "Invite a professional?"

"Don't do it," Sawyer warned. "Challenging Adler in boarding is like challenging a shark to a..." He paused, thinking. "A surfing competition."

"And how would a shark stay on a surfboard, exactly?" Jane asked, amused.

"By his fins," Sawyer said. "Naturally. Moral of the story: don't challenge a shark. Ever."

"Ever?" Lauren asked.

"Oh my god." Ryan let his head loll back, looking up to the sky. "It's on."

"It's on?" Lauren asked him. It was her turn to lean forward, a wry grin spread across her mouth.

"It's on."

"Are you sure?"

"This should be fun," Sawyer said.

"There's a little something you don't know about me," Lauren confessed, swinging her board beneath her with a wide, innocent smile.

Ryan raised an eyebrow at her. "A secret?"

"It's about to be revealed," she said, lifting a gloved fist before bursting her fingers forth—a magic trick guaranteed to blow his mind.

Ryan leaned back, the bunny hill giving way to a thousand trees beneath their feet. Jane leaned against him, and out of the corner of his eye he could see her smiling.

"Was this a setup?" he asked under his breath, the cold burning his cheeks.

"Like *you* need a setup," Jane told him, her temple nestled against his shoulder.

"And that would stop you?"

Jane bit back a smile, eventually replying to his question, "Not a chance."

Jane sat wide-eyed in the powder as Lauren sailed down the hill, tailing Ryan like a champ. Lauren had mentioned that she had boarded before, but she never said that she could keep up with the best of them. Before Jane was able to snap her left foot into her binding they were gone, leaving her and Sawyer in their snow spray.

She watched them until they were mere blips on the hill, then glanced over to Sawyer. He was lying against the snow like a fallen angel, his arms stretched out, looking like he was trying to get a tan.

"How long has it been since you've done this?" she asked.

Sawyer lifted his head to look at her, his chin pressed to his chest.

"Three seasons," he told her. "I'm going to eat it." He grinned up at the sun, and for a moment she considered just sitting there with him—the two of them in a single spot all morning, enjoying the view, relishing the company. But that would have been desperate and obvious: two things Jane Adler wouldn't allow herself to be.

She smiled, adjusted her hat, and rocked onto her toes.

"Later, alligator." She offered him a salute.

He was up on his board before she could gain ten feet on him. She was still trying to get her bearings when something snagged her jacket and pulled her backward. Sawyer missiled past her, only to throw her off balance, Jane's arms shooting out behind her; she winced when she connected with the ground, but she was laughing a second later. She couldn't help it, because just ahead of her, Sawyer flew forward, rolling down the mountain before skidding to a stop with an audible yelp.

Sitting outside the lodge beneath a multicolored umbrella, April spotted Ryan and Lauren first. They slowed at the bottom of the hill, each of them bending down to unstrap one leg, then sliding back in the line that would take them up the mountain again. April couldn't help but crack a smile as they pushed each other around. Their obvious flirtation raised her spirits. They laughed a bit too loudly as they waited in line, standing a bit too close together, Lauren pestering him by tugging at his zippers, Ryan reciprocating by pulling her hat off her head.

She spotted Sawyer and Jane fifteen minutes later, both of them looking significantly more unbalanced than their counterparts. They were laughing as well. Jane slapped snow off the back of his coat as Sawyer slid farther ahead. She lagged behind, fumbling with the strap that kept her foot in place, pushing off the snow to catch up to him. She reached for him with both hands, and he offered her one of his arms, then pushed off to propel them both.

Something twisted within April's chest. She waited for Sawyer to glance in her direction, to at least check to see that she was there, to make sure she was okay. Her prayers were answered when he craned his neck toward the lodge while standing in line, lifting a hand to wave at her after spotting her on the porch. April forced a smile, lifting a hand in return, but being acknowledged didn't soothe the burn of jealousy.

She pictured herself getting up, bolting down the lodge steps and across the snow. She was sure she could make it before they got on the lift again, and when she'd reach them, she'd shove Jane hard enough to make her hit the ground. Chewing on a nail, she hunched her shoulders and glared at Sawyer's back. A pair of neon-clad skiers sat at the table next to her, their cups of coffee steaming like a pair of smokestacks.

"They only found him because someone out there reported seeing a bunch of wolves," said one of the men, his ski jacket a painful lime green. "And then yesterday, there was some kind of incident."

The second skier took a careful sip of coffee. "Up here?"

The first guy nodded, blowing across the top of his drink, the horizontal line of steam wafting away from him, sending that heavenly aroma in April's direction. "Just shy of the Ridge Runner. Looks like someone decided to take a detour."

The second skier made a face like he'd just tasted something foul. "Stupid."

"Yeah, no shit. Probably a couple of dumb kids. It's all closed off if you go up there."

"They found a body?"

April furrowed her eyebrows.

Neon guy shrugged. "Like they'll tell you that, right? Though I kind of doubt it. Seems like they'd have to shut down the entire run, if not the entire mountain."

"So how do you know it was wolves? They could have just hit a tree, right?"

The first guy lifted his paper cup of coffee as if toasting the lift at the base of the hill. "See that guy working the chair?" April tried to be casual as she glanced toward the lift. Jane and Sawyer were still in line. "He's got a mouth on him. Mentioned that the ski patrol found blood. A lot of it."

"Shit," the second skier responded. "But someone would have heard."

"Not if it was after hours, and you know how these guys go up at the last minute."

Skier One frowned, shaking his head. "Lesson learned..."

April cleared her throat softly and rose from the table, suddenly uncomfortable. What if there *were* wolves? What if Sawyer decided to be an idiot and go off-trail like those other people had? She stepped inside the lodge, considering waiting at the base of the lift to warn the group of possible danger. But that would just make her look like an ass, like she was looking for excuses to ruin their good time. She frowned as she approached a long line inside, the noise inside the lodge nearly deafening with how crowded it was. She needed to soothe her nerves, and an overpriced cup of hot cocoa sounded good.

By the time she finally got her drink she had decided that no, she wouldn't say anything about what she'd heard. They only had two more days up here after this one, and she was determined to suck it up and be a good sport for Sawyer's sake. She knew the cabin was for sale, was well aware that Ryan was moving to Europe to be some fancy slope reviewer. For all she knew, she'd never see Ryan Adler again. And despite feeling bad for Sawyer losing touch with a friend, she couldn't help but feel a little satisfied. They were about to start a new life together, and she didn't need the poster boy of perfection hanging around and screwing it up.

It had become unbearably cold during their last hour on the slopes. The clear blue sky that had warmed the hills throughout most of the day had become overcast, clouds rolling across the crest of the mountain, settling over the resort, and blanketing it in frigid shadow.

"Just one more time," Ryan pleaded. "It'll be quick, I swear."

Lauren cast a glance at her friend while Jane stood next to her, her teeth chattering, her gloved hands pressed firmly over her hat-covered ears. "I feel like I'm dying," Jane whined. "*Please*, let's just go to the car, okay?"

"But Lauren wants to go up again," Ryan protested, shooting Lauren a look. "Right?"

Lauren gave both of them a guilty smile while Sawyer looked on, shoulder to shoulder with Jane. "Maybe a little," Lauren confessed. "But it *is* cold."

"You guys are ridiculous," Jane complained. "Give me the keys; I'm going to the car."

"Just go to the lodge," Ryan suggested. "You and Sawyer find April, have some coffee. Chill out for half an hour while we go up one more time."

Jane winced at the suggestion. Spending time with Sawyer and April was awkward enough, but having coffee with them, *alone*—she bit the inside of her cheek to keep herself from slamming her fist into Ryan's arm for even suggesting it. She tensed when Sawyer's gloved hand slid up her back and stopped on top of her shoulder.

"Come on," he said, "let them have their fun."

"The lift operator won't let you up anyway," Jane assured him.

"He will if I give him a twenty. Besides, who could resist this face?" Ryan caught Lauren by the cheeks and squeezed, her lips puckering up like a goldfish. Lauren smiled through her contorted face, and Jane couldn't help but crack a smile.

"Fine, whatever," she sighed. April would ask them if they had a good time and Sawyer would tell her how hilarious it was when they both fell flat on their backs and laughed into the sky, and April would just stare and scowl and shoot daggers through her eyes. Then Jane would shrug awkwardly and say, "Eh, it was okay," and April would know she was lying. There was no winning with this scenario.

Lauren faltered, noticing Jane's unease. She caught Ryan by the wrist just as he was about to slide back to the lift. "Hey, maybe this isn't that great an idea after all," she began.

"What? Why?"

"Let's just go home," Lauren continued. "Pop in a movie or something." Jane watched as Lauren gave her brother a wink, admiring the girl for knowing how to get exactly what she wanted. Ryan hesitated, his hand still in hers, and eventually caved to the proposition. If there was one thing Ryan loved more than snow, it was the provocative look on Lauren's face.

"Fine," he relented as Sawyer unstrapped his board from his feet.

"I'll go grab April," he announced, turning away from the group.

As soon as his back was turned, Jane sighed, her breath steaming ahead of her, wishing he'd just forget April, wishing that Sawyer were giving *her* a look—the kind that suggested they go back to the cabin, cozy up, and get warm together.

The Nissan's heater blasted them as they snaked down the mountain, stuck behind a slow-moving minivan, its rear end covered in dozens of bumper stickers. Ryan amused himself by reading them aloud, then settled into grumbling each time the van hit its brakes ahead of the slightest curve. By the time they made it back to the highway, the sun was setting fast. The sky had grown dark around the edges, the sun casting long shadows across the road when it managed to shine through the gloom. Turning onto the road that would lead them back to the cabin, they rambled over weatherworn potholes, the Xterra catching a particularly brutal one beneath a front tire. Ryan cringed, muttering a curse beneath his breath as the car lurched. This road had always been bad, but it seemed worse this time around.

With a good three miles to go until the final turnoff, Jane leaned forward in the passenger seat, squinting at something against the glare of the sunset. Ryan slowed the car, seeing it as well: a stain in the snow, the exact same type of blot they had seen the day before—a swath of red, as though someone had taken a giant paintbrush and made a crimson stroke across the ground.

"What the hell," Ryan murmured, the Nissan rolling so slowly they all but crawled past it.

"That's the same one from yesterday," Lauren said from the back.

"Can't be," Ryan answered. "This one is closer to the cabin, and it snowed last night. It would have been covered over. This is fresh."

Jane twisted in her seat to look at Lauren, noticing that April's eyes were wide.

"Holy shit," April whispered to herself.

"What?" Sawyer asked, squinting at the dark spot against snow that was turning blue in the low light. "It's just some road-kill, right?"

"It's not roadkill," Ryan said. The car stopped. They all looked at one another before Ryan unbuckled his seat belt.

"Wait." Jane blinked at her brother, shaking her head in pro-test. "You're *not* going out there."

"Ryan…" Lauren was ready to join in Jane's campaign for staying in the car, but Ryan was determined. His door swung wide and he slid out of the vehicle. A moment later the back pas-senger door opened and Sawyer followed him into the dusk.

Jane rolled down her window. "*Both* of you," she said, her tone surprisingly stern. "Get back in here."

But Ryan was too intrigued to listen. He'd always been drawn to stuff like this, turning dead animals over with a stick when he was a kid, picking up bleached bones off the forest floor with his bare hands. And Sawyer had been even worse. He had scared his mother half to death when she found a dead bird stuffed in their freezer between two pints of Blue Bell ice cream, frozen solid in a ziplock bag. Ryan's boots sank into the snow, a good three inches of powder beneath the crust. He crouched down, only a few feet from the red streak that decorated the landscape.

"Goddamnit, Ry!" Jane was livid, her irritation diluted by the occasional gust of glacial wind.

"We saw the same thing yesterday," Ryan told Sawyer, "far-ther down the road." He looked up, searching around the base of the trees for a carcass.

"Animal?" Sawyer asked, his hands deep within his pockets.

"I guess." Ryan shrugged. "But where are the remains?"

"Better question," Sawyer cut in. "What the hell are these tracks?"

Ryan straightened, shaking his head at the strange footprints. "What the fuck?" he said. "These would have had to have been made by something, I don't know..."

"Pretty damn tall," Sawyer finished.

The indentations in the snow were distinct. The long, skinny tracks were suggestive of bare feet, but with only four elongated toes leaving deep rifts in the snow. Ryan didn't like it. From what it looked like, some mutant hillbilly was stalking the woods, killing whatever he could find to sustain himself through the winter. He'd have to keep Oona in the cabin, play it safe, but Oona would go nuts being cooped up like that. He had brought her out here so she could have a good time, and now he had *this* to worry about.

"Maybe someone was hunting," Sawyer suggested. "Isn't it some kind of season right now?"

"Turkey, I think," Ryan told him. "We heard a gunshot yesterday."

"Well, there you go." Sawyer dropped his hands to his sides, satisfied with that answer.

"But these tracks..."

"Weird shoes," Sawyer said.

"Are you kidding?" Ryan shook his head at that. "These aren't *shoes*, man."

"No." Sawyer took a backward step. "Haven't you seen those highly attractive Five Finger shoes people are wearing these days? Just because they aren't appropriate for snow doesn't mean some genius didn't wear them while hunting wild turkeys with his backwood chums."

"Really?" Ryan gave Sawyer a skeptical look. "A hillbilly in *Vibrams*?"

"It could have been Bigfoot," Sawyer said. "It could have been the abominable snowman."

"You know they have a show about Bigfoot?" Ryan asked, turning away from the tracks and back toward the car. "Like, these guys genuinely believe they're hunting the damn thing. They think it's a science."

"But what if they're right?"

"What? That Bigfoot exists?"

"Sure." Sawyer shrugged. "Explain those tracks. Maybe it does. There's a logical explanation for everything."

"Yes," Ryan said. "I agree. Logical. Like hillbillies wearing toe shoes."

"Or maybe it's a Realtor wondering what the hell we're doing in that cabin while the new owner is a state away or something."

"And they're hungry." Ryan grinned. "So they're hunting wild turkeys near the property, camping in the trees, wondering how to politely ask us to leave."

The car door slammed shut. Jane was coming for them. Sawyer patted him on the shoulder, encouraging Ryan to head back to the car. It was cold, and they were about to be reprimanded. Ryan stood there for a moment longer, his eyebrows furrowed at the swath of gore, before stepping back onto the muddy road.

"What are you trying to do?" Jane demanded. "You're an ass, you know that?"

"It's closer to the house," Ryan told her. Jane snapped her mouth shut, blinking at the stain her brother had just been inspecting. She rushed behind him as he continued toward the car, crawling back into her seat and slamming the door behind her before he could get around the Nissan's front end.

They drove the rest of the way in relative silence. But Ryan couldn't get it out of his head. Something, or some*one*, was out there, and close to the cabin. It made him uncomfortable. It wasn't safe.

CHAPTER FIVE

Ryan and Jane had only three balls left on the table—the blue two, the red three, and the burgundy seven—while Lauren and Sawyer had six. Lauren leaned over the table while Ryan lined up a shot, a mischievous smile dancing across her lips. She tugged down on the hem of her T-shirt to distract him, her cleavage perfectly lined up with his shot. Jane chuckled as she picked at a slice of leftover chocolate cake, giving Sawyer a dubious look.

"Your teammate is cheating," she told him, licking a smear of frosting off a fork tine. "You should both be disqualified."

"It's okay," Ryan said, bending over the table, his chin close to the Kelly green felt. "I'm undistractable."

"*Undistractable* isn't a word," Sawyer told him.

"It doesn't matter," Ryan said, pulling back the pool cue before forcing it through his fingers. The cue ball cracked against the red three, forcing it into the corner pocket with a muffled thump against the table's bumper. He straightened, squared his shoulders, and made an announcement: "They're only boobs."

"*Only*," Lauren snorted, snatching her pool cue from against the wall.

"Once you've seen a few dozen pairs," Ryan teased, "you've seen them all. Now, if you don't mind, take your shot. I'm ready to win this thing."

Jane took a seat on the leather sofa that flanked the wood-paneled wall, her gaze shifting from the game to the girl at the couch's far end. April had been coiled into its corner for the last hour, not saying a word, looking forlorn.

"Oh, *come on*," Ryan complained, motioning toward Lauren. She was climbing on top of the table, her hair in a wild ponytail, her eyes brimming with determination. "Does someone have a rule book?"

"Shut up, boyo," Lauren told him, tossing her hair over her shoulder before squinting down the length of her pool cue, the tip of her tongue curling over the corner of her upper lip.

Jane bit back a laugh and glanced to the girl beside her. "Are you okay?" she asked. April wasn't Jane's favorite person by a long shot, but seeing her looking so down made Jane feel guilty for having such a good time.

April forced a smile and nodded faintly. "Yeah, I'm fine."

"Are you sure you don't want to play?" Jane motioned to the pool table. "You can take my spot."

"I suck at pool." April slid her hand across the leather cover of *Dracula*. Jane smiled at the book.

"Did Sawyer ever tell you that he read that book like a dozen times?"

"This one?" April peered at the novel in her lap.

"Well, not that one specifically, but yeah. He had this tattered paperback he'd take with him everywhere. He just about cried when the cover fell off."

"It was a tragedy," Sawyer told them. "I never did get a replacement copy."

"Take that one," Jane told him, nodding to the novel in April's lap. "There's no way you'll finish reading it before we leave here anyway," she told April. "It took me nearly two months to get through it."

"Is that the unabridged version?" Sawyer asked, stepping over to the girls to take a look at the hardback. "It *is*." He was pleased.

"It's an old copy, I think it has some Old English or Elizabethan in it or something..." Jane said.

"I guess that's why it doesn't make any sense?" April said, and Jane chuckled in commiseration. The old-timey language had given her a headache too.

"Hark, fair maiden!" Ryan sidestepped the pool table and saddled up to Lauren with a flourish. "Thou art beautiful, but a lousy cheat."

"I play to win, Count." Lauren batted her lashes at him.

"And I live to drink," Ryan shot back, "and must drink to live!" He seized her in his arms and she squealed as she fell back in a dip, Ryan exposing his teeth vampire-style before biting her neck.

Jane held back a laugh as Lauren tried to hide her blush, looking back to April with a faint smile. "Would you like some tea?" she asked.

April shook her head.

"I'll take some," Sawyer said.

"A beer?" Ryan asked, raising an eyebrow at his sister. When she made a face at him he jutted out his bottom lip and batted his lashes.

"I thought you only drank blood, Vlad."

"Blood and beer," Ryan clarified.

"You're going to get fat. That stuff is full of carbs."

"*Blood* is full of carbs?"

"Beer, genius."

"Chocolate cake, though..." he countered.

"Shut up," she told him, gathering up Lauren's cake plate on her way to the kitchen.

"What?" Ryan blinked, feigning offense. "That's the second time I've been told to shut up in a thirty-second span. When did we all get so hostile?"

Jane wrinkled her nose at him and stepped out of the room. There was a crack of pool balls a second later. Lauren shrieked, apparently under attack yet again.

The plates clanged against the counter as Jane left them beside the sink, grabbing the kettle off the stove. Holding it beneath the tap, she peered at Oona. The dog was sitting at attention in front of the kitchen door, seemingly staring at her own reflection in the glass without moving a muscle.

"Are you okay, Oona?" she asked, but the husky didn't respond to her name. "Do you need to go out?" It was a question Oona knew well, one that usually resulted in excited tail wagging. But again, the dog did nothing. It was almost as though she hadn't heard Jane at all. Placing the teapot back on the stove, Jane turned on a burner and slid dirty plates onto the dishwasher's bottom rack. Concerned, she approached the kitchen door to squat next to her brother's pet, placing a hand on the dog's back.

Oona reeled back, her teeth bared, and Jane jerked her hand away, her heart thudding in her throat. She fell backward, putting distance between herself and the growling dog by pushing away with her feet. She could hear Ryan in the hallway. He yelled Oona's name and she immediately backed down, ducking her head in guilt.

"What the hell just happened?" he asked as he came into the kitchen, extending a hand to his sister while his eyes remained on his dog.

"I don't know," Jane replied, her voice shaking, unable to help the tears from springing to her eyes. Ever since she was a kid, she'd cry when she was scared or angry, as though processing an excess of emotion at once was too much for her to handle.

"Are you okay?"

"I'm fine," she insisted. "Just freaked out. I thought she wanted to go outside, and then she just turned on me."

Ryan crouched in front of the husky, catching her by the snout so he could look her in the eyes, then snapped his fingers and pointed her out of the kitchen. Oona bowed her head and slunk away, utterly harmless in her stance.

"I just scared her," Jane confessed, her gaze snagging on Sawyer, who was now standing in the mouth of the hallway, a concerned look veiling his features.

A second later Oona was barking in the living room—a less-than-friendly snarl that rumbled from the depth of her throat.

"What the *fuck*?" Ryan stomped across the room. Jane clasped her hands together, steadying their tremor as she offered Sawyer an embarrassed smile.

"Are you all right?" he asked softly. Jane nodded, waving her hand as if dismissing the whole thing. Sawyer took a step closer, his fingers sweeping across her hand before he retracted his touch, startled by Lauren's voice behind them.

"Um, guys?" Lauren stepped into the kitchen with an expression Jane couldn't read. "I think I know why Oona's flipping out. There's something outside. April just saw something out the window."

The four of them made a beeline back to the game room. April stood next to the couch, her arms wrapped around her waist, her nose an inch from the glass. Oona leaped onto the sofa, growling beneath her breath before expelling another bark.

"What was it?" Ryan asked, flipping the light switch next to the outside door. The light illuminated a plain concrete slab; nothing but a barbecue grill and a couple of loungers folded up against the side of the house.

"Deer," April said. "Something was chasing them."

"A wolf?" Sawyer asked, giving Ryan a questioning glance.

"Could be." Ryan shrugged, but April shook her head in response.

"It looked big."

The group stared at one another for a long moment, then turned to look out the window again. Oona whined and jumped off the couch, stopping in front of the door, waiting to be let out.

"Don't you dare," Jane warned. "It could be a bear or something."

"It's not a bear," Ryan said. "They're hibernating."

"Well, what else could it be?"

"Hold on to her collar," Ryan commanded.

"What?"

"Hold on to Oona's collar," he repeated. "I'm opening the door."

"Oh my god," Lauren said from behind her hand.

"No," Jane protested, but she hooked her fingers beneath the husky's collar anyway, knowing that if Ryan went through with it, Oona would be out that door before anyone could stop her. "Ryan, don't," she said. "What if it's dangerous?"

"The only thing dangerous out here are wolves, and they're scared of people," he insisted, throwing the dead bolt. "Did you put anything in the outside trash can? They probably smell food."

"Yeah," Lauren said under her breath. "They smell food, as in *us*."

"I didn't throw anything out," Jane told him. "It's all inside."

"If they're scared of people, what's the point?" Lauren asked. "Just leave it."

"They're scared of people, but they may not be scared of dogs."

"So keep her inside!" Jane snapped, but the door swung open before she could insist any further. Oona tried to run, nearly jerking Jane's shoulder out of its socket. She whined as her owner stepped outside in a short-sleeved T-shirt and stocking feet, his breath puffing out in front of him. Sawyer moved toward the door before a little plea escaped Jane's throat. "Tom, stop."

Sawyer turned to look at her. She gave him a beseeching look, but before Sawyer had a chance to react—to either succumb to her request or defy her and step outside—Ryan was requesting his help.

"Sawyer, there's a flashlight in the laundry room," he said. "Grab it, would you?"

Sawyer offered Jane an apologetic frown before stepping past her, disappearing down the hall.

"God," Lauren groaned, shivering as the cold poured into the room. "This is like a goddamn horror movie." She forced a laugh, but she sounded more spooked than she was letting on.

Jane's attention wavered to April, blinking when she noticed that the girl wasn't looking out the window anymore, but was looking right at her—*staring*. Jane swallowed against the lump in her throat, her stomach sinking to the floor. Sawyer jogged back into the room, flashlight in hand, and stepped onto the patio. He swept the flashlight across the expanse of night, illuminating tree trunks and snow.

"There," he said, holding the light steady. A set of reflective animal eyes flashed in the distance, but they were too far away to identify.

"We scared it off." Ryan nearly sounded disappointed.

"Damn." Lauren snapped her fingers. "And here I was hoping we were all going to die."

"Get back inside," Jane demanded. But the guys didn't budge, still scouring the landscape like a couple of Boy Scouts. "Jesus, Ryan!" She was annoyed now. "Oona is about to take my arm off!"

The guys rambled back inside and Ryan locked the door behind them. The air inside the room instantly grew warmer, and Jane let go of the husky before rolling her shoulder with a wince.

"That was completely stupid. What if it *had* been something dangerous?"

"Then it would have eaten me," Ryan said. He pointed the flashlight at her, turning it off and on like a strobe. For a moment everyone was silent, and then both Sawyer and Lauren laughed while Jane continued to scowl, contemplating worst-case scenarios. Finally, Sawyer picked up his cue stick and broke the tension.

"Rack 'em up, boys and girls," he said. "Best two out of three."

Sawyer padded down the upstairs hallway with a glass of water in hand, passing every single door until he reached the room he and April were occupying. It was dark, everyone already in their rightful rooms, exhausted by a long day on the slopes. Sawyer had nearly cracked a joke about their room placement when Ryan had led them down the hall the day before, but he understood the reasoning behind it; nobody wanted to hear them get it on in the room next door. Had Jane still been with Alex, Sawyer would have wanted them as far away as possible—down the hall, if not in a motel room twenty-five miles away.

April was already on the pullout sofa, Stoker's *Dracula* in hand, the sheets pulled up to her chest, squinting at the pages with an exceptional sense of intensity as Sawyer stepped inside. "I don't know how you did it," she said. "This is impossible to understand."

"It's not *that* bad, is it?" He held the glass of water out over the comforter, waiting for her to take it. April leaned forward and grabbed it, frowning.

"Water?"

"There was only diet soda left. Figured you'd want water instead."

She grimaced and took a drink, wrinkling her nose at him before placing the glass onto the end table next to her side of the bed.

Sawyer slid beneath the covers and glanced her way. "Are you going to read for a bit?"

April contemplated it, then shook her head and closed the book with a muffled slap. "It's giving me a headache." She handed it to him, and Sawyer gingerly plucked it from her fingers, smoothing his hand across its leather cover. "It's your gift, anyway," she muttered.

"So? You can still read it."

"I'd rather watch the movie," she told him, readjusting her pillow before lying down.

Sawyer shrugged and slid the book onto a table that housed a lamp, his fingers lingering upon the embossed leather for a moment longer before turning off the light. The moon had reflected off the surface of the snow the night before, sending shards of cold blue light through the slats of the blinds, but tonight was as dark as pitch; the sky was heavy with clouds, casting the darkest shade of black across the cabin, the hills, the trees. Sawyer adjusted his pillow beneath his head, then pulled the covers up to his chin and closed his eyes.

"Sawyer?" April's voice cut through the quiet of the room.

"Yeah?"

"You still love me, right?"

He reflexively furrowed his eyebrows, as though April could see his expression through the darkness, but his heart knotted within his chest. It was the question he'd been trying to answer since they had arrived—since before that—the question that unspooled inside his head every time Jane was within arm's length, cooking or laughing or simply standing there doing nothing at all. He had almost kissed her when they had stood together in the kitchen. He had wanted to grab her by the waist and lift her onto the counter, his mouth rough against hers. He had yearned for the freedom to take advantage of the emptiness of the downstairs rooms, to sneak away behind a closed door and make frantic, muffled love to the girl he had never truly given up. But he had made himself let the opportunity slip through his fingers.

"Of course I do," he replied, blindly reaching across the bed to catch April by the hand. Once he found her, he leaned over and pressed a kiss to the corner of her mouth.

"Okay," she said softly. "Just checking."

Sawyer gave her hand a squeeze and fell back onto his pillow, closing his eyes against the thud of his own heart.

It could have been ten minutes or two hours when he blinked awake. April was nudging his shoulder, whispering his name as she tried to pull him out of sleep.

"Sawyer," she hissed. "Wake up."

Rolling onto his back with a muffled groan, he released a groggy sigh under April's continued prodding.

"What?"

"I keep hearing something," she whispered. She was sitting up, wide awake. Despite the darkness around them, he could see her silhouette. "I heard it last night too. I can't sleep."

"It's just animals," he told her, turning onto his side. "Just block it out."

"I can't!" she huffed. Her words were but a breath, but against the blanket of silence even the slightest whisper sounded like a scream. She jostled him again. "Sawyer."

"*Jesus*, Ape."

"I'm serious!" she insisted. "I think Oona is outside or something. Go check."

"Oona's in the house," he grumbled, regressing to an eight-year-old response and pulling the sheets over his head.

"If Oona's inside that's even weirder," she whispered. "Because there's *something* out there. I can hear it on the deck." When Sawyer didn't move, she huffed. "Fine, but the driveway is right below us. Don't blame me if someone breaks into your precious Jeep."

Sawyer loved that Jeep. It had taken him months to track down the perfect model on AutoTrader. Once he did, he obsessed over his new car for weeks, washing it every weekend, Armor-Alling the dash until it glinted in the Denver sun. He shoved the blanket away from himself and sat up with an irritated groan. "Really?" he asked. "You think someone's going to break into my car *out here*? I swear to god…" He forced himself to his feet, blearily stalking across the room to the window. Parting the slats of the blinds, he squinted into the night.

"If it's so unlikely, why are you up?"

"So you'll go back to sleep," he insisted, letting his hand drop from the window. "There's nothing out there, like I said."

"I'm telling you, I *heard* something."

Pulling his hand across his face, he gave a frustrated sigh.

"Fine," she said. "Whatever." Throwing herself down onto the mattress, she yanked the sheets up to her shoulders.

"I'm sure you heard something," Sawyer told her, trying to be compassionate despite his irritation. April was the lightest sleeper he'd ever met. Since they'd moved in together, he'd had to stop using the ceiling fan in the bedroom because it rattled, the space heater because it ticked; he'd gone so far as to remove the wall clock because she insisted the click of the second hand was equivalent to a sledgehammer when the room was quiet. "We used to hear animals out here as kids all the time," he told her. "I can't exactly go out there and ask them to shut up." Leaving the window, he started to move across the darkened room. A moment later, a flash of pain ignited his senses, the sofa bed shuddering against his impact. Sawyer rolled onto the mattress in muffled agony. "Fuck!" he hissed, his right pinkie toe throbbing beneath the pressure of his hands.

"Christ," April whispered, crawling across the bed. "Are you okay?"

Sawyer didn't reply, too busy fighting back reflexive tears of pain. His toe was throbbing like a tiny heart.

"Is it broken?" She pulled his hands away from his foot. "Turn on the light," she told him. But just as he stretched his arm out toward the lamp, a loud thump sounded overhead.

Their attention snapped up to the ceiling.

"I *told* you!" she said, slapping her hand over her mouth as soon as the words burst from her lips. Sawyer shushed her, his eyes pointed skyward. They sat motionless for a good thirty seconds, both of them holding their breath, staring at the ceiling, waiting for the next noise to rouse them from their stillness. But the sound didn't return.

"There were these guys at the lodge," April told him after a moment. "They were talking about how the ski patrol found some blood in the mountains. Like, I guess they were worried that someone was eaten by wolves or something."

Sawyer allowed himself to fall back onto his side of the bed, his eyes shut tight against the gnawing burn of his foot.

"Do you think that's what that stain was?" she asked. "The one we saw in the snow on the way back up here?"

"No."

"But what if it was?"

"Then there would have been cops." He sighed. "Right? Cops? Because there would have been a dead body. But there weren't any cops up on the mountain, Ape."

"How can you be so sure? The mountain is huge."

"I'm just sure." Rolling over, his face pressed into the mattress. "Jesus Christ." He cursed the pain, his words muffled against the sheets.

But April was too wrapped up to worry about Sawyer's toe. "What about the noise?" she asked.

He pressed his hands over his face at the amount of throbbing heat radiating from his foot. He'd probably broken the damn thing, and now he'd be grounded for the rest of the trip. Ryan was going to be pissed, and Sawyer would be stuck in the cabin for the rest of the weekend. "Goddamnit," he whispered.

April went quiet for a moment, then eventually spoke again. "Are you okay?" Her hand slid across his shoulders, rubbing his back. "Want me to get somebody?"

"I'll be fine," he said through clenched teeth. "I just need to sleep it off."

Again, April paused in thought before replying. "You're right," she said. "It was probably just an animal." Crawling across the bed, she slid on top of him, rolling him over to straddle his hips. "And now we're both wide awake." He could make out the outline of her raised arms as she pulled her T-shirt over her head, tossing it aside.

"Ape," he said, his throat dry. She silenced him by pressing her mouth to his, her teeth tugging at his bottom lip.

"Let me take your mind off that foot," she proposed. Wriggling on top of him, she caught the hem of his shirt, then gave it an upward tug.

"They'll hear us," he insisted, trying to roll her off him, but she squeezed her knees against his hips, refusing to budge.

"So let them hear us." She arched backward to fully expose herself, sliding her hands down her breasts to her hips, grinding against him.

Sawyer closed his eyes, trying to relax, unable to help the sudden ache between his legs. April hooked her fingers beneath the waistband of his pants, giving them a downward tug. He exhaled a throaty breath as she eased down onto him, his fingers coiling against the curve of her backside, letting himself drift when she started to move: rhythmic, slow, her breath coming in soft gasps.

He sat up, his arms twining around her, his mouth against her neck. Her nails trailed up and down his back as he buried his face in her hair, inhaling the scent of shampoo—Jane's shampoo, the same scent he'd breathed in when he had first pulled Jane into his arms. Jane's face flashed against the backs of his eyelids, her head tilted back, as April moved on top of him. His heart quickened when April's soft moans drifted from between Jane's lips, his mouth traveling across the slope of her shoulder, Jane's name on the tip of his tongue—

He tensed. This was the very reason he had kept his distance for so long—he wasn't over Jane. His stomach flipped.

"Ape," he whispered, trying to catch April's attention, but his uttering her name only made her increase her pace. "April." He caught her by the hips, trying to hold her still as he began to wither inside her.

"Tom." The nickname slithered past her lips, and as soon as it hit his ears he went limp, his heart hitching in his throat. Nobody called him Tom but Jane. It was their thing, their history. But April didn't notice him tense beneath her. She continued to move, slithering her hands across his chest.

He caught her by her biceps, crushing her down into the mattress, their roles suddenly reversed. "Stop," he told her, catching her hand as she reached for his hair. He pushed it away, rolling off her, pulling his pants back up. April was left lying there—naked, stunned. But it didn't take her long to regain her bearings.

"Are you fucking *kidding* me?" she asked, full volume now. "Since when do you pass up a screw?"

"Will you keep it down?" he asked, nearly pleading. "You're going to wake everyone up." Pulling the sheets back up to his chin, he closed his eyes, determined to fall back asleep despite the pounding of his heart. But she wasn't having it. Grabbing the sheets by their hemmed top edge, she pulled them away from him with a jerk.

"Answer me," she snapped. "What the hell is this?"

Their eyes locked. He was the first to look away.

"I knew it," she hissed, sliding off the bed and stomping through the room. She snatched her shirt off the floor like a matador waving a cape at a bull. "This is why you didn't want me to come up here with you, right? So you could fuck her instead of me?"

"I don't know what you're talking about." He was shooting for indifference, fending off the nausea that was clawing its way up his throat. April was right: he yearned for a random run-in in an empty room, just him and Jane, so he could apologize and maybe, just maybe, she could forgive him for leaving, for losing touch and letting her go. He wanted the secrecy, wanted the torrid affair with the girl he still pined for. He had been forced to give her up: first for an education, then for some asshole who had swept her off her feet, and so he'd moved on too. But when Sawyer had learned that Alex had cheated, a part of him wanted to break the bastard's jaw; the other part wanted to drop everything, move to Arizona and heal Jane's hurt. It didn't matter that he and April were together. It didn't matter that he'd given her a ring.

Again came the guilt, the question of whether he even loved April at all—because if he did, why would his first instinct be to run to someone else? He hated himself for it; had vowed to keep himself in check; purposely avoided Jane in conversations with Ryan, kept blowing Ryan off when it came to getting together again. But she just kept coming at him, worming her way into his thoughts, forever in the background, forever waiting like some phantom he couldn't shake.

April yanked her shirt over her head and threw open the bedroom door, making as much noise as she could as she marched toward the bathroom. Sawyer knew it would come to this. He knew from the moment they had gotten together but had tried to convince himself that he was wrong. April would take Jane's place in his heart, and when the news of the baby came, for a moment she had. Sawyer pictured himself as a husband, a dad, and even if his thoughts circled back to the girl from his past, all he'd have to do was look into his child's eyes and remember that April had given him this new life, this new purpose to exist. Because what could have been more powerful than that? He had gotten cocky. A final trip up to the cabin? Sure, why not? What could possibly happen, especially with April on his arm?

But what happened had been inevitable. He saw her, he touched her, he smelled her, and he was addicted all over again. Jane made him weak, desperate. She broke his will. But he had waited too long, tying himself to April forever. And now Jane would never want him, and April would never take him back.

Ryan peered into the darkness as he lay on his side, listening to a muffled one-sided argument taint the otherwise peaceful quiet. He considered getting up, making sure that all was well with his closest friend, but he decided against it, not wanting to get involved. Ryan was a believer in fate. Everything happened for a reason; nothing was random or left to chance. He and Jane being born at the same time; the implosion that had become their family life—all of these things had to happen to lead him to where he was now—with his sister, his best friend, and Lauren, a girl he hardly knew but was starting to need. They all had to take their own journeys, be it together or alone. He could only hope that Jane and Sawyer would journey together...and that Lauren would agree to visit him in Zurich.

He tried to make out the words, listening for the master bedroom door to creak open, for Jane to stick her head out into the hall. But the dispute came to an abrupt conclusion, and silence overtook the house once again. He relaxed, didn't move as he continued to listen and think. His move to Switzerland was part of his fate, a fate that would remove him from the life and people he knew. Maybe that distance was just what he needed to get his head on straight, to get over the fears Jane had so often encouraged him to let go of. He wasn't sure that he and Lauren would work out, but for the first time in his life he actually wanted to try. He wanted to let her in, to *not* push her away the way he had pushed Summer. Because who knew how that relationship would have turned out if he hadn't been so afraid?

He peered at the ceiling when he heard the same thump on the roof that he had before the argument had erupted. Oona stirred at the foot of the bed but didn't rouse, exhaling a loud breath through her nose before emitting a muffled bark in her sleep. Ryan went through the possible animals that could make it up onto the roof—various foxes, possibly a cougar. As a kid, his dad had taught him that porcupines could climb trees, and they had caught one doing just that as they rode the snowmobile up and down the driveway while waiting for Thanksgiving dinner one year.

He closed his eyes, wondering just how hard Jane would scream if she saw a giant quilled rodent fall from the roof.

CHAPTER SIX

Clyde hardly heard his cell buzz over the iron drone of Megadeth. Pushing through an alcohol-induced haze, he rolled onto his stomach—soured by more than a dozen guzzled beers—and tumbled four inches to the floor from the mattress pushed into the corner of his spartan room. He hefted himself onto his hands and knees, dirty blond hair hanging around his face in a curtain. The phone continued to vibrate and chirp while he crawled across a floor littered with dirty laundry and trash. Just as he groped for the phone, it fell silent, going to voice mail. Less than fifteen seconds later, he heard Pete's cell scream in the opposite room. He rolled onto his back, let his phone tumble from his grasp, and fell back into a dizzying post-bender slumber, because there was no better cure for a hangover than sleep.

But he jerked awake a second later, Pete's voice cutting through a killer guitar solo. "Man," Pete said. Clyde peeled his eyes open, then squinted despite the room being mostly dark. Pete steadied himself against the doorjamb, his face a mask of postdrink nausea. "Fuck, wake up, dude," he said, daring to release the doorframe before stumbling headlong toward Clyde's currently vacant bed.

"Get off my bed, man," Clyde groaned.

"Get up, dude," Pete replied.

"I'll get up if you get off my fucking bed, man. You don't do that."

Pete forced himself off the mattress, wobbly on his feet. "Do what? Listen, hey..."

Clyde crawled back across his floor, climbed onto his bed, and immediately collapsed face-first into his pillow.

"Clyde." The name was nearly a whine. "We're fucked, buddy. Totally fucked."

A muffled syllable drifted from the folds of Clyde's sheets, a "what?" squelched by a pillow in dire need of replacement—its body shapeless and flat, its sham stained with hair grease and sweat.

"Hey, did you hear me?" Pete kicked at one of Clyde's still-shoed feet. Without warning, Clyde rolled over and launched the dirty pillow at his roommate with surprising force. Pete stumbled backward, nearly tripping over a pile of clothes before his shoulder caught the wall. After regaining his footing, he said, "Guess what?"

"What?" Clyde asked begrudgingly.

Pete ambled over to Clyde's window, shoving the curtain aside to reveal the darkness of the morning. Fat flakes tumbled past the glass.

"Aw, *shit*," Clyde hissed, then clapped his hands over his face. This was just what they needed. They hadn't partied in nearly a week, holding out as the meteorologist fumbled every forecast. They'd finally had enough, ending up at the liquor store, where, lo and behold, there was a sale on thirty-sixers of brew. Deeming it a sign from God himself, they proceeded to get epically plastered while playing Xbox and listening to Metallica's *Master of Puppets* on repeat. And now it was *snowing*.

"We got called in," Pete announced, holding his fist up to his mouth, fighting back a diaphragm-rattling belch. "Side roads off the highway," he said. "We've got an hour."

"What time is it?" Clyde murmured, trying to sit up.

"Four thirty."

"Goddamn." He winced against the taste of his own mouth. "Coffee?"

"I'll make some," Pete said. "I need some fucking Tylenol."

Clyde sighed unsteadily, then pulled his hand down the length of his face before letting it fall to the bed. He was tempted to call in, but the resident road crew was small, and that would leave the others high and dry. Clyde liked to think of himself as loyal—not the kind of guy to screw over the other guys on the team.

Dragging himself into the bathroom, he leaned over the sink and splashed cold water onto his face. He was still dressed from the night before, so all he had to do was grab his coat and hat and charge into the snow. Clyde's plowless pickup was parked just yards from the house. It was a pain in the ass to detach the plows after every use, so the boys took turns—one truck would be street ready while the other was left with plow and chains. It saved them a hell of a lot of time on mornings just like this, mornings when the wind was so cold it made their bones ache and their eyes sting. Clyde winced against the chill as he marched toward his pickup, his head throbbing, his brain swollen, his stomach sour. He had to pause next to the front fender, anticipating the inevitable as sickness curdled at the back of his throat, but after a few deep breaths, he regained his bearings and climbed inside the cab.

He drove around to the back of the house, headlights cutting across the darkness, illuminating Pete's old Chevy and the self-built carport next to it where they kept all their gear. Clyde's plow was parked beneath the lean-to structure, bright yellow paint chipping off ten-gauge steel. He had helped his dad paint it decades before, just before Christmas. His mother had picked out the color—yellow being her favorite. Parking so that his high beams shone against the carport's shoddy construction, he rolled down his window and stuck his head into the cold, expertly lining up the truck so that the plow would slide into place. Satisfied with his position, he cranked the stereo and reached into the glove compartment for a smoke. Despite his pounding headache, music helped wake him up, and at the moment being awake was more important than being comfortable.

Lighting his cig, he sucked in a lungful of smoke and slid out into the predawn darkness, snowflakes glittering along the sides of the carport that would more than likely collapse in on itself before next winter. He busied himself at the pickup's front bumper, Slayer coiling through his open door. When the CD paused between tracks, a low-octave moan caught his attention. He raised an eyebrow, jamming his arm into the truck to crank down the music. A shadow cut across the wooded backyard, Clyde catching the movement from the corner of his eye. "Hey, Pete?" Another moan sounded in reply, and Clyde couldn't help but grin. "You okay, buddy?" he asked, looking back down to what he was doing, his cigarette dangling from the swell of his bottom lip. "You want to hand me the socket wrench from the tool chest?"

The moaning continued, only to be cut short.

Clyde glanced up, blinded by the high beams, unable to see a thing beyond the truck's front bumper. "Pete?"

Nothing.

He sighed, took another drag off his cigarette, and flicked it into the snow. "You suck at holding your liquor, man," he said. He stepped out of the headlights and could hardly see a thing. His eyes fought to adjust to the sudden darkness, but all he could make out were the windows of the house—illuminated from the inside out—and the interior of his truck, brightened by the weak glow of the dome light above the dusty dash. He ducked inside the truck, turned up the music to a low roar, and stepped around to the bed of the pickup. Stopping next to the toolbox mounted flush against the back of the truck's cab, he shoved the heel of his hand against a push-button lock, sending one of the box's two metal lids bouncing upward on its spring. A tiny light blinked on, Clyde's menagerie of tools glittering in the anemic yellow glow. He rifled through the mess, haphazardly shoving his precious gear this way and that.

"Socket wrench, socket wrench," he mumbled, as though chanting the tool's name like a mantra would make it spring from the pile of chrome-plated metal. "Son of a..." It was nowhere to be found, and Clyde's mind bounced to the last time he couldn't find a piece of equipment. Pete had borrowed his Dremel tool, and it had been Clyde who had found it in the tool chest on the back of Pete's truck. He slammed the lid of his box closed and marched across the yard toward Pete's Chevy, nearly tripping over a fallen branch on his way. He cursed beneath his breath as he regained his footing, grabbing the branch by its brittle wood and tossing it aside.

The branch came back at him, landing just shy of his boots.

"Pete?" Clyde blinked, squinting into the dark. "Hey, stop fucking around, man. Where's my ratchet?"

Nothing.

"Whatever," he muttered, popping Pete's toolbox open, and there it was, the tool Clyde was looking for. "You know, I don't care if you use my shit," he announced, grabbing the wrench and turning back to his own truck. "But it sure as hell would be nice if you'd put stuff back where you found it. It's called common courtesy."

Another moan, this one phlegmy, like a death rattle deep within a chest.

"I should pay your mom a visit," he continued, stepping back around his front bumper. "Complain about how she raised you in a barn before giving her a nice Clydey-boy screw." Pete hated mom jokes. It was one of his pet peeves. And yet there was nothing beyond the drone of Clyde's music. Not a "fuck you," not a witty quip in return. The lack of a comeback suggested that Pete was somewhere out there in the dark puking his guts out. "Pete? You gonna survive?"

He slid the ratchet onto the hood of his truck. Curiosity getting the best of him, he stepped back into the inky early morning, snowflakes drifting across his line of sight. He did a double take when he spotted someone standing in the darkness a dozen yards away, but it sure as hell wasn't Pete. The guy was tall and toothpick skinny, and while Clyde couldn't see much of anything it almost looked like the stranger was naked—there were no lines to suggest the fold of jeans or the padding of a winter coat. The silhouette reminded him of the sick pictures Pete had showed him once; naked men and women with their hair shorn standing in long lines, numbers tattooed onto toothpick arms. But there was something about the guy standing a dozen yards away that didn't sit right; his arms were too long for his body, and that head…it was massive, like one of those old-timey water babies in a circus freak show.

"What the shit?" he whispered, blinking a few times to try to get a better view. As he was about to take a step forward, a crash behind him made him jump out of his skin. He reeled around, his gaze snagging on his freshly crumpled hood, as though something heavy had landed on it—but there was nothing there. The music played on while one of his headlights flickered, then cut out. His heart thumped in his chest beneath the rush of adrenaline, but his reflexes were still dulled by the alcohol that tainted his bloodstream. Impaired judgment had him weighing the fact that his truck hood was wrecked over the shadow figure that loomed in the distance. He'd made a move toward the pickup when he was shoved backward as though something had lunged at his chest, the air rushing from his lungs, the seat of his jeans skidding across the ground.

He froze, stunned, unsure of what had just happened.

Something leaned into his line of sight, but he couldn't make out what it was. The headlight shone behind it, throwing the figure into silhouette, its gaunt body nothing but bones and sharp angles. *The devil*, he thought. *Lucifer, in the flesh.* Panicked, he began to crawl backward, the snow burning the exposed skin of his hands. But before he got more than a few feet away, he bumped into something behind him, something that emitted a deep, rumbling growl. The thing in front of him pulled its arm back, the silhouette of a giant four-fingered hand held aloft, the palm shovel-like with thin, rangy digits jutting out. Clyde opened his mouth to scream as the hand swiped through the air, black talons catching the light, but he gurgled instead. His eyes widened as hot blood bubbled from his neck. His hands flew to his throat, trying to keep the blood from spilling, but it poured across his fingers.

He fell onto his back, gasping for breath, staring at the house just a handful of yards away, a house that was safe and warm. Just then, he saw Pete casually step across the kitchen, a fresh pot of coffee held in his hand, oblivious to what was going on just outside. Clyde reached out, praying to God that his friend would sense that something was wrong, that he would stop to look out the window. But he didn't.

As soon as Pete disappeared from view, the two…things that loomed above Clyde stared down at him, and while he couldn't see what they looked like, the distinct scent of urine over the hot metallic aroma of his own blood sent him into a panic. He tried to scramble to his feet despite his injuries, but one of them lunged forward, its teeth tearing into Clyde's shoulder. He choked on his blood as he tried to cry out, his efforts drowned by the wail of guitars, the banging of drums. His entire left side felt like it was on fire. He rolled onto his injured shoulder in a feeble attempt to cool the burn with the snow as he clawed at the ground, trying to skitter away from his attacker. But as soon as he turned away, he felt a viselike grip catch his leg. With a single blink, Clyde stared toward the house, trying to scream but unable to catch his breath, praying for salvation, sure this couldn't really be happening. And then he felt the ground slide out from under him as he was jerked backward, the cabin suddenly gone as he was pulled into the trees.

Pete couldn't hear anything above Megadeth's wail, so when he finally saw the creature standing in the mouth of the kitchen, it was far too late for him to run. The skeletal thing filled the entire doorway, leaning down to duck through the threshold, its spiderlike arms bending at unspeakable angles as it pulled itself into the room. Clyde's lidless travel mug slipped through Pete's fingers and crashed to the floor, hot coffee sloshing across his boots. Despite the monster's size, the thing's height was far from its most disturbing attribute. Pete choked on the air in his throat as he stared at its black marble-like eyes sunken deep into an overly large head, an impossibly wide mouth full of thick, yellow teeth inside its skull. *Impossible*, he thought. He tried to breathe and cry out all at once, backing himself into a corner as the thing advanced snorting through a nonexistent nose at the scent of freshly brewed coffee, a scent that mingled with the blood smeared across the monster's face and arms.

Pete pressed himself against the wall and squeezed his eyes shut, the most arbitrary thought careening through his brain: *Jurassic Park*. It had been his absolute favorite movie as a kid. He had been so obsessed with it, his parents hadn't had the heart to return the VHS tape back to the rental place, and after months of late fees, they bought it instead. Now the adult Pete stood glued to the kitchen wall, a warm trickle of urine dribbling down his thighs, convincing himself that if he didn't move, if he didn't breathe, if he didn't make a sound, the hellion in front of him wouldn't realize he was there, just like the T. rex in the movies. But even with his eyes closed, he could hear the thing coming closer. He could smell the blood, refusing to believe it was the blood of anyone he knew. When he finally opened his eyes, he was standing face-to-face with a grinning demon, the thing's broad teeth mere inches from the tip of his nose.

When the creature lifted a hand of long, bony fingers to Pete's face, he couldn't help the muted whine of terror that escaped his throat. With his cheeks in its grasp, sharp claws digging into his flesh, the savage canted its head to the side, seeming to study the horrified expression that Pete could feel twisting across his face. It was staring at the thud of his pulse just below his jaw that pounded in time with the drumming of his runaway heart. Pete cried out as it lifted him from the floor by his head alone, his legs dangling, his neck feeling like it was about to tear away from his torso, his boots kicking the wall behind him as he struggled to get free.

And then Pete went involuntarily still, a sensation he couldn't quite place spreading from his stomach out to his limbs—hot and cold all at once. Suddenly he crumpled to the ground as the creature pulled its free hand away, and for a moment hope speared his heart. It was letting him go. He was going to survive. Like a shark, the thing had come to realize that Pete wasn't its rightful prey. But its fist clung to something long and gray—something that felt like it was tugging on Pete's insides like a rope or a string.

Before he had enough time to process the scope of what was happening, the monster began to eat, pulling entrails out of

Pete's belly like an unbroken cord of sausage. A scream ripped its way out of his throat. Pete shot out an arm and grabbed at the strand of slick viscera, jerking it backward in a gruesome game of tug-of-war, as he fought for what was rightfully his, fought the horrific feeling of himself literally *unraveling* from the inside out. The savage ceased its chewing, seeming bewildered by the fact that its gutted game was fighting back.

But Pete was fading. Black spots bloomed in front of his eyes. The burning crawl of blood loss snaked around the inside of his skull and squeezed his brain. He pitched to the right, rolling onto his stomach in an attempt to catch a breath, but he choked instead, inhaling the blood that was splashed across the linoleum. It was his blood. *His* blood. Everywhere. So much of it he could see his own reflection in the deep burgundy beneath him, his own expression of baffled terror echoed back at him, but twisted as in a funhouse mirror.

His diaphragm gave way to an unnatural rattle and a sob ripped its way out of his chest as he saw a matching pair of alien legs enter the kitchen, the sound muffled by a wet tremor of a growl as the two creatures began to fight. He stared at their sinewy legs as they dodged each other.

His world went black as they snarled at each other, the sound reminding Pete of hog hunting with his pop. The kitchen table turned over next to his head. The refrigerator shook as one of them fell against it. Dishes crashed to the floor above the sound of Clyde's music droning from across the house, Pete's wheezing breaths coming in short bursts now. Before he could summon up another cry, something grabbed him by his neck, yanked him upward, and gave him a vicious shake. And despite the wail of the music, the last thing Pete heard was the snapping of his own neck.

Jane squinted against the sun that filtered into the room, rolled onto her back, and rubbed the sleep out of her eyes while Lauren remained motionless beside her. She would have liked nothing more than to stay in bed for an hour longer, still tired from the night before—she and Lauren had stayed up long after crawling into bed, whispering across the sheets about Ryan and Sawyer and the weird way April had looked at Jane during their game of pool, April's expression teeming with bad vibes. And then there had been the fight. Both Jane and Lauren had lain breathless in the dark, their ears straining as hard as they could. Jane had nearly crawled out of bed to peek into the hall, but Lauren had stopped her, grabbing her arm and giving her a shake of the head.

"Don't," she'd whispered. "What if she sees you?"

Jane had nearly rolled her eyes at the suggestion. *So what?* she thought. *Let her see.* Jane wasn't the one making a ton of noise in the middle of the night, waking everyone up. But Lauren was right. If Jane had been caught eavesdropping, it would have caused even more drama. And yet, long after the argument had subsided, nearly an hour after Lauren had fallen asleep, Jane remained wide awake, contemplating tiptoeing down the hall and pressing her ear to the very last door. She imagined sneaking downstairs to find Sawyer sitting in a dark living room, staring out the large picture window that overlooked the mountains and trees. He'd turn to look at her when he heard her approach, they'd stare at each other for a long while—breathless, silent—and then his face would brighten like the moon lighting up the night.

But no matter how hard she tried, she couldn't will herself to feel good about the anger she'd heard from down the hall. Lauren would have reprimanded her for being so "nice," so "fair," but Jane couldn't help it. Nobody liked being in the middle of an argument, especially not when it was on display for everyone to hear. She was sure Sawyer was miserable, embarrassed, uncomfortable, and there was nothing about that that made her happy. Her incessant thoughts had afforded her a little over three hours of sleep, but the host wasn't allowed to sleep in. She had breakfast to make; she was sure the boys would be itching to go back up the mountain.

Sitting up, she grabbed her discarded socks off the floor and pulled them onto her feet. She shivered against the cold, rubbing her arms as she made her way toward the window for her first look at the world. She paused to pull a sweater over her head, her fingers snagging in the tangles of her slept-in hair, and then she blinked at the view. There wasn't a speck of green as far as the eye could see. It had snowed overnight, and it had snowed hard.

A childlike thrill speared her heart as she rushed across the carpet to the bedroom door, opening it quietly despite her excitement, not wanting to wake her friend. She took the stairs two by two, skidded to a stop in the hall, and marched into the kitchen without a thought to her appearance. Despite her love for the summer, a fresh coat of snow always left her excited. And she pictured her and Ryan building a giant snowman on the porch just outside the kitchen door.

Her wide smile faltered before it altogether disappeared as she rounded the corner. Sawyer stood at that very door, his back to her, looking out onto fresh powder. He held a steaming mug between his hands, and there were a couple of backpacks at his feet. It looked like he was contemplating an exit despite still being in his pajamas, just out of bed, his hair a mess. He eventually turned to offer her a tired smile. A moment later he looked away.

"Remember the winter break when we got stuck up here?" he asked. "Your dad was so pissed."

Jane frowned at his tone. She could hear it in his voice; something was wrong. Stepping across the kitchen to the coffeemaker, she poured herself a cup. The coat of snow on the deck's railing was at least six inches thick. She looked back to him and his bags.

"Something happen?" she asked. She hated the way his shoulders slouched. They had had a great time the day before, and now he was standing there, wounded, looking out onto the landscape, apparently yearning for escape.

"Yeah," he said quietly. "I guess you could say that."

"What?" Jane asked, her question almost a whisper.

Sawyer shook his head. "I fucked up." He shrugged, took another drink. "Nothing new."

She pressed her lips into a tight line, trying to refrain from a full-fledged interrogation, but it was hard. Her curiosity had kept her up half the night, and now it was back with a vengeance, but there was more to it than that. The bags at his feet turned her stomach. She didn't care what April did, but Sawyer couldn't leave. This was their last visit up here, none of them sure when they'd be able to get together again next. After this, the cabin would be gone forever. After this, Ryan would pack his own bags and offer her his usual salute and toothy ready-for-adventure grin before giving her a hug and walking into an airport terminal. Her heart quickened at the idea of it—losing this final opportunity to be together, losing her last chance to make things right with the boy that she'd lost so long ago. She couldn't bear to look at him, her sinuses flaring with her sudden urge to cry. "I heard," she said, keeping her voice as steady as possible, staring down into her mug, the scent of java doing nothing to soothe her nerves. "What was it about?"

He sighed. "Jane, can we—" His mouth snapped shut, cutting his sentence short when April marched into the kitchen, fully dressed, looking like she'd been up for hours. Jane turned to face them, her mind reeling with those three cryptic words. *Can we what?* She watched April wrap a scarf around her neck while standing at the mouth of the hall, staring at her beau. And for the first time that weekend, Jane was seized with a genuine pang of animosity toward the stranger standing in her childhood mountain getaway. She wanted to grab the ends of that scarf and pull them so tight around April's neck that her perfectly pale complexion turned an ugly shade of blue. She wanted to openly roll her eyes and ask her where it was that April planned on going in such weather, and then banish her to the upstairs study like the unwelcome little bitch she was.

But rather than spitting out the profanities that were dangerously balanced on the tip of her tongue, she squared her shoulders, took a breath, and forced a smile that filled her with self-loathing. "Good morning," she said, the spirited tone of her own voice ringing in her ears. She was a hypocrite. A liar. A two-faced fake.

"Morning," April murmured, failing to offer Jane a smile.

Jane turned away, silently carrying her mug of coffee down the single step that led into the living room, giving the couple some room while her own hostility simmered just beneath her skin. April didn't care whether she offended anyone, scowling at virtual strangers, dodging conversations, spending entire days at ski lodges in some pathetic attempt to derail everyone's good time. She was the one who stormed through halls in the dead of night, slamming doors, waking up the house, and Jane was self-effacing enough to still be *nice* to her. Jane glared at her own reflection in the window, disgusted with her own tolerance.

"What are you doing?" she heard April ask. "Admiring the view?"

"We're snowed in."

"That's not my problem."

Jane frowned at the landscape. An empty deer feeder stood a handful of yards away from the living room window, half-buried.

Their dad used to drive more than twenty miles to buy bales of alfalfa during the summer, back when the cabin was used during every break she and Ryan had from school. They'd pile the feeder full, and Jane would spend hours watching deer meander outside the window—sometimes with babies, sometimes with fuzzy antlers atop their heads. During one winter, right before Christmas, one of them was bold enough to wander onto the deck. It had nearly startled their mother to death. Mary Adler had looked up from the dishes and stared straight into a buck's big black eyes. When she had screamed, the animal took a flying leap off the deck's icy stairs. Their dad had been hysterical about it all day, swearing it had been the funniest thing he'd ever seen.

"What do you want me to do, Ape?" Sawyer's tone was steady, soothing. He was blessed with the ability to keep a cool head in the most strained of situations. His composure had always made Jane feel safe; if the world were to suddenly catch fire, Sawyer could pacify her until it consumed them both.

"All I know is that we're leaving," April said. "Today. This morning."

"How?"

"I don't know. Figure it out. Why don't you go wake up your friend, go plow the road? Speaking of..." Her words tapered off.

Jane looked back to the kitchen just in time to catch Ryan's entrance. His hair was wild, sticking up in every direction. He shielded his eyes against the glare of the snow, then greeted the fighting couple with a few gravelly words: "Plow it with what, my dick?"

Jane looked away, biting back a bitter laugh, a flare of vindication igniting at the pit of her stomach. Ryan had a way with words. He was rough when it was called for, and he never hid his true feelings; they were twins, but complete opposites, like yin and yang.

"We've got two days left, remember?" Ryan reminded them. "It'll take us two days of this awesome vacation to shovel the drive, and maybe then, if we're lucky, we'll be able to get our asses back to civilization." The sound of a mug being pulled from an overhead cabinet. "But don't count on it." Coffee pouring into a cup. "We may be stuck here till spring."

"What?" April asked, alarmed.

"He's kidding," Sawyer assured her.

"Am I? Have you looked outside? Remember the winter break when we got stuck here for two weeks?"

"I'll try the Jeep," Sawyer resolved. "Throw it into four-wheel drive, see what happens..."

"You're delusional." Ryan laughed. "I bet there's two feet out there. Even if you get to the bottom—"

"I'll try it," Sawyer insisted.

"We really have to get home," April added, as if trying to fool them into believing that this attempt at a sudden departure had nothing to do with her, but with circumstances beyond her control.

Jane peeked into the kitchen just in time to see Sawyer leave. April followed him a second later. Ryan was left standing in front of the sink. He caught sight of his sister out of the corner of his eye and shot her a look.

"Did you hear them last night?" Jane asked quietly, making her approach.

"I heard *her*," he said. "Fucking maniac. I knew it the second I set eyes on her."

"Knew what?"

"That she's as crazy as a bag of cats."

Jane bit her tongue, taking a sip of coffee.

"I have my radar set to batshit. I can smell a psycho from a mile away."

"She didn't seem that—" Jane snapped her mouth shut, cutting herself off midsentence. No. She wasn't going to defend that chick, especially not to Ryan.

"What?" he asked. "That bad? Don't bullshit me. You saw it too. I *know* you did. If she thinks they're going to make it out of here today, it's proof of her insanity."

"I'll make breakfast," Jane told him, not wanting to talk about it anymore. If the conversation continued, it would only be a matter of time before she lost her cool and burst into tears. Abandoning her half-drained cup, she turned to the fridge. "Maybe you should go help him."

"Help him do what? Get stuck? Pretty sure he's got that covered." Ryan took a seat at the dining table.

Standing in front of the open fridge, she closed her eyes, her heart flipping inside her chest.

"The *moment* he told me she was coming, I just had this feeling," he continued. "Like, 'Well, that's it, there go our plans, shot to hell before they ever had a chance.'"

"Then you should have said something," she said softly, pulling a carton of eggs from the refrigerator.

"Like what?"

"Like 'Don't bring her.'"

"Right, because that would have gone over great." He grumbled into his mug, shaking his disheveled head. "This trip was doomed from the start."

"Then why are we here?" Jane asked. Ryan blinked up at her, surprised by the insistence in her tone.

"What do you mean?"

"I mean that if you *knew* this was going to suck, why did you still want to go through with it? Why couldn't we have done something else?"

"Like what?"

"I don't know, anything. He could have come out to Phoenix."

"Great idea," he said under his breath.

"We could have driven up to Denver."

"And you would have agreed to that?" he snapped, snorting at the idea of it. "I would have said, 'Hey, Jane, let's go visit Sawyer up in Denver,' and you would have said, 'Oh, great idea, let me pack my bags'? Bullshit, Jane. I've been trying to get us together for *years* and you've been evasive every time. Oh, no, you can't, you have stuff to do for school. Oh, it's bad timing. Oh this, oh that, oh dear sweet Jesus, not Sawyer Thomas."

She swallowed against the lump in her throat as her eyes burned.

"The only reason you came up here was because it was our last chance," Ryan said, the edge in his voice evening out, skirting around apologetic. "The only reason I was able to talk you into it was because of Zurich, and even then you hesitated. Even then you had to invite someone to come up here with you as a security blanket."

Sweeping a hand across her cheek, she cleared her throat, fighting like hell to keep her composure. "And you regret that I did, right?" she asked. "You regret finally meeting Lauren. I can tell by the way you can't keep your eyes off her."

"I don't regret meeting Lauren," he confessed. "Lauren is fucking amazing."

Jane stared into the sink, her fingers gripping the edge of the counter.

"But you know what?" he asked.

"What?"

"I sort of resent it."

A flurry of anxious butterflies erupted around her heart. *Resent?* Her gaze shot across the kitchen. Ryan was looking right at her, his expression shifting from unsteady to justified, as though he'd just unearthed some terrible secret.

"It's true, then," he said steadily. "There was an ulterior motive. You knew what was going to happen, that we were going to dig each other. How ironic that I should meet a girl I actually like weeks before packing up my shit and moving halfway across the world."

She clenched her teeth, suddenly hating him. "And you?" she asked, shooting a quick look toward the hallway to make sure nobody was eavesdropping before narrowing her eyes and glaring at her brother. "*You* didn't have an ulterior motive?" she hissed, keeping her voice down.

"Oh, I certainly did," Ryan confessed without missing a beat. "But that got as screwed up as this whole trip, and I hate to tell you, but that isn't my fucking fault."

She looked away from him, taking a steadying breath. He was right; it wasn't his fault. It wasn't anyone's fault. Things were just twisted, too muddled to ever get back to the way things were—back when she and Ryan and Sawyer were the Three Musketeers, always together, always laughing, never lonely or angry or unsure.

"You're right," she said after a long while. "He *will* get stuck."

"He's already stuck," Ryan said to himself.

"You should go out there with him. If he's going to leave, at least it'll give you more time—"

Ryan shoved himself out of his chair. "There are plenty of rooms. She didn't mind spending an entire day alone in the fucking lodge, but now she can't sulk on her own in here? What's the difference?" He crossed the kitchen to meet Jane at the sink, turning her to face him by looping his arms through hers and pulling her into an unanticipated hug. Jane sighed against his shoulder, mutely shaking her head at their situation. "I love you," he told her.

Lifting an arm to press the hem of her sleeve to one of her eyes, she eventually stepped out of his embrace and grabbed the carton of eggs from beside the sink. "How many do you want?" she asked, sniffling.

"Three," he said.

Jane looked up at him, forced a smile.

Ryan stared at her for a moment, then gave her shoulder a squeeze and turned away, wandering down the hall.

"This is fucking crazy," Ryan concluded while waddling through the snow, careful not to kill himself as he descended the deck stairs. "This snow *and* this idea. What the hell happened anyway?"

Sawyer plunged his hand into the precariously balanced powder on the railing, pushing it overboard. "I don't want to talk about it."

They rounded the corner to spot the Nissan and Jeep, heavily frosted, the tires half-buried in the drift.

"Dude." Ryan gave an incredulous laugh, motioning to the vehicles to punctuate the scenario's insanity. There was no way this plan was going to work.

"Didn't your dad have some sort of plow attachment for the snowmobile?" Sawyer asked.

"Like twenty years ago. He doesn't come up here in the winter anymore. He never got over that winter break."

"Then why did *we* come up here? You didn't think it was possible that *we* could get snowed in?"

Ryan held up his gloved hands. "I checked the forecast. I checked the damn thing like a half dozen times. You want a bullshit job? Predict the fucking weather."

"Look." Sawyer sighed. "I wouldn't care if it was just us, you know? But she's driving me insane."

"You want to tell me what happened?" Ryan asked, punching holes in the snow with each step. "Or are you going to cryptically whine about it for the rest of the weekend?"

"Just help me, okay?"

"I'm *trying* to help you. Want me to call her a cab? Request an airlift?"

Sawyer finally reached his Jeep and drew his arm across the hood. A thick blanket of white slid forward, exploding just beneath the front bumper.

"There's no goddamn way," Ryan said. "This isn't going to work."

"Are you sure that plow isn't in there?" Sawyer nodded toward the garage.

"I didn't see it. It isn't as though Pop was ever exactly handy, you know? He doesn't have some epic supply of usefulness stashed away for times like these."

Ryan continued to shuffle down the driveway toward the road, leaving Sawyer to knock snow off his car. He stopped at the crest of the hill, looked down the length of the drive—a good quarter of a mile, its rough surface and various potholes completely invisible beneath a blanket of white. Had there not been trees on either side of the road, it would have been impossible to tell it was there at all.

"This is insane," Ryan said softly, then raised his voice, craning his neck to look back toward his friend. "Even if you do get down there, you still have, like, five miles to the highway, and that highway is going to be *closed*, man. You're going to fly off the road and kill yourself."

But Sawyer didn't reply. With half the Jeep uncovered, he waded to the other side.

"Since when did you stop caring about life?" Ryan asked. "I know things are complicated, but say yes to the future. Be reasonable."

"Hey, Ry?" Jane's voice came around the side of the house, clear as a bell in the silence of a fresh snowfall. Ryan looked toward the cabin. He couldn't see her, but he knew exactly where she was—hanging halfway out of the kitchen door, wincing against the cold.

"Yeah?" he called back.

"When you're done, can you check for alfalfa under the deck and put it in the deer feeder if it's there?"

"Are you kidding?" he mumbled, but replied before she had a chance to ask him again. "Yes, dear," he chimed, then plodded back toward the cabin just in time to watch Sawyer pull open the driver's-side door. He had to give it a firm tug before it gave, frozen to the doorframe. Sliding inside, Sawyer banged his shoes together, trying to loosen the snow from the treads of his boots and folds of his jeans.

"I'm trying to help you," Ryan told him. "It was a miracle getting her up here." He nodded at the cabin, at the voice that had just spooled across the blanket of snow. "You do realize that, right?"

Sawyer kept his silence.

"And since when do you not answer me when I ask you a question, anyway?" Ryan asked, clumsily adjusting his trooper hat with gloved hands. "I mean, I respect your privacy and everything, but since when did we get to that point?"

The Jeep's engine rumbled to life.

Sawyer leaned back in his seat and sighed.

"You don't want to talk about it." Ryan held up his hands. "I get it. But you realize you're making a huge mistake, right? You do realize that this crazy shit…" He waved a hand at the house. "It's just going to get worse, yeah?"

"It's called responsibility," Sawyer said. "Maybe you've heard of it."

"You mean the stuff it takes to run a successful business?" Ryan quipped back. "Yeah, I've heard of it. But responsibility doesn't have to take over your life."

"No?" Sawyer raised an eyebrow at his friend. "Is that why you're moving? Because it hasn't taken over?" Sawyer stepped on the gas, revving the engine. Ryan stepped away from the car as Sawyer swung the door closed.

"It's part-time," he said, raising his voice, trying to yell through the window glass and over the engine's roar. "What you're getting into is full-time for the rest of your goddamn life." The Jeep started to roll backward, crunching snow beneath the back tires.

Sawyer gave it some gas, leaving deep tire tracks in the driveway. Backing up onto the road, he pointed the Jeep down the steep grade. The e-brake zipped into place. Ryan watched his childhood friend slide out of the car and trudge around its front, using the Jeep's tracks as a thoroughfare as he marched back toward the house. Ryan blocked his way when Sawyer reached the end of the tracks, his hands held up, wanting to say what he had to say before Sawyer went back inside.

"Listen, you're my best friend, all right?"

"Don't," Sawyer warned, pushing Ryan's hands away from his chest.

"You don't have to do this. A kid doesn't have to come with vows anymore."

"Ryan, move," Sawyer said, but Ryan refused.

"I'm not moving until you hear me out, because this shit has to be said."

"Nothing has to be said. What's done is done."

Ryan shook his head. "What does that even mean?"

"Just move." Sawyer tried to step around, but Ryan moved in the same direction.

"*What's* done?" he asked. "You told me you were going to wait; you were going to think it through."

Sawyer grabbed him by the shoulders and moved him to the side before stepping around the Nissan's front bumper, trudging toward the deck.

Ryan peered at Sawyer's back. "Hey," he called out to him. Sawyer paused, looking over his shoulder. "What the hell did you do?"

Sawyer shook his head and looked away, ascending the stairs while Ryan was left to glare at the trunk of a tree.

Sawyer stepped back inside the cabin, tracking snow across the floor. He snatched his backpack off the ground and threw it over his shoulder, the duffel bag following suit. Jane was standing at the kitchen island, a whisk in her hand, a chrome mixing bowl sitting in front of her. She blinked at him, her expression blank. Sawyer stared at her, frozen in place, his brain telling him to say something, to apologize yet again, but his vocal cords constricted, refusing to make a sound.

"Are you really leaving?" Jane asked, her expression unreadable.

"It isn't my call," he croaked past the dryness of his throat. "I'm sorry. Everything is just…"

Jane nodded, looked down. "Yeah," she said. "I know."

He stared at her, wanting to ask what that meant, wanting to know what it was she knew. But before he could gather up the courage, April stepped into the kitchen and shot Jane a look: a smile so disingenuous that it turned Sawyer's stomach.

"Thanks so much for having us," April said, her tone painfully insincere. "We had a blast."

Jane's expression wavered. He watched her indecision flicker across her face like bad reception, challenging her soft-spoken nature as she tried to smile in return.

"We'll see you again," April told her. "At the wedding, for sure."

Sawyer's heart pulled into itself like a snail backing into its shell. For half a second he felt like the world had reversed its orbit. April stepped through the open kitchen door and out into the snow, leaving Sawyer silently reeling in her wake. When he dared to glance back up at Jane, she looked a little paler than before, her green eyes glinting in the morning sun. He hadn't wanted the news to come out this way, hadn't even told Ryan for fear of how he would react, especially after what Jane had gone through with Alex not more than a few months back. Sawyer had kept his engagement to April a secret from the person who knew everything about him. Ryan even knew about the baby six weeks ago, and back then Sawyer had still been unsure about how he felt about what his life had become. And the first thing Ryan had told him hadn't been "congratulations" or even how Sawyer had just screwed up in the biggest way possible, but "Don't marry her." It was classic Ryan, a warning born of his own insecurities. And so when Sawyer asked April to become his wife two weeks later, he hadn't brought it up in conversation with Ryan.

But now it felt like keeping that secret had been all for nothing. He was waiting for it, waiting for Jane to tell him she never wanted to see him again, waiting for her to tell Ryan, so Ryan could tell Sawyer what a huge mistake he was making. How stupid could he possibly be?

"I'm sorry," he said, then turned, not wanting to hear her reply, not wanting to see her face, not wanting anything but to get away, to crawl into the Jeep and drive.

By the time he stepped off the deck, April was halfway to the car and his dismay was slowly shifting gears. He couldn't help but think that maybe Ryan had been right—April *was* a mistake. Because what kind of a girl stooped so low as to break such important news in such a cold, calculated way? What kind of a girl was willing to destroy his dearest relationships because she was pissed?

As Sawyer approached the Nissan, Ryan's arms were crossed over his chest, his expression grave. His friend's disappointment was apparent. Sawyer stopped in front of him, dropping the duffel bag into the snow.

"I have to tell you something," he said. "Because April just made shit a lot worse, and if I don't tell you, you're going to hear it from Jane."

"You already asked her," Ryan said flatly, and while Sawyer shouldn't have been surprised that Ryan had figured it out on his own, he was still caught off guard. He opened his mouth to speak, to explain, but Ryan shook his head as if to say *forget it.* "It's your life," he said. "It was screwed up of me to try to stand in your way. I'm sure she's great."

Sawyer frowned at Ryan's resignation. Something about it felt finite, like his closest, truest friend was giving up on him, like Sawyer had just traded a best friend in for a wife. "Don't do that," he told him.

"Do what?" Ryan asked. "Finally stop being a dick and start being supportive? What else is there for me to do?"

"You'll always be a dick," Sawyer assured him, staring down at the snow.

"I should probably try to fix that, or I'll end up turning into my dad."

"Probably."

"So, sorry for being a dick," Ryan muttered. "Just give me a chance to get back into the country before you run off to Vegas or something, all right? I want to see Elvis marry you. I at least deserve that much."

"The Chapel of Love for the ceremony and a Barry Manilow concert as the honeymoon," Sawyer agreed.

They both went silent then, staring at the ground between them, shifting their weight from foot to foot as the cold bit at their cheeks. Finally, Sawyer moved in to give his best friend a parting hug. "Tell Jane I'm sorry, all right? It wasn't supposed to be this way."

"Yeah, I know."

"Hey, good luck with Lauren. Who knows, right?"

Ryan smirked.

Sawyer turned to walk the narrow tire trail toward the Jeep. The question of whether the Jeep would make it through the snow was irrelevant now. They *had* to make it, because Sawyer couldn't go back inside that cabin again. Not after April's announcement. Not after the way Jane had looked at him, wounded, betrayed.

Slamming the car door shut, he clicked his seat belt into place, shifted into first, and released the parking break. April sat in the passenger seat, pissed off, not speaking—silence he was sure to miss a few minutes from now, when she'd grow tired of the silent treatment and launch into another tirade. Easing the Jeep forward, snow crunched beneath the tires. Ryan appeared in the side-view mirror, watching them descend the steep grade.

The distance between them grew.

When the Jeep slowed, Sawyer gave it some gas. It continued to ramble forward, but eventually had to stop. He put it in reverse, backing up to reveal a pile of snow he'd pushed forward with the bumper, a good two feet tall, compacted and barricading them from going any farther.

Ryan was right. They were going to end up dead.

April said nothing despite the wall of snow ahead of them, and for a moment Sawyer wondered whether she realized how unachievable this was. Maybe that was why she wasn't saying anything—because she *knew* it was impossible. Maybe she was stewing in her own defeat, ready to tell him to forget it. But

Sawyer wasn't going to forget it—not after what she'd pulled back there. She wanted to go, so they'd go. Passive-aggressiveness had slithered into his bloodstream, infecting him like a disease.

He shoved the Jeep into first, revving the engine. In the rear-view mirror, Ryan put his hands on top of his head, his mouth moving. Sawyer couldn't hear him, but he knew exactly what Ryan was saying. *You've got to be kidding.* But Sawyer wasn't kidding.

He floored it.

April gasped.

The Jeep hit the bank of snow and rolled through it, but more snow gathered in front of the car seconds later. They had advanced only a couple of feet before they were stuck again, and this time Sawyer couldn't back up. With one pile of snow behind them and another one ahead, they were trapped.

"Are you crazy?" April screeched.

"This was your idea," he reminded her, trying to stay calm.

"Right," she said. "This is all *my* fault, you bringing me here…"

"Bringing you here? Are you serious?"

"Go around it," she demanded, motioning at the blockade of snow ahead of them.

"You practically begged me to bring you."

"Yeah, well, big fucking mistake," she said. "It won't happen again, I assure you."

Sawyer bit his tongue, deciding to focus on how to get the Jeep down the road, but April refused to let up.

"Like I want to hang out with your preppy-ass friends any-way." She scowled. "It's like spending a weekend with Donnie and fucking Marie."

Sawyer closed his eyes, trying to keep his cool.

"It's gross," she told him.

He blinked at her.

"Gross that you associate with people like that." Her bottom lip quivered and she looked away, as if ashamed of the judgment that had just dripped from her tongue. "I'm sorry that I'm not as perfect as Jane Adler," she said softly, tears streaking her cheeks.

Sawyer opened his mouth to speak, but her culpability robbed him of his fire. He looked straight ahead, staring through the windshield and an endless expanse of snow, his guilt so heavy it was suffocating him, burning him up from the inside out. He unzipped his coat and pressed his face into his hands, momentarily overwhelmed by the silence that surrounded them.

"Here," April said, her voice quavering with emotion.

Sawyer let his hands drop to his lap and blinked at a ring attached to a silver chain in the palm of her hand. It was an old ring he had had since high school, one that was far too big for her to wear, but he had given her as a placeholder for her real engagement ring once he had the cash to buy it. He didn't move, afraid to take it, scared to know what that would mean. Would he ever see her again? Would he be shut out of his child's life?

"You can give me the real one when you buy it." She wiped a cheek with the sleeve of her coat. "If you decide you still want to buy it." She dropped the ring into his hand and looked away again. "I'm sorry that I'm such a bitch. I just want to go home, okay? Please just take me home."

His heart twisted as he closed his hand around the ring, sliding it into the pocket of his coat before looking back to the unnavigable road ahead. "I don't know if I can, Ape," he confessed quietly.

"Just…please try," she pleaded. "I can't go back in there. I'm not going to. There's no way."

Sawyer could relate to that. He didn't want to go back in there either, not without erasing the last fifteen minutes from everyone's memory. He reversed again. There wasn't enough distance between them and the car-made mogul to plow through it, so he turned the wheel to the right instead. They'd go around.

He heard something behind them—a yell. Ryan was waving his arms over his head. Jane was standing next to him, her oversize sweater hanging off her like a sack, her colorful pajama pants a circuslike contrast against the whiteness of snow. Sawyer hit the brakes, suddenly realizing what Ryan was screaming about, but it was too late. The Jeep slid down the slope of the driveway, then suddenly lurched forward, the right front tire sinking lower than the rest.

"Shit," Sawyer said, freezing in place. But with no possibility of reversing, he kept the Jeep rolling; it was forward or nothing. April sucked in a shaky breath as the front tire pulled out of the divot while the back tire replaced it. He cursed his decision of veering right rather than left. Left would have given him a better view of what he was doing. Right just had him guessing what was coming.

"Roll down your window," he said.

April did as she was told, a startled expression veiling her features, a cold blast of air coiling through the car's interior.

"I need to know if I'm clear."

"I don't know," she said, her bottom lip trembling again.

"Ape, come on. I need your help."

"Clear of *what*?" she asked.

Frustrated, he leaned forward, his chest pressed against the steering wheel. The trees were close to the passenger side now, threatening to knock off the side-view mirror. Ryan was skidding down the road behind them, sticking to the tracks they'd made. Sawyer reluctantly rolled down his window as his friend slid to a stop beside the car.

"You can't go any farther," Ryan told them, breathing hard. "You're at the edge of the runoff."

Sawyer slammed the Jeep into reverse, but the tires just spun, kicking up dirty snow onto the road.

"I'm not going back in there," April whispered, her gaze pleading for Sawyer to keep trying.

"You're stuck," Ryan said. "There's no way out of here."

That was when April started sobbing.

Sawyer blinked at the girl next to him, surprised by her response. There was no question that she would resist hiking back up the driveway, but he couldn't help but stare as she shook her head in insistence, her fists pounding against her knees, a full-fledged temper tantrum—something he had yet to witness in the six months they had been together.

"No no no *no NO!*" she yelled. "I'm not going back in there! I want to go home!"

Ryan leaned through the window, trying to reason with her. "Even if you get down this road, you're never going to make it to the highway."

"Why don't you mind your own business?" she wailed. "I don't even *know* you."

"Jesus," Sawyer said.

"If you don't drive, I will," April cried into her hands. "Just stay here with your friends, okay? I don't want to be here anymore."

"Okay, just give me some room," Sawyer told Ryan. Ryan opened his mouth to say something, but Sawyer shot his friend a look. "I can't handle this right now," he confessed. "Ryan, move." And then he stomped on the accelerator.

The Jeep lurched forward.

Ryan jumped back.

The right tires sank low and April's eyes went wide. One of her hands instinctively pressed against the dash while the other held the armrest of the door.

"Oh my god," she yelped, but Sawyer pressed on toward the inevitable, and the inevitable came quickly. The Jeep sank low, every nerve in Sawyer's body buzzing as he felt the left tires lift off the ground. April screamed as the car tipped against the embankment. Sawyer's mind reeled, wondering why the hell he had just done what he'd done, wondering if this stupid move had been some subconscious sabotage to stay here longer now that April's ring was in the pocket of his coat, now that he was free. The Jeep tipped over, pinning April's door in place as she bawled.

They were stuck for good.

April's breath came in gasps. She stared at the boy in the driver's seat, speechless, as Sawyer tried to keep from falling on top of her. After a bit of effort he shoved the car door open and pulled himself out.

"Holy shit," Ryan said, his hands on top of his head again, assessing the situation. "Holy shit, dude. Holy *shit*. You just wrecked your car," he marveled, unable to peel his eyes away from the leaning vehicle. "Your baby. Your pride and joy."

Sawyer stared at the Jeep for a long while, as though suddenly realizing exactly what he had done. And then he shrugged. "Yeah, I did. Didn't see *that* coming, did you?"

April cried out for help as Ryan laughed, exasperated. Sawyer stepped back to the car and helped heft her up and out of the vehicle. April tumbled out of the window, slipping on the snow. She sat there for a long moment before Ryan extended a hand to her, trying to help her up; but she refused, too stubborn to admit that she had lost. Still sobbing, she eventually righted herself, but rather than walking uphill toward the cabin with the boys, she pointed herself downhill instead.

"Where are you going?" Sawyer asked her.

"Home!" she yelled back.

Sawyer tipped his head up to the sky—*God save me*—and groaned. Ryan paused in his ascent and stood next to him, looking back at April as she stumbled through shin-deep powder.

"Are you going to get her?" he asked.

"No," Sawyer said. "Let her walk it off."

Ryan shrugged and turned back up the hill, he and Sawyer slogging through the snow.

"I can't believe you actually asked her," Ryan said after a while.

"I don't want to talk about it," Sawyer said. "Seriously, don't ever bring that up again."

CHAPTER SEVEN

April wiped at her eyes as she stumbled through the snow. She cursed herself for crying, the cold air stinging her cheeks as she staggered into the featureless landscape. Swiping at her eyes with her sleeves, she swallowed her sobs, wondering whether she had overreacted; maybe what she had sensed between Sawyer and Jane had been nothing but her own jealousy, insecurity, imagination. It wasn't as though she'd caught them in the shadows of an empty room.

But the way he looked at her, the way his voice went softer when he spoke to her; it made April's heart ache. She could see it plainly on Jane's face: she and Sawyer were sharing some hidden secret.

The snow was deep, nearly up to her knees in places, but she was determined to keep going, if only until her heart untwisted itself. She had no idea how she was going to face any of them again. She'd embarrassed herself, especially with Ryan, sobbing like some hysteric. But the emotion had overwhelmed her—a deluge of frustration that had splintered into temporary insanity. And now Sawyer's Jeep was stuck in a ravine, they were snowed in for God knows how long. Those people wouldn't want anything to do with her again. And Sawyer...

Another sob burst from between her lips.

The way he had taken back the ring, no protest, no anything—Sawyer wouldn't marry her now. She had seen the look on his face, uncertainty veiling a ghost of relief. She had shown him the darkest part of herself—the anger and jealousy that occasionally took hold of her, consuming her like a fire. It had startled him, and now he'd call the whole thing off, baby or not.

With the snow as deep as it was, each step was an effort. Her expectation of reaching the highway began to dwindle. Her toes began to burn. She wondered whether this was how it felt to be lost, alone, spiraling toward some inevitable fate. The endless expanse of white, the silence, the solitude were overwhelming. She stifled another cry, twisting to look over her shoulder. The road leading up to the cabin was gone, and she wouldn't have had any idea which direction she had come from had it not been for her tracks. But it was that path that pushed her forward despite the cold. When Sawyer became worried enough, it would be easy to find her. And that was what she wanted. Despite her anger, she wanted him to see how far she'd stalked away from the house— that distance representing the hurt he'd caused. She wanted to hear him call her name, to follow her into the emptiness, to grab her by the shoulders and shake her, a classic black-and-white movie moment. *Damn it, April, don't you know I love you?* And then she'd crumple in his arms. All would be forgiven. She'd apologize, beg him to take her back.

A spark of irritation bit at her heart. He should beg her to take *him* back. This was his fault. He was the one who had made her suspicious. Narrowing her eyes against the glare of the snow, she pushed onward, defiant. Despite her thick woolen socks, her feet burned inside her boots. Her hands hurt, and she cupped them over her mouth and blew against the thinness of her gloves. Glancing over her shoulder again, she saw movement. A spark of elation warmed her from the inside out. He was coming to get her.

If she hadn't seen the shadows shift behind her at that very moment, she would have started back toward the cabin despite her reluctance. She was starting to freeze, but he was on his way, and she was going to make it as difficult as possible for him to catch up to her. The harder it was for him, the more overjoyed they'd be to be back together.

She picked up her pace, pushing off trees, throwing her weight forward, making her footfalls swifter. There was a clearing ahead and she pictured it in her head—summertime, an expanse of grass and wildflowers. If they had only waited seven months from now, they could have come to the mountains when it was warm, packed up a picnic lunch and walked to this very clearing, a baby tucked into the crook of April's arm. Sawyer would have brought his guitar. They would have flown kites and woven dandelions into crowns and done all the hippie bullshit that made April roll her eyes. Yet somehow, standing in the cold, seeing the clearing covered in snow, she yearned for warmth, for bologna sandwiches and lemonade and a semblance of family that, up until then, she had never had. A picnic in the mountains didn't sound so bad as long as he was by her side. She was tired of being damaged. She was ready to let it all go.

She turned back toward Sawyer. Despite their differences, she *did* love him, she *wanted* to get married, she was glad the baby was his.

But there was nobody behind her. The shadow she'd seen shifted every now and again was still there, lurking. Was he just watching her, making sure that she didn't go too far?

"Sawyer?" She called the name into the silence, nothing but the howl of wind high up above.

The shadow froze when her voice left her throat.

"Sawyer," she repeated. "Please...I'm sorry. That was crazy. I just...this trip has been hard for me. I got overwhelmed." Her feet were really hurting now. She could hardly feel her toes.

Her nerves buzzed when the shadow shifted once more, because it wasn't the same shadow she'd been watching. She swallowed against a wave of anxiety. Sawyer wouldn't have come out here alone. It was probably Ryan. They had been following her all this time. But why hadn't she heard them talking? Why had they let her come this far?

Because it's not them, she thought.

Worst-case scenarios spiraled through her head. She had wandered onto someone's property and the landowner was a psychopath, horror-movie insane. Maybe he lived out in the middle of nowhere because out in the middle of nowhere there wasn't anyone around to hear the screams. Maybe some maniac had heard her yelling Sawyer's name, had followed her out here, and was waiting for the perfect time to strike. That was where the blood along the side of the road had come from—some crazy killer ready to slit her throat.

"Hello?" Barely a whisper.

She was an idiot. She should have sucked it up, marched back to the cabin, locked herself upstairs for the rest of the weekend. Her breath hitched in her throat. A third shadow shifted beneath the shade of the trees.

"Sawyer?" The name quavered, fear punctuating its syllables.

No response.

It wasn't him.

She turned away, her breaths coming in gasps now. Those shadows were blocking her way back to the house. She started to walk again, determined to put distance between herself and the trees. Maybe her stalker would back off, not wanting to come into the clearing. Maybe if she screamed loud enough Sawyer would hear her back at the cabin. He and Ryan would find her. They had to. She couldn't be that far away.

Unable to help herself, the tears came again.

The cabin had settled into an uncomfortable silence. Ryan sat at the table, his chin in his hands, while Jane kept herself busy in the kitchen. Sawyer was alone in the living room, nursing a cup of coffee, staring at a blank television screen, while Lauren spent some time on the deck smoking, then went back upstairs. The tension was stifling, and Ryan considered opening all the doors and windows to air the place out, wondering if the cold would shock them all back into some semblance of normalcy.

It had been ten minutes since he and Sawyer had left April outside, and Ryan could relate to her need to get away. He'd spent most of his life shutting down and clamming up. But he couldn't help the seed of worry from sprouting in the pit of his stomach. It was cold out there, and the clouds were rolling in fast.

Ryan glanced over to Jane when she sighed and poured a fresh mug of coffee. She looked tired, ravaged by a revelation that hurt more than she had expected. He could see it on her face—the emotional scar that she had tried so desperately to heal freshly opened and bleeding. Jane turned to look at him, forced a broken smile when she realized he'd been watching her the entire time, then took a seat next to him at the table with a downturned chin. Her eyebrows furrowed together as she tried to understand it, trying to figure out how to make things right again. But Ryan doubted there was a way to do that now. Their group had been fractured beyond repair. If it hadn't been for the snow, all that would have been left to do was to pack up and go home.

"I was going to make another dinner," she started.

"Don't," he said. "Just take it easy."

"We still have to eat," she protested, staring into the steam of her coffee cup.

The wind picked up outside, howling through the trees. He watched the pines closest to the deck bend against the railing. Jane closed her eyes as if contemplating something.

"When did all of this get so screwed up?" she asked quietly.

Ryan shook his head, sliding his hand across the table to squeeze her fingers in reassurance. Everything was going to be okay. It had been years before, and it would be again.

"I guess I just..." She hesitated, scoffed at the thought that rolled through her head. "I was stupidly hopeful, you know?" She lifted her gaze to look at him. "As much as I hate to say it, I think you should go find her."

He could see it in her eyes—she didn't want April back any more than he did, but the weather was taking a bad turn. The wind was pushing the clouds fast across the sky. In another fifteen minutes the sun would be blotted out entirely. Pinching the bridge of his nose, he drew his hand across his face. He predicted yelling, lots of slamming doors. It would be like Mom and Dad all over again. He slid her mug over to himself, took a swig, and rose to his feet.

"You should talk to him," he told her, nodding toward the living room. "He feels like shit."

"What am I supposed to say?" she asked him.

Ryan tipped his gaze toward the ceiling. "Just tell him you don't hate him. Don't forget that when you and Alex shacked up, Sawyer was the first to congratulate you. You think he was happy?"

Jane frowned. "And you think he's happy now?" she asked, daring to look her brother in the eyes.

But Ryan didn't hold her gaze for long. The sound of a zipper being pulled upward had his attention drifting across the kitchen to Sawyer.

"I'm going to go bring her in," he told them. "Last thing we need is someone catching pneumonia."

"Don't," Ryan said. "I'm going right now."

"I'm already dressed," Sawyer protested.

"You're going to go out there and as soon as you find her there's going to be another fight," Ryan warned. "You'll get stuck out there and then the *both* of you will have pneumonia. Let me go."

Sawyer frowned, looking unsure. He looked to Jane for reassurance, and she slowly offered him a nod.

Ryan waited for Sawyer to step back into the living room before giving Jane a look. *Talk to him.* And then he turned down the hallway and walked up the stairs.

He paused when he saw Lauren sitting on the sill of the bay window in the upstairs hall. After what he had watched transpire between April and Sawyer outside, he was overwhelmed with the urge to confide in her, to let her know that, yeah, she had his attention. An odd sensation twisted his stomach as soon as she looked his way. It was nerves. He hadn't felt nervous around a girl in years.

"You okay?" he asked, and she offered him a faint shrug before twisting her hair. He paused next to the window, his shoulder against the wall. "What?"

"I feel bad," she confessed, looking out onto the trees. "For Jane, I mean. Learning about it like that." She paused, meeting Ryan's gaze. "Did you know?"

Ryan sucked in a breath. Being clued in to the seriousness of Sawyer and April's relationship but *still* having chosen to shove Sawyer and Jane into the same house for four days made him feel like shit. It had been a selfish attempt to lift some of his own guilt for taking the merger, more money, the move—because if Sawyer could only take his place, he wouldn't have to feel so bad for leaving Jane behind.

"Really?" Lauren asked, taking his silence as a yes. She gave him a severe look, as if judging him by that single indiscretion. It made him numb, like he couldn't have screwed up any more even if he had tried. "Did you *want* this to happen?"

"Of course not," he said somewhat curtly, then looked down at his feet and shook his head. "Of course not," he repeated, his tone softening. "I never wanted any of this. But I'm an idiot. I thought I could change things."

"How?"

"I don't know."

"You're lying," she said, sliding off the windowsill to stand in front of him, nearly chest to chest. "It was a chivalrous gesture," she said. "It says a lot about your character. But you're right, you're an idiot. This shouldn't have happened. This is bad all around."

"I'm self-indulgent, irresponsible."

"You don't need to degrade yourself, Ryan."

"Then what?" he asked, chewing his bottom lip.

"Just make it right. Sit them down and explain it to them. Apologize." She offered him a smile, lifting a hand to slide her fingers along the curve of his jaw. Ryan's stomach flipped. He closed his eyes, then caught her hand in his, giving it a light squeeze, trying to sequester the butterflies that had unfurled their wings inside his chest.

"I want this to work," she whispered, her breath caressing the shell of his ear. "Us, I mean. I want to see where this goes. But I need you to fix this, you understand? I need to know you have that in you, because if Jane can't trust you with her heart, I certainly can't trust you with mine."

"Ren." He whispered her name, the tips of his fingers dragging along her arm. She tilted her head as if to listen, allowing the swell of her bottom lip to brush against his. "I'll fix it, but April's still outside. I have to go find her."

Lauren leaned back, putting an inch between them before she offered him a quiet laugh. Taking a backward step, she motioned to Ryan that he was free to leave, but it was the last thing he wanted to do. He yearned to kiss her, to have that first intimate moment right there by the window, the snow in the foreground, the both of them standing in his favorite place. But it couldn't be. Not then. So he did the next-best thing. Lifting her hand in his, he pressed his lips to her knuckles before releasing her fingers. He turned away from her, pointing himself toward his room.

He paused when he heard her speak.

"I'm coming with you," she said. "Give me two minutes." And then she ducked into the master bedroom, and he couldn't help but smile.

CHAPTER EIGHT

Jane and Sawyer watched Ryan and Lauren step into the snow from the open kitchen door, Oona following her master. Tracking people in the bitter cold was what Oona had been bred to do, but as soon as the trio reached the deck stairs, the dog hesitated, looking back to the cabin. Confusion washed over Ryan's face as his dog vacillated between staying and going.

"Maybe it's too cold," Jane suggested, but she knew that was impossible. These dogs raced the Iditarod. They trekked across Siberia. There was something more to Oona's reluctance—something that made Jane uncomfortable. It was enough to make her want to pull Lauren and Ryan back inside, refuse to let them go, but it didn't change the fact that April was out there somewhere and it was growing colder by the minute.

Sawyer had insisted he go out to search with Ryan and Lauren, but Ryan had protested. Both he and Lauren were already dressed in their gear and ready to go, while Sawyer's stuff was out in his Jeep halfway down the drive. Allowing Sawyer to accompany them would have slowed down the search party, and the snow was starting to fall. Sawyer had eventually relented; leaning against the kitchen island, he pressed buttons on his phone as if a certain combination would magically grant him a bar or two of service.

Jane watched him try again to send a text message to April's phone, only to have it fail like all the others. She looked away, her attention veering back to the dog.

Oona whined at the top of the steps, watching her owner continue without her. She barked as if telling Ryan to stop, then lay down in the snow and put her snout on her paws, offering up a pair of puppy-dog eyes.

"Come on back inside," Jane said. But the dog didn't respond. Jane shook her head and closed the door, left to stand in a hauntingly quiet house. Sucking in a breath, she narrowed her eyes at her long-abandoned coffee cup upon the counter, then swigged the cold dregs like a shot of tequila.

"Aren't you hot?" she asked. Sawyer was still wearing the jacket he'd pulled on earlier that morning, as though somewhere in the corner of his mind he was planning on spontaneously getting up and walking out.

Sawyer's gaze wavered from his phone down to the secondary jacket he'd brought with him—much lighter than the one he had worn snowboarding, insubstantial against what was going on outside.

"Well, you're making me nervous."

A faint smile crossed his lips, assuring her that he remembered that particular pet peeve. She couldn't stand it when people kept their coats on with no intention of leaving. It made her anxious, as though the situation hinged on her every word. Abandoning his useless phone on the island, he unzipped his jacket and shrugged out of it, dropping it on to one of the dining table chairs before returning to his original spot. Jane's attention snagged on his faded black Sisters of Mercy shirt, almost hating him for bringing that particular shirt with him—he must have remembered, must have known.

"Is that what I think it is?" she asked, staring at a well-worn logo against faded black cotton—the outline of a star behind a featureless profile. But he didn't have to respond for her to know it was the very shirt she had stolen from his room, the one she had slept in after their first night together while his parents had been out of town. Jane had loved that room. It was an extension of its owner, smoky and mysterious, the walls plastered in torn-out magazine pages and band posters. She would sit at his desk, picking dried wax from the varnished top while he played her his favorite songs, stuffing CD after CD into his crappy stereo. That room had always been dark, the red curtain hanging heavy over his window, choking out the daylight. He had books about medieval warfare and music theory; stuff she could hardly wrap her mind around, but she'd flip through them while lying on his bed, inhaling a deliciously noxious mix of cigarettes and candle smoke. Jane had walked away from that relationship with a lot of things: a love for the strange and unusual, a weakness for the scent of clove cigarettes, and an ache in her heart whenever she heard one of the hundreds of songs he would play for her on a loop. But she'd given back that T-shirt. Even after a dozen washes it had held his scent, so she folded it up, tucked it into a box, and mailed it to Boston a few weeks after she had lost him to the world. It was a decision she regretted, a decision that tied her heart into a knot with the shirt's sudden reappearance.

"Same one," he replied. "A little worse for wear."

Jane looked to her hands. "Why did you bring it?"

Sawyer held his silence for a long while, then pushed away from the island and stepped back toward the table. She watched him dig through one of his pockets before returning, the quiet jingle of metal hitting tile sounding when a ring tumbled from the palm of his hand. She stared at it for what felt like an eternity, knowing that ring as well as that T-shirt. It was the one he used to wear on his thumb—the one she used to spin when they held hands.

She shook her head, not understanding what he was trying to say.

"She gave it back," he said "Told me to give her a real one if I still wanted to."

Jane bit her bottom lip, wanting to reach out and touch that old memento as though doing so would somehow bring back the past. "And are you going to?" she asked softly, afraid to meet his gaze. She pressed her lips together in a tight line, shaking her head. "Sorry, that's none of my business."

"Isn't it?"

She blinked up at him, suddenly desperate to reach out, to grab his hand and crawl under his arm.

"Did *you* want to get married?" he asked, pushing his hair behind his ears.

She swallowed against his question, frowning at the floor. "Yeah, I mean…" She raised a single shoulder up to her ear.

"It felt like the right thing to do," he said. "Until it didn't."

Sawyer had a way with words, always knowing what she was thinking, like magic. Ryan was Jane's rightful duplicate, but Sawyer could decipher her like no other. He could reach inside her head and expose her innermost secrets with a phantom hand.

"It was my idea," he confessed. "And it may have been a mistake, but what can you do?"

"But why?"

"It felt like the right thing."

"The right thing," she echoed, her chest suddenly feeling Tin Man hollow. Sawyer Thomas wasn't the marrying kind. He was like Ryan in that sense—free and exuberant, with a bright future ahead of him. He was passionate about his work, and he'd worked hard to get where he was. Jane swallowed against the slow-growing realization of what "the right thing" must have meant. She had teased her own brother more than a few times, insisting that the only thing that would ever tie Ryan down was accidentally knocking someone up.

"Please tell me that doesn't mean what I think it does," she whispered. Sawyer had just scored his dream job, had moved into a new apartment. From what Ryan had told her, he was happy in his new life. But now it was unclear where that happiness had come from; had it been because everything seemed to be falling into place, or had it been because of April and the promise of a family?

She stepped closer to him, gathering enough courage to grab his hand. Her heart lurched when he squeezed her hand in response.

"Don't think less of me," he told her. "This wasn't the plan. You always told me I was good at making the right choices, remember?"

She did. She had told him that very thing inside an airport terminal despite her breaking heart. Jane offered him a weak smile, on the verge of tears. She couldn't decide whether she was upset because his dream had been derailed, or because her secret desire had just been rendered impossible.

"But then I got to wondering, why not me?"

Jane pressed her lips together, trying to keep her composure. "Why not you…?"

"Yeah, why not? People get married, they have kids; that's life."

She wanted to protest, to insist that he wasn't regular people. Sawyer Thomas didn't get married, didn't have kids. He was supposed to remain eternal and perfect while everyone else moved on, got hurt, grew old with age and regret.

"I'm happy for you, Tom," she told him, but she could see he wasn't convinced.

"Yeah, I can tell." He cracked a smile. "Overjoyed."

"Sorry, it's just a lot to take in. As long as you're happy. This is what you want?"

"Wanting and getting aren't the same thing," he told her. Dipping his chin enough to catch her gaze, he offered her a brave smile. "Right?"

"What does that mean, exactly?"

"Are you really going to make me say it?"

"I don't know." She swallowed against the lump in her throat. "Maybe."

He shook his head and looked away. She could see it in his face: he wasn't buying in. Despite all of his opportunities to corner her—the night in the kitchen, up on the mountain, on the chair lift where nobody would see, and now—he restrained himself. Admitting that he had held himself back would undo his effort. It would render all that willpower invalid.

"You said this may be a mistake," she said. "What does that mean?"

"It means it may be a mistake," he said. "You've made those yourself."

Tears stung the backs of her eyes. She needed to tell him, confess that despite the heartache, she was *glad* she'd caught Alex cheating on her.

I still love you.

It screamed inside her head, knocking against the sides of her skull, fighting to break free. But she couldn't tell him, not after what he'd confessed. There would be no breaking up the wedding, no last-minute confession, no running away into the sunset. Because now there was a baby, and a baby was the most important thing.

"Do you regret it?" he asked. "Marrying Alex, sharing the time with him that you did; you loved him, didn't you?"

She swallowed against the lump in her throat, winced on the inside, getting his point. "I did," she confessed. "Once."

"So you know where I'm at," he said quietly. "You understand."

She laughed, tears finally spilling over her bottom lashes. She swiped at her cheeks, looking up to the ceiling, trying to squelch the sob that was trying to claw its way out of her chest.

Sawyer leaned forward to catch her chin in a tender grasp, the pad of his thumb sliding across her cheek. Her nerves buzzed beneath his touch. "We learn from our mistakes," he told her. "You're stronger for what happened to you, and if this blows up in my face..." Sawyer's expression twisted in apologetic uncertainty. "*C'est la vie.*"

"But I want to *protect* you." The words tumbled out of her before she could stop them, her entire body going rigid with the declaration. A mixture of shame and embarrassment crashed over her, threatening to suck the air out of the room. But before she could wilt with mortification, she was disarmed by Sawyer's smile. His grin was wide, so effervescent and beautiful that it nearly broke her heart. It was the smile she remembered from so long ago, the very smile that had made her fall in love with him, the expression that had haunted her for so long. His eyes glinted with a look she'd longed to see for years—adoration, an overwhelming ebb of affection just for her.

She nearly jumped when Oona barked outside. Could they already be back? Her gaze met Sawyer's, and for a moment she felt like her world would crumble if she didn't kiss him one last time. She could see it in his eyes—he knew what she wanted, knew what she was thinking. But instead of edging forward, instead of tilting his head just enough to let his mouth brush against hers, he gave her hand another squeeze and let it go.

"I wanted to protect you too," he admitted. "But you know what I wanted even more?"

Jane shook her head, looking away.

"I wanted you to live."

With those few carefully selected words, Jane was rendered speechless. And within her silence, she loved him more than ever.

Trudging down the slope toward Sawyer's crippled Jeep, Ryan still couldn't believe Sawyer had done what he'd done. He'd be surprised if the Jeep's axle wasn't bent to hell, and the car was most certainly going to need a face-lift on the passenger side. Sawyer had never been a fan of conflict, so tipping the car the way he had had been a bold move; it had *looked* like an accident, but Ryan knew better. And while the answer to Sawyer's problem had been an extreme one, Ryan couldn't help but feel proud of his usually calm friend for letting go of all that pent-up aggression and allowing the moment to be what it had to be.

With the weather being as cold as it was, Ryan assumed that April had crawled back into the car for warmth, but when he and Lauren peered through the windows the car was empty, which could only mean one thing: she was out there somewhere, nearly half an hour in the freezing cold in nothing but a pair of jeans, a stylish coat, and boots nowhere near appropriate for the snow.

"Shit," Ryan said.

"How long has it been?" Lauren asked.

"Long enough," he said, sweeping the perimeter to see if April was just shy of the vehicle somewhere. She could have wandered off to go to the bathroom, or maybe she'd gotten bored and decided to take a walk before coming back. Only one thing was certain: up here, frostbite set in fast, and if April was suffering from it, he had no idea how they'd get her to a hospital.

He froze when he heard Oona bark behind them. He turned to see whether the dog was following them, but the husky was nowhere in sight.

"April?" Lauren yelled into the wind, but received no reply. They looked at each other, then picked up the pace as they continued down the road toward the base of the hill. They hadn't taken more than a few additional steps when Ryan caught movement in the trees.

"Look," he said, pointing out a shifting shadow.

"Thank god." Lauren breathed a sigh of relief.

"Hey, April, come on," Ryan called out to her. "It's fucking *freezing* out here."

But rather than a moody bride-to-be stepping out of the trees and into the road, what sounded like a guttural purr reverberated against frozen pines. Ryan and Lauren looked at each other.

"What the hell was that?" Lauren asked, her eyes wide. She stepped away from the trail April had left and moved to the edge of the road.

"Don't." Ryan caught her by the sleeve. It was an animal, and it could attack if it felt threatened. "We need to go back."

"What?"

"What do you want to do?" he asked her. "Fight whatever that is with your bare hands?"

"It's probably just an elk or something."

But elk didn't move like that, and they certainly didn't purr.

Something about that shadow set Ryan's teeth on edge. His nostrils flared as he pulled Lauren back. "Do you smell that?"

Lauren inhaled, grimaced, and lifted her gloved hand to her nose and mouth as soon as the scent hit her. The air was stifling, heavy with the stench of blood and death.

"Come on," he said, pulling Lauren along. He didn't have a clue as to what he was going to grab for protection back at the house, but anything was better than nothing. Lauren dragged her feet behind him, her breath puffing out from beneath her scarf. He let go of her sleeve, giving her some leeway, but the moment he did she caught his hand in her own. Their eyes met, and though half her face was obscured by her scarf, he could tell she was spooked.

"Don't be scared," he said.

She narrowed her eyes at him defiantly. "I'm not sca—"

The crack of a branch stalled her words.

A tree shuddered in the near distance, snow falling from pine needles in fat clumps, as though something was climbing upward at a rapid pace. Ryan shook his head as they stood watching, unable to put together what kind of an animal would be big enough to shake a tree like that.

"You're right," he said, his breath steaming out ahead of him. "It's probably an elk. Rubbing its antlers or something..."

"And the smell?" she asked, taking a backward step up the slope.

Ryan didn't reply. He couldn't. He didn't have the answers, and he was getting a bad feeling, like they were in the wrong place at the wrong time.

"Come on," he said, his grip tightening around her hand.

"But April..." She looked over her shoulder as he dragged her along. And then she stopped dead in her tracks, refusing to budge as she stared back down the road.

Ryan spotted what had caught her attention right away. It was impossible to miss—a long black scarf slowly rolling across the road, carried by the strengthening wind.

"She's there!" Lauren said, and then, just like that, Lauren let go of his hand and started to run, not back toward the cabin, but down the road.

Ryan's heart lurched inside his chest. Every nerve stood on end.

"Lauren, wait!"

He wasn't sure what had come first: his words or his stumbling steps. He was running after her, kicking up snow behind him; but that moment of hesitation, the moment it had taken him to process what was happening, had given Lauren a head start, and the girl was quick. She leaped through the snow like a gazelle, bolting toward the scarf that was encrusted in white, determined to find the girl they were looking for regardless of what may have been out there.

For a split second, Ryan wasn't sure what he was so afraid of. They were making plenty of noise; they'd scare any animal that was out there away. But that sour feeling in the pit of his stomach wouldn't let up. It was a feeling that had saved his ass more than a few times, the most memorable being an avalanche in the French Alps that had buried four boarders but had spared his life. After that, he had never doubted that feeling again. Jane had called it a sixth sense. Premonition. A mental alarm that sounded when something wasn't quite right.

Lauren reached April's scarf and plucked it off the ground with a gloved hand. Ryan slowed his steps a few yards shy of where she stood, both of them searching the trees for its owner. Ryan's breath caught in his throat when he saw that same shadow they had seen earlier shift behind the pines. He froze, realizing just how close it had come to them, but Lauren didn't hesitate. She stepped to the side of the road, the scarf dragging on the ground.

"April?" She took another step forward before a rasping growl stopped her dead.

Ryan's eyes went wide as the shadow breached the perimeter of the trees—not a man, not an animal, a *thing*, ashen as though it had frozen to death in the cold. Ryan choked on his breath as the creature leaped forward, landing in the center of the road just shy of where Lauren stood, blocking her way back to him. Its long, angular body hunched over as it crouched like a gargoyle, the knobs of its spine jutting out of its back, crosshatched by a menagerie of scars. Ryan instinctively stumbled backward, his heart stuttering. Whatever the thing was, it was a good foot taller than him, all sinew and bone.

Lauren let out a scream, but she squelched it fast. She shot Ryan a terrified look, her eyes begging him to tell her what to do. But he couldn't process what he was seeing. This was impossible, like one of those horror movies that made him throw his hands up and proclaim it was all crazy and improbable and it could never happen; how could something be scary if it could never be true? But there it was—a creature standing in the gray daylight as if to mock his skepticism, as if to say, *See? Nightmares* do *exist.*

And then, as if to mess with his already blown concept of what was real, that skeletal thing darted away, dodging back into the safety of the trees that lined the road.

Lauren stood frozen, her eyes impossibly wide, her chest heaving beneath her coat.

"Fucking *run*," he told her, and they both fell into a sprint. His instinct was to save himself, to run ahead and survive, and once his legs started pumping, the impulse to keep running was nearly too strong to fight. He had to get back to the cabin, had to get to safety, had to get to Jane, had to get out of there. But Lauren...he couldn't leave her. This girl. This wonderful, mind-blowing, beautiful girl. Rejecting the urge to keep running toward safety, he slowed enough to twist around, his arm extending out behind him, reaching for Lauren's hand as she stumbled toward him, kicking up snow.

They charged up the driveway, fighting the slope, Ryan pulling Lauren along as she began to lag, her legs sinking deep into the powder. "Hurry up!" he urged. The longer the monster stayed gone, the louder the cacophony of a group moan that rose from the trees. He couldn't believe it. It sounded like there were dozens of them. A dozen of these fucking nightmares calling one another, announcing that they had found their next meal. Ryan's eyes went wide as the moans grew more insistent, more vicious as they rattled deep within those things' throats. He gave Lauren a yank, spooling his arm around her back as he tried to rush her along.

Lauren stumbled, falling forward, sinking into the thick blanket of snow. He tried to grab her by the arms as she struggled to right herself, their breath coming in quick, quaking gasps. Ryan's jaw dropped when the creature took a flying leap back into the drive, every sinewy muscle in its body pronounced beneath a thin sheath of skin. He skittered backward, nearly losing his balance in the process, groping at the girl before him, his mind screaming *get out of here, get yourself off this fucking hill.*

Lauren scrambled to her feet as the thing watched from a safe distance away, and for a moment Ryan was mesmerized by the size of its teeth, each one as wide as two fingers put together, tapering off to a terrifying point. Those teeth were predatory, stained by the blood of its kill; but rather than four canines set between two rows of incisors, there were a good dozen fangs jutting out of an impossibly large mouth. The way its maw hung open reminded him of an anglerfish. It was watching them, as though relishing the horror that wafted off them like a pheromone, as though enjoying the cadence of Lauren's quiet, weepy gasps as she struggled to right herself.

Ryan's heart lurched to a stop when the thing squatted deeper into the snow, its muscles rippling beneath hairless gray flesh, a grotesquely wet rumble resonating from deep within its throat. It canted its head to the side, its huge mouth giving it a perpetual smile. Its black marble eyes flashed in the pale morning light.

Midscramble, Lauren froze in place when a second creature stepped out of the shadow of the trees, that same frothy snarl vibrating against the hollow of its throat. This one was closer, having stepped out from the trees less than ten feet away, its soulless eyes fixed on Ryan, its teeth so big they were forever exposed.

Ryan was as rooted in place as Lauren was, both of them suspended in a pocket of breathless horror. But just as the closest hunter was ready to pounce, Lauren's cry pulled the savage's attention away.

"Get away from him!" she screamed. The battle cry would have made sense if Lauren had some sort of weapon to defend herself, but she stood empty-handed, armed with nothing but her own fearlessness.

The creature appeared almost startled by her defiance. It lurched backward, then twisted around and bolted back into the trees. Ryan watched Lauren's determination melt into what could have only been stunned surprise, his own heart clamoring for freedom from his chest. She turned to look at him, bewilderment written on her face. For a split second she almost seemed to smile, proud of herself, but Ryan shook his head.

No.

This wasn't over.

Run.

He reached for her hand, unable to breathe, about to choke on his own pulse as the creature down the slope of the drive launched itself forward.

He heard the thing bolt up behind them.

His eyes locked with Lauren's, her expression frozen in time like a snapshot. But her gaze didn't reflect the horror he felt. Behind wisps of flaxen hair, she looked mystified, as though unable to believe where they were, what was happening, what would inevitably become of them both.

Her hand was torn from his grasp as she was snapped backward. He stared wide-eyed as the thing threw her onto her back, Lauren kicking her legs at the oncoming horror, trying to scare it away with her screams. She planted her foot against one of its bulbous knees—nothing but a ball-shaped joint suspended between two leg bones—jamming her heel against it as hard as she could, but rather than forcing it to stumble, she made it angry instead. Ryan continued to stare as the hellion reeled back, its mouth open impossibly wide, and then charged her. Ryan's brain screamed for him to help her while his instincts urged him back up the road. *You need a weapon*, it shrieked. *You can't fight that thing with your bare hands.* The creature's jaws snapped just inches from Lauren's face as she shoved it backward with her feet.

Ryan's gaze snagged on the snowboard on top of Sawyer's Jeep. But the Jeep was downhill, and Lauren and the creature were between him and the car. He turned uphill, started to run again—there were three more on top of the Nissan. If he could get back to the driveway, he'd have something to swing at that fucking thing.

Lauren gave a bloodcurdling scream.

Ryan's heart ceased to beat.

No, he thought. *Nonono!*

He reeled around, hardly able to process the scene. There was blood. So much blood. Lauren was still kicking at the thing above her, but with only one leg. Her other leg lay motionless in the crimson snow, detached, the foot twisted at an impossible angle. The creature grabbed her flailing limb, crouched low to the ground in a pool of gore-drenched snow, and, in a move that was a gruesome imitation of a sex act, lifted Lauren's hips before burying its mouth in the massive, gushing wound below her pelvis. Its black eyes locked onto Ryan as it fed, challenging him as sucking noises punctuated the short-lived silence, broken by Lauren's final scream.

Oona was going nuts out on the porch, her bark a mixture of alarm and aggression. Jane stopped at the kitchen door, her hand on the knob, hesitating. Since Oona had turned on her the night before, it was a wise idea to let the husky calm down.

"What the hell?" Sawyer murmured, watching Oona lose it as she jumped up onto her hind legs, her front paws pounding the redwood railing, shoving her nose through the slats of the deck. But despite her apparent eagerness to get at whatever was out there in the trees, she refused to bound down the stairs and toward the road.

"I don't know," Jane said, her face twisting with worry.

Every hair on Sawyer's body stood on end when he heard the wail.

"Oh my god." Jane tore the door open, running into the snow in her socks. Sawyer followed her, his hand clamped around one of her arms, the cold biting at his skin as he held her back.

The screaming continued, impossibly loud for the fact that they couldn't see where it was coming from. Jane was already crying, panicked, and despite the yell belonging to a female, she was yelling Ryan's name, weeping it into her hands. Sawyer's heart rattled in his chest, sure the screams were coming from April, sure that something terrible had occurred. Maybe she had stayed outside so long because she had hurt herself. Maybe she had stepped into a snowdrift or stumbled down the embankment into the ravine that flanked the drive and broken her leg.

Sawyer tried to pull Jane back inside, pushing through his own fear, his pulse thudding in the hollow of his throat.

"What are you doing?" Jane squealed, shoving Sawyer away from her, trying to get around him, but he wouldn't relent, blocking her way.

"Go inside," he told her.

"What? No!"

"Go inside, Jane!" Sawyer yelled, turning to run down the steps. He stopped when Jane's hands clamped over his wrist, squeezing it tight. "She needs my help," he told her, tearing his hand from her grasp, then bolted down the stairs, running past the Xterra and toward the road where his Jeep sat incapacitated deep in the drift. He all but collided with his best friend as Ryan took the bend, his eyes wild, his expression unreadable.

"Get back inside," Ryan choked, frantically shoving Sawyer backward. But the screaming hadn't stopped. It was weaker, but he could still hear it. Sawyer grabbed Ryan by his wrists, swung him around so they exchanged positions.

"What the hell is going on?" he demanded. Where was April? Where was Lauren? Why the hell did Ryan abandon them? All he had to do was take a few steps down the driveway to see what was happening. Breaking free of Ryan's grasp, Ryan clawed at the fabric of Sawyer's T-shirt, desperately trying to stop him.

"No!" he yelled. "Get the fuck *back*!"

"Did you find her?" Sawyer shouted in return, panic seizing his throat, but he stopped short when he reached the driveway. A dozen yards away, there was a huddle of what looked to be naked men, their corpse-like skin glistening with splotches of red. They were shoving one another, fighting over a kill. He couldn't wrap his mind around the amount of blood that was splashed across the snow between them. And then there was a girl, cracked open like a gourd, steam rising from her exposed entrails. Something in his brain clicked, identifying her—*April*. It was April, torn apart, his unborn child ground down to nothing between a demon's teeth. But a flash of blonde hair upon red-painted snow snapped him back to reality.

It was Lauren.

Sawyer stood frozen in place, his mouth agape, his eyes fixed on the one creature that had stopped contending with the others and was now looking right at him, its nightmarish fangs clacking together. It canted its head to the side like a curious dog, that gruesome grin slathered in blood.

Sawyer lurched backward when Ryan groped at his shirt, both of them stumbling up the stairs. But Sawyer wasn't ready to go inside. Despite his terror, he had to get out there, had to find April. He shoved Ryan away, trying to get around him, only to have Ryan push him in return.

"Get off me!" Sawyer yelled as they struggled, Ryan forcing him toward the open door while Sawyer fought to escape his grasp. Amid the panic, Oona let out a snarl, convinced her owner was under attack. She reeled back, her teeth bared, and bit down, her teeth sinking deep into Sawyer's skin. But, teetering on the edge of what felt like insanity, he hardly noticed the dog chomping down on his forearm. Shoved inside the house, he watched Ryan throw the dead bolt into place. A flimsy lock wasn't going to do a goddamn thing against the monsters outside—but it sure would do its job if April came stumbling up the porch steps and tried to get inside. She'd be locked out. Doomed.

He stared at the lock, sure that lock was sealing her fate, torn between the safety of the group and the safety of the woman who carried his child. She was out there somewhere, hiding, waiting for it to be safe before she bolted toward the cabin. She was smart. Resourceful. She'd come back. She had to come back.

He snapped out of his daze when Ryan grabbed him.

"Jane, get in the pantry," Ryan yelled.

Wearing a look of terrified confusion, Jane jumped at the order and blindly did what she was told, her eyes brimming over with frightened tears.

Ryan shoved Sawyer away from the door and across the kitchen. They scrambled into the walk-in pantry at the mouth of the hallway, Jane already inside, wide-eyed and terrified, her face a mask of bewildered dread. Oona ran in behind them, her tail between her legs, and Ryan slammed the door closed, searching for something to use as a barricade, but there was nothing. All the shelves were secured to the walls, immovable.

"What happened?" Jane asked, her voice shrill with fear. "Where's Lauren?" When Ryan didn't answer her, Jane's dread bloomed into hysteria. "*Where's Lauren?!*" she screamed, clawing at her brother's chest, trying to move him away from the door. Sawyer caught her by her arms, pulling her back. She thrashed against his grasp, twisting as she attempted escape, the blood from his fresh dog bite smearing across her arms as she tried to wriggle free. "Tell me where she is!" she demanded, her tone crackling with a desperate rage Sawyer had never heard before, one that made him feel numb. "Let me go!" Jane screamed, trying to escape Sawyer's grasp. "I need to go get her!"

A flash of Jane running out into the snow: those things falling onto her, snarling, fighting over which one of them got the best piece of his first love. His stomach twisted, the sudden burn of nausea threatening to double him over where he stood.

"No," he said.

Lauren was dead.

"You can't."

She was *dead*.

"We need to stay here." His voice cracked.

April was still out there. Scared. Alone.

Ryan pressed his back to the door and slid down it, his head in his hands.

"She's gone, Janey," Sawyer said, his voice warbling with emotion. "Lauren's gone."

Jane stood motionless in his grasp, as though the life had gone out of her within a blink.

Sawyer's heart twisted, burning in his chest, his wounded arm throbbing in time with his pulse. He looked away, unable to stop picturing April out there, freezing, hiding from those things. But he couldn't go out there. If he did, Jane would follow. Jane twisted away from him, crashed to her knees, and sobbed into Ryan's shoulder. Her cry tore through Sawyer, punching him in the heart.

"What happened?" she sobbed. "What happened to Ren, Ryan? What did you do to her?" She shook him, trying to get a response.

"Wolves," Sawyer said, his throat dry, closing around that lie. But it was all he could do to keep everything from falling apart. "A pack of them. It wasn't his fault."

"Then why are we in the pantry?" she screamed. "Why aren't you going out there to get April?"

He swallowed against the questioning. How was he supposed to answer that?

"You're lying!" she wailed, turning on her brother again, her fists beating against his arm. "Why aren't we going out there? Why are we locked inside like this?"

Again, there was no response from Ryan. He was catatonic, lost in his own grief, drowning in guilt.

"What was it?" she asked, turning her attention to Sawyer instead. "You saw it, didn't you?"

Sawyer shook his head faintly. "I only saw them for a second. I was too busy looking..." *at Lauren.* His words faded before he could finish.

She turned her attention back to her brother. "Tell me what happened," she sobbed. "Please."

Finally Ryan spoke, a reply so ominous it made the hair on Sawyer's arms stand on end.

"If I told you what happened, you would never leave this room again."

CHAPTER NINE

He was trying to make sense of it, but all Sawyer kept seeing was that thing staring at him, those giant teeth clacking together as it stood in Lauren's blood. There had been a pack of them, whatever the hell those things were, and while they had been grouped together, they had fought one another, suggesting a definite pecking order. But he couldn't see past Lauren's body, cracked open, dying.

But when he had set eyes on her, he hadn't seen Jane's blonde-haired friend, but April Bennett, the girl he'd met in a vintage record store, the girl who had been reading the back of a Bauhaus album when he had spotted her from across the shop. She had disappeared while he flipped through vintage new-wave vinyl, and when he stepped out onto the sidewalk with a paper bag full of records tucked beneath his arm, she was smoking a cigarette just outside the door. To say that he hadn't been smitten by her would have been a lie. Only a few months ago, he could hardly restrain himself from undressing her with his eyes. Now he couldn't help but picture that body lying out in the snow, probably in a place where he and Jane and Ryan used to run and dig and pretend that they were lost in the woods, nobody but the three of them left in the world.

That was his worst fear.

April was volatile, but she wasn't stupid. He reassured himself that she would have found a place to hide. Maybe she was in the Jeep, curled up in the foot well and waiting for someone to find her.

"We can't stay in here," he finally spoke. "We need a plan." Because despite his own terror, he had to find her. He had to save his child.

"There is no plan," Ryan said toward the floor.

"We have to make one," Jane cut in. It was impressive, the way her face was going through emotions like a flickering light-bulb—horrified one second, grief stricken the next. But she was keeping it together. "We just need to figure out what to do," she said. "We'll be okay..."

"We'll be okay?" Ryan laughed bitterly. He looked up for the first time since they'd scrambled into that tiny room, his eyes hard. "You have no fucking idea. You have no fucking *clue*."

Jane's composed exterior wavered. Sawyer could see Ryan's severity eating at her, singeing the fine-spun fibers of her self-control. "That's why you need to tell us what you saw," she told him. "We can't fight them if we don't know what they are."

"And what are you going to do, Jane? Are you going to teach them how to color inside the lines?" Ryan asked her. "Are you going to teach them how to bake a fucking cake?"

"*Hey.*" Sawyer's voice snapped Ryan to attention. They locked eyes, challenging each other. "Don't take this out on her. This isn't anyone's fault."

Ryan's expression went sour. He looked down at his hands, holding something back, and then those hands covered his face again. Guilt. It was so heavy Sawyer could taste it.

"We can't stay in here," Sawyer repeated. "April is out there, right? We have to go look for her. Or at least *I* have to go look for her. You guys can stay here but I can't."

"You go out there and you're dead," Ryan said flatly. "I know you saw them. April isn't out there. If Lauren didn't make it, neither did she."

"Why?" Sawyer clenched his teeth at the insinuation. "Because you liked Lauren better?"

"Because it's not goddamn logical. How can she be out there, Sawyer? She was wearing jeans and a designer coat, for fuck's sake. If they didn't get her, the cold already has."

Sawyer lunged forward, grabbing Ryan by the front of his coat, jerking him up to his feet before slamming him against the pantry door with a snarl. Jane gasped at the sudden barrage of movement, her hands flying out to grab Sawyer's shoulders.

"Don't!" she yelped, but it only made Sawyer shove Ryan again.

"Say it again," Sawyer challenged, releasing Ryan's coat a second later, disgusted.

"You guys, stop." Jane stared at them both with wide, glassy eyes. "We can't turn against each other."

Sawyer shook his head. "You're giving up? Is that it?"

"No," Jane answered for him. "He's not. Nobody is giving up."

"I'm not going to die in here," Sawyer assured them, taking a backward step.

"Nobody is going to die..." She faltered when she realized that she was wrong. Someone had already died. Lauren was gone forever, and according to Ryan, April didn't stand a chance. "Ryan?" Her bottom lip trembled. "We're not going to die out here, right?"

Ryan said nothing.

She tried to compose herself, but her shoulders lurched forward, giving way to a stifled sob. "I have to go back to work. The kids don't have a sub. I need to at least call in..."

"Jane." Sawyer reached out to her, his hand grazing her shoulder. It hurt to look at her, hurt to know that he couldn't do anything to soothe her nerves. "It's going to be okay," he told her. "I promise."

"Okay," she whispered. "Okay. It'll be okay."

Sawyer let his head fall back, staring at the ceiling. Maybe Ryan was right. Maybe there was no way out of there—no possible way they could make it. It was hard to believe that just that morning, less than an hour before, his biggest problem was the wrath of an angry girl. But now, the fabric of the world had changed, reality had shifted, the impossible had become possible.

The blink of an eye.

A snap of the fingers.

Just like that, and everything was different.

Ryan had lost track of time. He knew where he was, knew what he had seen, but he couldn't for the life of him remember how he had gotten back inside the house, whose idea it had been to pile into the pantry, or what they were waiting for. Because they *were* waiting; otherwise, they would have moved.

Jane had crumpled into a corner. Sawyer was on the opposite side of the room, more than likely contemplating April's fate—a fate that Ryan hadn't been very delicate about. He felt guilty about putting those images in Sawyer's head, but his lapse in sympathy was far outweighed by the way Lauren had stared at him, almost bewildered by the fact that her life was over, that Ryan just stood there not doing a damn thing, because there was nothing left to do. But he could have done *something*. He could have run at that fucking thing, pummeled it with his fists. Maybe he would have scared it off, bought them a few extra seconds, been able to drag Lauren up the road. Maybe if he wouldn't have been so goddamn scared he could have helped her. But he hadn't. And now the three of them were sitting in a pantry because of him, rather than fighting.

"Remember why it took us so long to get up here?" he finally asked. Both Jane and Sawyer looked up with matching expressions—they were surprised to hear him speak. After such a long silence, his own voice made his skin tingle. "The last time we were supposed to come up here was two winters ago, but Jane refused to come up. Remember why?"

"That guy," she said. "The cross-country skier. It was in the news."

"It wasn't just one guy," Ryan said. "They focused on the one guy because he was a pro, an Olympian, not some amateur on his day off. He did that shit for a living. There were four other people with him."

"I don't remember that," Jane confessed quietly.

Ryan shook his head, tapping a finger against the floor, punctuating his point. "We nearly called this one off too."

"Wait." Sawyer sat up from his slouch, squinting at Ryan from across the room. "What are you saying?"

"I'm saying that we're not supposed to be here."

Jane and Sawyer looked at each other. He could see it on their faces—they weren't getting his point.

"The cross-country team," he continued. "They were missing for nearly a week. They found the guy dead, found *all* of them dead. They went off the designated trail, which was no big deal because the guy was a pro. And then they found the entire team dead in a snowed-over pass."

Jane's eyes went wide. She shot a look at Sawyer, then looked back to her brother. "What happened to them?" she asked.

Ryan shook his head.

"What?" she insisted.

But Ryan remained silent.

"No," she said, her tone stern. "You can't just bring something like this up and not finish. What happened to them, Ryan?"

"They thought it was an animal…" he said, sounding almost desperate.

"They were *eaten*?" Jane's tone rang with alarm.

"Holy shit," Sawyer whispered.

"And you still brought us here?" She was on the verge of hysteria. "You still brought us here, Ryan? You *knew* there was something out there and you dragged us up here anyway?" A sob wrenched its way out of her chest. "How could you? Lauren's *gone*," she cried. "She's gone."

"Animal attacks happen all the time," Sawyer said softly, trying to calm her down. "There's no way we could have known, Janey. They're so rare…" But his nerves were buzzing. Those skiers hadn't been eaten by wolves or bears or anything of the sort. The hellions lived out in those woods. This wasn't the first time something like this had happened.

"It was a one-in-a-million chance," Ryan told them, searching for a sign of understanding, of forgiveness. "One in a billion, Janey."

"Well, congratulations." Jane's words hitched in her throat. "You won…the fucking…lottery."

"These things…" Ryan hesitated. "They're like out of a nightmare. They're impossible. They can't exist. They're huge, like seven or eight feet tall. Skinny but strong. They can jump like cats, climb trees…"

Jane's eyes grew wider with each detail, her expression a mask of horror.

"And their teeth…"

"Their teeth," Jane whispered, her bottom lip trembling at their mere mention.

Ryan fell silent, staring at the floor, seemingly overwhelmed by his own description, as though listing off their traits somehow solidified that the things he had seen outside were real.

Finally, Jane spoke into the quiet.

"So it's true, then… We *are* going to die."

Sawyer watched Ryan ease the pantry door open a crack while he pulled Jane into the farthest corner of the storage room. He stood in front of her like a sentinel, feeling her breath hot against the back of his neck as she jabbed her fingers through the belt loops of his jeans. Had it been any other time, he would have savored being so close, but his attention was on Oona, on thoughts of getting to April. The husky stuck her snout against the crack of the door.

Ryan shot a wary glance over his shoulder. Sawyer could see it in the way he was clinging to Oona's fur—he was preparing himself for the worst. If the coast was clear, Oona would come get them without incident. If the creatures had somehow gotten inside the house—climbed through broken windows, scavenging for food—she wouldn't come back at all. Leaning in, Ryan pulled the dog into his arms, momentarily burying his face in her neck. A second later he pulled the door open and let her scramble into the kitchen, allowing her to escape without giving himself enough time to reconsider.

They waited in a silence so oppressive Sawyer had to concentrate on breathing just to get enough air. He was anticipating a terrible yelp, a crash of pots and pans against the floor, a window breaking, or that god-awful clacking of monstrous teeth. His arms broke out in gooseflesh as he pictured one of those creatures catching Oona in its jaws, shaking her like a dog shakes a toy.

Jane moved behind him, shifting her weight from one foot to the other. He glanced back at her and she gave him an embarrassed look.

"I need to go," she whispered.

Sawyer nodded in mute understanding and turned his attention back to Ryan, still crouched beside the door, waiting for his beloved pet to return with good news. Sawyer swallowed against the lump in his throat, the backs of his eyes suddenly burning at the flash of a childhood memory: crawling into the backseat of a car, needing to pee five minutes later. It was something he'd never get to experience as a father—the frustration, the annoyance, the amusement of a little boy who looked just like him, or a little girl who looked just like April, begging him to pull over. There would be no trips to the toy store, no birthday parties at Chuck E. Cheese's. He would never get to freeze in the late-October cold, standing on a sidewalk just beyond a stranger's front door, watching his kid trudge up the front steps, a plastic pumpkin floating just inches from the ground. He wouldn't get the opportunity to pull into a McDonald's drive-through and buy a Happy Meal—a secret he and his mini-me would keep from Mom. And the old *Fraggle Rock* episodes he had started collecting the day after April had given him the news—he'd never watch those now, his arm around a little kid, a bowl of popcorn between them both, because Ryan was right—the odds that April was still alive out there were slim to none.

Just when he felt like he was about to lose it, Oona stuck her snout into the crack of the door and blew air through her nose.

"Thank god," Ryan said, letting the pantry door swing wide, both hands plunging into Oona's fur. "Good girl."

"Can I go?" Jane asked from behind Sawyer's shoulder.

Sawyer nodded and stepped aside, and Jane slunk out of the pantry, wary as she disappeared down the hall. He followed Ryan into the kitchen, looking around the place for signs of anything strange, but the cabin appeared untouched—just as they had left it about an hour earlier. If they hadn't known any better, it would have been easy to pretend nothing had happened. The only difference between now and then was that it was snowing again, big fluffy flakes the size of silver dollars falling from the sky.

And Lauren and April were gone.

Sawyer approached the kitchen door, his fingers pressing to the glass, feeling the cold it was holding back. If those savages hadn't gotten to April yet, the cold would have done her in hours ago. He told himself that she was dead, that she *had* to be dead, because the idea of her still being alive out there was too much to bear. If he'd just been less rough with her, she wouldn't have stormed off on her own. If he'd just insisted that she come back inside, Ryan and Lauren wouldn't have gone to get her. Lauren would still be alive as well.

He nearly jumped when Ryan's hand fell onto his shoulder.

"Stop thinking about it," Ryan told him.

"Easy," Sawyer said softly.

Ryan shook his head, assuring Sawyer that he knew his request was next to impossible, but he was right: They had to focus on facts, not assumptions, and the only thing they knew for sure was that the three of them needed to get out of there; they needed to get to safety. The sooner they could come up with a plan that wouldn't get them killed, the sooner they could find April and bring her home.

Sawyer turned away from the door, and for the first time he realized just how many windows were in the cabin. Those things could come crashing through the glass and end them all. "It isn't safe in here," he said. "We can't stay in here like this."

Ryan nodded, looking around as if coming to the same realization. "It doesn't help that this place is massive either," he muttered. "Pops didn't consider what a pain in the ass it would be to secure this place in case of an apocalypse."

"What if we choose a room?"

"What, like the pantry? It took us less than an hour to start going nuts in there."

"We should at least board them up," Sawyer insisted. The idea of just sitting there *waiting* for something to happen was insane.

"With what?" Ryan asked. "Furniture?" He glanced down the hall to see if Jane was there, then took a step closer to Sawyer, lowering his voice. "Those fucking things tore one of her legs off like it was nothing. You think they aren't going to be able to get in if they want to?"

"So what are we supposed to do, just wait for them to come get us?"

"We'll gather up a bunch of supplies, stick to one area, and if they come, then we'll have to fight."

"Fight." Sawyer gave Ryan an even look. They were both thinking the same thing: how in the world were they going to fight those things? Sawyer hadn't seen the exchange, but if they had been able to rip one of Lauren's limbs from her body it meant that they were impossibly strong.

"Look, everything has to have a weakness. Those pieces of shit have an Achilles heel; we just have to find it."

Jane stared at herself in the guest bathroom mirror. She looked tired, haggard, as though she'd been up for days. Dropping her gaze to the sink, she turned on the cold water. Her hands were shaking badly.

She had imagined herself in bad scenarios before—a lone gunman trudges through the halls of Powell Elementary, his sights set on Ms. Adler's second grade class. She had envisioned herself blocking the door with her desk, then grouping everyone in a single corner, all of them low to the ground, soft whimpers of fear slithering across the linoleum floor. Despite it being no match for a gun, the pepper spray in her purse had made her more confident. If anything did happen, at least she had some way of defending herself.

The pepper spray had been a gift, still in her purse upstairs. After she had an incident in a parking garage with an inebriated bum, Ryan had picked it up for her at a sporting goods store. He had offered to buy her a gun, insisting that it was no big deal, that he'd drive her out to the gun range a couple of weekends in a row, that they'd get her a license to carry a concealed weapon, but guns scared her. She had watched one of her uncles aim through a scope and shoot an elk dead during a hunting trip when she was a kid. Ryan had been there, running toward the carcass as fast as he could after their uncle said it was safe. Growing up in Colorado, hunting was a part of life. Every other restaurant had a stuffed head mounted on the wall, proclaiming the majesty of the Rockies by displaying the dead. The Adlers eventually stopped going to their father's favorite barbecue joint because of all the taxidermy on the walls. Jane had burst into tears over a plate of pulled pork, insisting that the deer that hung over the fireplace in the center of the dining room looked sad, like it had been crying for its mother when it had been killed.

She splashed water onto her face, remembering her father's toughness. He would have told her to put her war face on—this was no time for tears, but time for defense. Jane looked into her own eyes, water sliding down her cheeks, her bangs wet, slashing across her forehead like war paint. Her fingers tensed against the edge of the sink. Whatever was out there wasn't going to win. She wouldn't let them. She didn't care how big they were, how vicious—Ryan and Sawyer were her family, and nobody fucked with Jane's family.

Shoving herself away from the counter, she stepped out of the bathroom and launched herself up the stairs, taking them two by two. In the master bedroom, she grabbed her purse and dug through it, sliding the pepper spray into the back pocket of her jeans, then moved across the room to the large armoire against the far wall. The snow was dazzling in the enormous window that overlooked the mountains, and her heart twisted inside her chest when she stared out onto the white landscape. April hadn't been that bad. Jane had been quick to judge her, blinded by her own resentment, as though April had stolen something from her, when that hadn't been the case at all. Jane wished she had tried harder to make her feel more comfortable within the group. She wished she had prodded her for conversation, had asked her about her likes and dislikes, had tried to be her friend. But now April was out there somewhere, potentially huddled beneath a pine, hoping to God that someone would come for her. Jane couldn't help but feel that was partly her fault. Her eyes filled with tears at the thought before she squared her shoulders, glaring at her own reflection in the window.

"Stop it," she hissed. "Get it together." Ryan and Sawyer needed her. There were only three of them left, and all three of them had to get out of there alive. She looked away from the trees, pulled the heavy doors of the armoire open. The scent of cedar wafted out of its interior, enveloping her in a smell that would always remind her of this cabin, of the forest, of winters and fire and the open air. There was a quilt folded in quarters at the bottom of the cabinet, a few matching pillows piled on top. Jane dropped to her knees and shoved both hands beneath the blanket, feeling around until her finger found the small hole at the base of the wardrobe. It was funny how parents thought they could keep hiding places a secret, especially from a pair of rambunctious twins. She hooked her finger along the edge of that hole and pulled. A small door whispered upward. Shoving her free hand into the hidden compartment, she felt her fingers kiss the cold surface of metal. Closing her eyes, she wrapped her hand around the barrel of her father's gun, drawing the pistol out of the dark. It was heavy in her hand, ominous despite its stillness. Carefully placing it beside her on the carpet, she stuck her hand back inside the compartment, feeling around for the box of shells she knew was there. But her heart tripped over itself when she grabbed the paper box by its top; it felt lighter than she had expected. The soft jingle of metal against metal had her tearing it open, horrified as a grand total of four hollow points rolled against a brown cardboard backdrop.

She gathered the box and the gun together and dashed out of the room, concentrating on the stairs, worried that the gun would leap out of her hands and shoot up the place. She found the boys in the living room, Sawyer staring out the window with his arms wrapped around himself, more than likely contemplating running out into the snow. Ryan sat on top of the coffee table, surrounded by a menagerie of kitchen knives like some part-time ninja. He looked confused, as if unsure what their exact purpose was. Jane stepped over to her brother, presenting the gun and the box of shells the way someone would present a king an extravagant gift.

Ryan blinked, then looked up at his sister. "Where did you get this?"

"Dad's bedroom," she told him. "The old armoire."

"Jesus," he said, taking the gun from her. "I forgot this was there." He slid the clip out of the handle, Jane's heart stuttering when she saw it. The clip was empty. They had four rounds. That was it.

"I can't just sit here and wait," Sawyer announced, turning away from the window with determination. "I'm going to find her."

Ryan's expression wavered between boldness and fear. "It's insane," he said.

"We have a gun," Sawyer reminded him.

"And what if it isn't effective?"

"And what if it is?" Sawyer asked. "What if April is out there and we can just shoot those damn things and bring her back inside? Will you be able to live with that?"

After a beat of hesitation, Ryan slid the rounds into the clip and replaced it in the handle of the gun.

"Fine," Ryan said. "Let's go before I change my fucking mind."

Jane's entire body prickled with nerves at the thought of it—both of them going out there, regardless of how many weapons they took.

"I'll go by myself," Sawyer told him.

"Like hell you will."

"Who's going to stay with Jane?" Sawyer's gaze paused on her, and she gave him as brave a smile as she could muster.

For a moment she wanted to insist that Ryan stay, if only to keep one of them safe. But letting Sawyer go out there on his own was suicide.

"I'll be okay," she said softly, fighting the urge to fall into another fit of terrified hysterics.

The boys shuffled out of the room to prepare themselves against the snow while Jane sank down upon the windowsill, trying to keep it together, her gaze fixed on the deer feeder in a small clearing just beyond the house. Ryan had tossed a bale of alfalfa into it just like Jane had asked, and a family of deer was slowly approaching, thankful for the food during such a storm. Jane leaned forward, her forehead kissing the glass as she watched them, their skinny legs punching holes in the snow. But her attention wavered when a single pine shuddered in the distance, followed by another, then a third. Her eyes went wide as snow fell from the trees. She opened her mouth to yell for the guys, but she couldn't catch her breath. The deer began to bound away from the feeder, suddenly alerted to another presence, but a smaller one lagged behind. Jane's palms hit the glass, as though knocking on the window would somehow encourage the fawn to hurry. Before she could give a startled cry, a monster leaped from the tree, pinning the deer down against the snow.

Jane screamed, stumbling away from the window, her hands pressed over her mouth. She could hardly process what she was seeing as her heart clenched behind her ribs, unable to believe how enormous the thing's teeth were, how utterly emaciated it was, before it was joined by a member of its pack. The newcomer shoved the first away from the deer, determined to claim the kill for its own, tearing into the animal's jugular as Jane continued to back away, wide-eyed, her breath escaping her throat in tiny, suffocating gasps. By the time Ryan skidded back into the living room, there were four of them fighting next to the feeder, snapping their jaws at each other, their guttural squeals loud enough to hear from inside the house.

One of the deer that had fled into the forest circled back, bursting into the clearing, terrified as it stumbled onto one of its own being attacked. And while the four creatures were busy fighting, a fifth bolted across the snow, catching the larger deer's neck in its jaws only to tear out its throat, blood fanning out across the ground as the deer bucked beneath its attacker, desperate to get free.

Jane muffled her cry with the palm of her hand as she twisted away, refusing to watch any more. Those things were impossible—*impossible*—grotesque abominations of skin and bone, exactly as Ryan had described them. She squeezed her eyes shut, willing away the knowledge that Lauren had tried to run, she had scrambled and screamed, she had stared into those gaping jaws during the last second of her life. Terrified and trembling, Jane slowly looked to Ryan, and she could see it on his face—he knew they couldn't go out there. They'd be dead within minutes.

A gun wasn't going to do a damn thing.

CHAPTER TEN

The sun, which had been absent all day, was now setting over an invisible horizon, and the endless gray that blanketed the sky grew heavy with impending night. But the oncoming darkness made no difference; visibility was nearly zero. She could see the deck's railing just outside the window, but beyond that, all that existed was a deluge of white. Of all the years they had lived in Denver as kids, Jane couldn't remember ever seeing it snow this hard in the city.

She could only imagine how deep Sawyer's Jeep was buried now, the tracks it had made that morning probably gone. The wind howled outside, blowing snow off the railing in waves. It was one of those storms people never forgot, the kind that refused to let up until the food and firewood were gone. They were going to die here. If they didn't starve, they'd freeze. And if those two fates didn't get them first, the beasts that lingered in the trees would.

Jane turned to face the living room. Ryan was sitting next to the fireplace, occasionally poking the last of a burning log. Sawyer sat on the couch, his gaze fixed on the gun she had found. It rested on top of the coffee table, loaded and ready next to the knives, though that gun didn't make her feel much better after the display she'd witnessed a few hours before. They were speaking in low tones, trying to come up with a plan, their conversation dwindling every time she got too close. And while a part of her wanted to be involved in every aspect of their escape, her maternal instinct pushed her into the kitchen, focused on what it would take to keep them alive while they were inside the cabin rather than what they would do once they left.

She moved past the pantry, knowing there was nothing of use in there. After an hour of sitting in that room, she could recite the contents of each shelf by heart, and none of it would take them out further than a few days. She entered the laundry room, pulling open the cabinets that had always served as a catchall, and Jane found everything from extra paper towels to a sealed five-pack of Colgate, but no food. She sat down on the floor. It was ironic. The last time she had swung by Costco, she had stopped in front of an end cap stocked full of emergency freeze-dried food. She had rolled her eyes at it, thinking about how ridiculous some people were with all of that end-of-the-world crap. And yet here she was, cursing herself for not buying that stupid box when she had the chance. It would have kept them sufficiently fed for weeks, long enough for help to come, or at least for some of the snow to melt from the road. All they had now was a few days' worth of groceries, all refrigerated—stuff she had bought to make dinner for everyone—and half of that stuff would be too far gone to eat in a few days, let alone in a week.

She pulled herself to her feet, then froze.

The light overhead flickered once, then twice.

Outside, the wind wailed.

Every muscle in Ryan's body tensed when the house went dim before blazing bright again. He slowly got to his feet, as if tiptoeing would keep the cabin from throwing up its arms and declaring a blackout. Swiping the gun from the coffee table, he slid it into the waistband of his jeans as a particularly violent gust of wind rattled the windows, sending the snow upward in ghostlike tendrils before releasing it back to the ground.

He hadn't seen a storm like this in years, and this certainly trumped the worst. He'd gone up to Whistler a few years before, hung around the Olympic Village, had a great time at the bars; then the weather took an ugly turn. A three-day snowboarding trip had turned into a six-day hotel stay, then another day trying to get things squared away at the airport. It had been a disaster, but at least it had been within the limits of civilization. That blizzard had nothing on the one that raged outside now. With it being as cold as it was, one good gust could snap frozen branches and take down trees.

Ryan wondered whether they were the only people left alive in the area, whether the town twenty-five miles away had seen the likes of these monsters or if these things stuck to the mountains, where they knew they could outnumber their prey. What if they were truly stuck here, everyone else for miles having been devoured, the highway closed, the roads snowed in?

There was another flicker, the electricity's lull humming in the silence. Where the hell had he left that goddamn flashlight? He ran down the hall and toward the game room, then stopped in the doorway, his eyes darting across the pool table they had left midplay. It had been Lauren's shot. Jane had gone to get something to drink...and April had caught something lurking in the dark.

It became clear in a flash—the animal they had seen out the window that night hadn't been an animal at all. It had been one of those things.

And it had been staking them out since they'd arrived.

The lights flickered again, then went out.

Jane scrambled to her feet and bolted down the hall, her heart thudding against her ribs, her fear of the dark suddenly stronger than her fear of taking a corner straight into the jaws of the enemy. But when she reached the living room, it was empty. Both boys were gone.

Panic seized her chest. Out of the corner of her eye she saw something move. Someone was out on the deck. She blinked, staring wide-eyed toward the figure. Was that Sawyer? Could he have possibly been stupid enough to go outside to smoke? She ran across the room, her hands pressing to the window. She balled up her fist and knocked on the glass. *What are you doing?* she wanted to scream. *Have you lost your goddamn mind?*

She fumbled with the lock when something rustled behind her. Veering around, she was ready to yell at Ryan about how Sawyer was about to get himself killed, but her words fell soundless when she found herself staring into the eyes of the man she was convinced was standing out in the cold.

Jane's stomach flipped.

"Where's Ryan?" she asked, because if Sawyer was inside, who was standing out in the snow?

Sawyer shook his head.

"*Where's Ryan?!*" she yelled, the world suddenly wavy with frantic tears. She turned away, unlocking the dead bolt, fear overwhelming logic.

"Whoa!" Sawyer exclaimed. "What are you doing?" He ran at her, catching her a split second before she pulled open the door. Jane thrashed against him, trying to fight her way free.

"Where's Ryan?" she wailed.

"I'm right here." Ryan caught his sister by her arm, trying to calm her down.

Looking back to the porch, she stared at the dark figure that was still lurking outside the window. Her heart crawled into her throat, threatening to choke her if the fear didn't asphyxiate her first.

"Oh my god," she whispered, suddenly afraid to move. Her eyes were locked on that shadow, unable to look away. She heard Ryan say something beneath his breath, felt Sawyer's arms tighten around her and pull her back. The shadow spun around, jaws pulled open impossibly wide. Its eyes were as black as tar, staring at them through the window as it slapped its claws against the glass.

Jane screamed, waiting for the demon to burst through the window. The thing stepped in front of the kitchen door, stood to its full height, its gray skin nearly blending in with the white background behind it. And just as she was sure it was going to come through the glass, it twisted in the wind and leaped over the railing.

"This is it," Ryan said, setting three white emergency candles onto the ledge of the fireplace, the glass glinting beneath the flashlight's beam. Sawyer had thrown a few extra logs onto the metal grate and was blindly tearing out pages of a magazine, frantic to keep the fire that had nearly extinguished itself from going out. Ryan lit the candles he'd found in the laundry room, but those tiny flames were swallowed by the vastness of the cabin.

Taking a seat next to a trembling Jane, he watched Sawyer twist glossy paper into ropes before shoving them beneath the wood. This was, in Ryan's opinion, the worst-case scenario. Without power the heater wouldn't kick on when it got cold, and the cold would come on fast. That, and they couldn't see a damn thing, but he doubted the darkness inhibited those creatures' ability to hunt.

Sawyer held a twisted piece of paper over one of the candles, waiting for it to ignite. The end caught fire, glowing in weird shades of blue and green. He leaned away from the flame, the quiet sizzle of firewood filling the silence.

"We can't be the only ones," Ryan finally announced. "There have to be other victims, right?"

"What difference does it make?" Jane asked quietly. With her arms wrapped around her legs, she stared into the fire, her mouth and nose hidden behind her knees. "We're stuck out here," she whispered.

Ryan couldn't argue her logic. "That thing had the perfect opportunity to attack, but it took off instead. Make sense of it."

Sawyer shook his head as the flames in the fireplace grew. Shadows danced across the walls.

"You know that has to be what April saw through the window," Ryan said. "It could have gotten us *then* too. We were outside, standing in our T-shirts on the back patio, but it didn't make a move." He swallowed, seemed to hesitate, then asked, "You think they're smart enough to stake a place out before they come in for the kill?"

Sawyer pulled the fire poker from its holder and nudged one of the logs. "Maybe they're afraid of big groups." The log shifted, spitting sparks up the chimney.

They all went silent.

"Maybe they're like wolves," Ryan said after a long while. "When wolves sense there's a threat within their perimeter, they get aggressive. Especially if something gets close to their den. Maybe someone was close to a cave or something, the storm came in, these things didn't have anything to eat so they just kept coming closer and closer to civilization. But what I don't get is, why haven't there been reports of dead people all over the place? I mean, that would make sense, right? If they're taking everyone in their perimeter out?"

They were pack animals, that was for sure; the way they had swarmed around Lauren had made that clear. Maybe the one on the deck *had* been scoping them out. Ryan shuddered beneath his sweatshirt.

They went quiet again, the fire licking at the sides of the fireplace. One of the logs popped and they all jumped. A spark flew onto the carpet. It glowed for a few seconds, then faded out.

"What if they haven't found any bodies because there haven't been any?" Jane asked after a long while.

"What about the skiers?" Sawyer asked.

"Maybe they got spooked and ran away." She went quiet for a moment, then lifted her head again as if in revelation. "That's why they're here," she whispered, her eyes going glassy. "When there's a storm like this, animals go into hiding. They're harder to find. And if that's what these things eat...deer and elk..." Her words faded.

"They're searching for food," Sawyer finished her train of thought.

A chill crawled up Ryan's spine. It made sense, and at this point it was the only thing that did.

"They're hungry," she said. "And we're the only prey they can find."

They tried to stay awake, tried to formulate a plan, but exhaustion gave way to hours of quiet. Trying to keep herself from falling asleep during her watch, Jane left the boys dozing in the living room and dared to venture into the kitchen. With the flame of an emergency candle guiding her way, she went through the motions of making coffee—filling the pot, stuffing a filter into the maker's basket, adding five scoops of Folgers before hitting the power button. She blinked at the machine when the power light didn't come on, convinced for a good five seconds that the stupid thing had died before rolling her eyes at herself. The routine was so ingrained in her blood that even an emergency candle did little to remind her that this darkness was involuntary. Exhaling a sigh, she settled on three glasses of water instead, returning to the living room a minute later, the candle precariously tucked into the crook of her elbow. Her father's Ginsu knives glittered in the firelight, all lying next to the revolver she had brought from upstairs. Ryan had shoved the pool cues under the coffee table, a few of them sharpened to deadly points, the rest awaiting honing just as soon as Ryan's watch began.

She set the glasses on the coffee table and moved back into the kitchen, pulling open the fridge's door. It was cold inside the house, but not cold enough to keep the food from spoiling. The unit harbored the dank scent of a refrigerator getting warmer by the minute. Grabbing the cake stand by its footed bottom, she pulled plates out of a cabinet and forks out of a drawer. Ryan still had half an hour to sleep before his shift, but he'd be hungry. None of them had eaten since that morning, and they had to keep their energy up. It was what Jane had put herself in charge of—making sure they were fed, rested, and ready when the guys decided it was time to go.

Sawyer stirred next to the fire when he heard her return. Oona's ears perked but she remained motionless, her head resting on Ryan's leg. Ryan was fast asleep under a blanket that had been draped across the back of one of the sofas, the hood of his sweatshirt pulled over his head, his back to the room.

Sawyer sat up and stretched with a wince.

Jane selected one of the knives on the coffee table, cutting into leftover cake. She offered Sawyer a plate with a halfhearted shrug.

"Thanks," he said, taking it from her.

"Kind of inappropriate," she said. "But we have to eat."

"Hey, I'll eat chocolate cake in any situation," Sawyer told her. He made an attempt to smile, but it vanished before it fully formed. Optimism was what would keep them afloat. She was trying to convince herself that if they made it through the night they'd be home free, but even if they made it through to morning, she could only imagine how much snow had fallen in the past twelve hours. It had been nonstop, and the wind was aggressive. If the weather didn't let up, there was no way they were going anywhere. She'd rather take her chances waiting for those creatures to break in than walk out into the wilderness with a guarantee of freezing.

"You know, two years ago, when we planned on coming up here, before that ski accident?" he said, cutting into his slice of cake. "Alex had something going at work and you told Ryan to come up here anyway, just me and him?"

She nodded toward her plate.

"I was the one who decided to postpone."

Jane glanced up at him, chewing the inside of her lip, not sure whether she was supposed to respond—whether she was supposed to ask why, or if silence was an acceptable response.

"I didn't want to come up here if you weren't here too. Despite everything."

She smiled faintly and looked back down.

"I'm still glad I came," he said quietly, frowning at his plate. "I know that's fucked up. It makes me feel shitty for even admitting it, because..." He paused, shaking his head at a thought. April. The baby. "I guess if this is the end...if this is what it took to wind up here with you guys..."

"Don't say that. If you hadn't come, this wouldn't have happened."

"Janey..." He lifted his eyes to meet her gaze. "If I hadn't come, I just wouldn't be here when it happened. It would have still happened. But I'd be in Denver calling Ryan's cell for weeks, and I'd eventually get into my Jeep and drive out to Phoenix, only he wouldn't be there."

Jane slid her plate onto the coffee table and stared down at her hands. Her chest constricted against Sawyer's words: *if this is the end.* She wanted to cry, wanted to apologize because suddenly it all felt like her fault. But her thoughts were derailed when Sawyer slid up onto the couch, cutting the distance between them.

"Janey, listen..." She could smell the chocolate on his breath. "Everything is going to work out. We're going to be fine."

She nodded without looking at him, but he caught her chin in his hand, gently tipped it up so they looked into each other's eyes.

"We're going to be fine," he repeated. "I promise."

But she could see it in his eyes: he didn't believe it. He was trying to convince her, to keep her calm, to keep her sane, but for Sawyer it would never be okay again.

His world was already gone.

CHAPTER ELEVEN

Ryan stirred from sleep, and for a moment everything was fine. They were at the cabin, the snow was great, Lauren was fantastic, and he felt good about the future. But every muscle in his body tensed when he heard Oona's growl beside him. He rolled onto his back, then sat up, only to be presented with Jane and Sawyer sleeping in front of the fire, tangled in each other's arms, knives strewn across the room, the cold starting to creep in through the windows, eating away the last of the cabin's heat. Pinching the bridge of his nose, he then let his hand fall from his face, his palm slapping the slick fabric of his snowboarding pants, and crawled toward the coffee table. The scent of baked chocolate roused a hungry rumble from his stomach, and he grabbed the spare fork that lay there, digging into the cake that was left on the covered stand. With a mouth full of chocolate and frosting, he rubbed behind Oona's ears, his gaze returning to his sister and best friend, unable to help the pang of sadness that flared in his gut. He should have tried harder, should have thrown himself in front of that creature to buy Lauren some more time. She had been incredible, the girl he had been waiting for, for so long, the girl he was convinced didn't exist at all, and he had let her die—no, he had let her be *torn apart.*

Another subdued growl resonated inside Oona's throat. Ryan froze midchew and blinked through the darkness. She was definitely at attention now, as though seeing something that Ryan couldn't. Swallowing the chocolate lump in his mouth, he stared through the living room and into the kitchen, his eyes wide.

The slight squeal of hinges reached his ears as the kitchen door slowly swung inward, and Ryan felt the cold almost immediately. Seeing the wind and snow blow inside proved that he wasn't imagining things; that door was genuinely open. Oona was staring at it too—her ears slicked back against her head, her snout wrinkling as she prepared to snarl.

The urge to warn Jane and Sawyer was almost overwhelming, but something kept him from making a sound. He held his breath and waited, praying that it had only been the wind, that the door hadn't been latched and it had finally given way to the air pressure outside. But why the fuck hadn't that door been locked? The idea of their having huddled inside this cabin, collecting weapons, considering how they were going to defend themselves while there was an *unlocked door* in the opposite room blew his mind. And then he remembered Jane yelling, Sawyer pulling her back, the thing on the deck. In their panic, nobody had realized the dead bolt hadn't been thrown back into place. And now Ryan was left sitting in the darkness of the living room, staring at it as it hung open wide, like a gaping mouth ready to scream.

The moment he saw something fill the doorway was the moment Ryan Adler was sure they were dead. Oona's defensiveness was suddenly squelched when the creature stepped inside. She ducked her head down, afraid, not daring to move from her master's side. Ryan, on the other hand, didn't move because he was petrified. With the fire to his back, his mouth hung open without sound.

One of the things that had murdered Lauren stepped around the kitchen island, sniffing at the air. Its stomach was emaciated, like that of a stray dog that hadn't fed for weeks. Long strings of saliva dripped from its wide jowls, glistening in the firelight. It sniffed the air with two holes that served as its nose, a gruesome purr rumbling deep inside its chest. Ryan's eyes widened as it began to pull out drawers, its nostrils flaring as it tried to sniff out food. Not having any luck, it finally pressed its huge skull to the refrigerator door, as if able to smell what was inside. With the fridge built into the cabinets, it didn't budge when the creature gave it a shove— not even a wiggle. The monster pushed it again, this time with more frustration. Nothing. Ryan watched this while trying not to choke on his own heartbeat, hoping like hell the thing didn't notice him sitting there beside the fire, praying that Oona didn't make a move, that Sawyer and Jane didn't bolt upright and start freaking out.

Swiping at the door, the flat of the demon's palm dragged across the refrigerator door, and its bony fingers hooked beneath the lip that served as the refrigerator's handle. It canted its head as if curious, considering this new discovery, and then pulled instead of pushed, revealing the treasure it was looking for. Ryan went numb, dread spiking his bloodstream.

They're intelligent.

That was why they hadn't attacked days before, when Ryan and Sawyer had stood outside just beyond the pool room. It was why the one on the porch hadn't burst through the glass when it had spotted the three of them standing inside in the kitchen. They were *smart*. They were weighing their options, considering the best plan of attack.

He nearly jumped when a glass jar exploded against the kitchen floor. Both Sawyer and Jane jerked awake. Ryan dared to move, pressing his fingers to his mouth, silently warning them not to make a sound. He could only hope that if that thing spotted them it would run away like it had before, but he wasn't about to take his chances.

The predator fumbled through the dark refrigerator with nails that had been made for climbing and tearing. It thrust its arm inside the fridge, drawing it out a moment later, inspecting a gushing milk carton crushed within its wide, clawed hand. Lifting its arm so that milk dribbled into its mouth, it whipped its head from side to side before flinging the carton across the kitchen, apparently disliking the taste. As soon as it ducked its head back inside the fridge, Ryan scrambled closer to his comrades. The fire blazed behind them, burning his back through the fabric of his sweatshirt.

Jane clamped her hand over her mouth, her eyes shimmering with panic that threatened to spill over. The terror crushed her self-restraint beneath its weight, and her whimper cut through the quiet of the room at precisely the wrong moment.

Her eyes widened.

Ryan's attention snapped to the hairless abomination in the kitchen.

It had heard, and it was staring directly at them, its gaping maw unhinged, the contents of the fridge at its feet. It lurched forward, its nails clacking against the floor. It stopped just shy of the single step that led down into the living room as if reconsidering an attack, the firelight reflecting in its cold black eyes, glinting off teeth too large to conceal.

Every nerve in Ryan's body stood on end. Foreboding buzzed along his limbs like an electric current just beneath the skin. Oona tensed beneath his arm, warning the creature to stay back with a growl. The thing swung its head around as though it hadn't been aware of the others in the room until that very moment, perhaps blinded by the fire behind them—but its eyes were locked on them now.

Ryan didn't stop to think.

As soon as it spotted them, he scrambled to the opposite side of the fireplace and grasped the fire poker, knowing that if he didn't make his move now he'd never have the chance.

The creature crouched down, the muscles of its legs coiling up like springs, and leaped forward, landing on the back of the couch like some monstrous bird. Jane screamed, shrinking back; she was the closest to it, directly in its path. It jumped after her, its feet thudding against the varnished top of the coffee table, chocolate cake and an assortment of knives spilling onto the carpet. Its jaws snapped at them, those teeth knocking together with a sickening pop, but it stopped short of the fireplace that blazed behind them. If that impossibly inhuman face could register emotion, Ryan would have sworn he saw a glimmer of fear in its onyx eyes.

But Oona didn't understand that the monster was frozen in place. Her lips pulled away from her teeth in a snarl and she bolted forward, protecting her friends. Latching on to the monster's long, bony arm, she tore at its flesh, shaking her head as if trying to rip the thing's arm from its body. The creature released a high-pitched scream, a shriek Ryan hoped wasn't a call for help. If even one more of these things showed up, they were dead. It reeled back, swinging the arm that was being attacked, tossing Oona across the room. The husky hit the wall with a yelp, but adrenaline had her bounding to her feet, diving back into battle without a second thought.

Ryan lurched forward.

The hiss that radiated from that gray-skinned monstrosity assured him that it was pissed, and he doubted Oona would survive another hit. Taking care of an injured person was one thing, but an injured dog—it was a near guarantee that she wouldn't make it. With the thing's attention on the husky, Ryan bounded at it, the fire poker held high over his head. He swung as hard as he could, bringing the protruding end down onto the monster's skull. The demon stumbled back as Oona fell on him, her jaws locking onto one of its legs. But the creature was too busy waving its arms wildly about its head to notice her attack. Ryan gave the fire poker a swift tug and it came free, a geyser of foul-smelling blood running down the monster's raw-boned back.

Sawyer dodged around both dog and owner, snatching the small ash shovel off its holder from beside the fireplace. He took a swing as Ryan pulled back, hitting the savage in its emaciated stomach with the sharp edge of the trowel. It emitted a guttural wail as it doubled over, but its cry was cut short when the fire poker came down onto its head for a second time, punching a twin hole in its skull. It veered around, sneering at Ryan, and he lost his grip on his weapon. Scrambling backward toward the fire, he felt the heat lick at his back; the creature rushed after him, stopping just shy of catching its prey for a second time. Extending a gangly arm to grab him, the thing pulled it back just as quickly, its rage transforming to frustration as it wavered from left to right.

Ryan winced against the heat, sure he would go up in flames if he couldn't put some distance between himself and the blaze. Sawyer swung the shovel again, striking the beast on the side of its head, but the hit didn't seem to faze it. It took a swipe at him with its giant hands, and Sawyer fell backward, crashing against the couch. He rushed to regain his footing, but the monster sprang forward, landing on the arm of the couch, looming over Sawyer as he cowered beneath the creature's cadaverous frame. Jutting its arm forward, it caught Sawyer by the shoulder as he attempted to bolt away. Rather than running, Sawyer gave a startled cry, twisting against the creature's grasp in a desperate attempt to run.

Ryan darted forward, not sure of his intentions, only knowing that he had to do something before his best friend was torn in half right before his eyes. But he came to a dead stop when a shot rang out. The room went silent beneath the piercing ring in his ears. Gun powder soured the air.

When the creature dropped to the carpet, it brought Jane into view, their father's gun in her trembling hands.

She couldn't bring herself to look away from it, hardly flinching when Ryan bolted out of the living room and through the kitchen, slamming the open door shut. Sawyer approached the creature at Jane's feet, still clinging to the fireplace shovel, ready to swing as he nudged it with the toe of his sneaker. Oona didn't want anything to do with whatever it was, dead or alive. She cowered in the corner of the room, watching everyone else inspect the body while she kept a safe distance from the thing that had slammed her into the wall.

"Jesus fucking Christ!" Sawyer yelled, dropping the shovel once he was sure it was dead. His hands flew into his hair as he backed away.

"The food is gone," Ryan announced, stepping back into the living room. He covered his nose and mouth a second later, shielding himself from the noxious stench of rotten eggs.

"Gone?" Jane turned her attention to her brother, startled.

"It raided the fridge, tossed it all onto the floor."

That left them with nothing but what was in the pantry, which wasn't much at all. She looked back to the creature at her feet, taking a couple of steps back. "It was hungry," she said softly.

"You think?" Ryan asked, his tone verging on sarcastic.

Pressing a hand to her lips, she felt another breakdown coming on, bubbling at the pit of her stomach like a witches' brew. She swiped at her eyes, looking away.

"What the hell is this thing?" Sawyer asked, refusing to approach it. "Look at the teeth." They were massive, predatory fangs stained a deep yellow.

Jane chewed on her bottom lip, considering an idea that was rolling around in her head, not sure whether it was ingenious or absolutely stupid. All she knew was that if more of those things showed up for a fight, she and the boys probably wouldn't be as lucky next time.

Taking a seat on the edge of the couch, she stared at the gun still held fast in her hands. "I think maybe we should use this to our advantage."

Neither Ryan nor Sawyer said anything, and while she didn't look up from the firearm in her grasp, she knew they were staring at her.

"Aren't there rubber gloves in the garage?" she asked, finally leveling her gaze on her brother.

"I think so," Ryan nodded, then shook his head just as quickly. "Rubber gloves for *what*?"

Jane slid the gun onto the coffee table, her fingers dancing on its edge. And then she swept the largest Ginsu knife in their arsenal off the carpet, inspecting it. Ryan slowly glanced over to Sawyer, a dark expression drifting across his face. And from the way Ryan's mouth turned up at one corner, she knew it was a good idea. It very well may have been a *great* idea. And it was all hers.

Sawyer couldn't believe they were going to go through with it. He and Ryan were putting all their weight into trying to get the monster up the single step and into the kitchen. Despite its emaciated look, the thing weighed a ton. Sawyer's fingers were on fire as he yanked on the blue tarp, the creature sliding along the carpet inch by inch as they dragged it, Sawyer's joints screaming against the tension as he leaned back and pulled.

The plastic sheeting slid across the hardwood of the kitchen far easier than it had across the plush carpet in the living room, and for a moment the boys stopped what they were doing, deliberating whether they wanted to do this in the kitchen or the garage. But the garage had a steep flight of stairs leading down into it. They'd have to make multiple trips after they hacked the thing to pieces—up and down the stairs with body parts. The kitchen was a better idea. The door was right there. All they'd have to do was open it and hurl the pieces onto the porch.

Jane took a seat in one of the dining chairs and covered her nose and mouth as the boys began to unwrap their gruesome package. Sawyer had seen his share of movies; he was waiting for it to twitch, to rear up and snap its teeth at them like a cheap jump scare. But the thing was motionless. He wrinkled his nose at the stench, not sure if it was the creature's blood that stank or whether the thing spent its free time rolling around in its own excrement.

Ryan made a face as soon as he unwrapped the tarp and that fetid smell hit him head-on. Jane murmured an "oh god" when the stink finally made it across the kitchen to where she sat. Ryan swept the butcher knife off the kitchen island, the blade glinting with cold winter light. Outside, the snow continued to fall. Sawyer decided to keep his skepticism to himself, trying to convince himself that this was a good, solid plan, their *only* plan. But if it continued to snow, their work would be under inches of powder before any of the others could sniff it out.

He watched Ryan lean in, hovering over the creature that had nearly taken them out, poking at the dead thing with the tip of the knife like a curious kid. The blade scraped across one of the creature's fangs, setting Sawyer's teeth on edge.

"Look at the eyes," Ryan said, noting the beads of onyx deeply set above those gaping jaws. "No eyelids. And the hands…" They nearly looked human, albeit flattened out, the fingers gruesomely crooked and long.

"Hurry up," Jane told them from behind a cupped palm. "It stinks."

"What's this supposed to accomplish again?" Ryan asked, seemingly hesitant to hack up the thing in front of her.

"They might have an aversion to the scent of their own blood, or the sight of their own kind dead somewhere. Some animals see the corpses of their own species as a sign of danger. They avoid it."

"And if these things don't avoid it?" Ryan asked. When Jane failed to reply, he looked back down to the corpse and took a breath. "Let's get this over with," he said, and before Sawyer could step back, he plunged the knife into the creature's chest. Jane gasped and looked away, but the blade hardly pierced the thing's flesh, striking the breastbone, leaving Ryan struggling to free the knife. A moment later he straightened out of his crouch, cleared his throat, and made an announcement. "I'll be right back," he said. "I need to get the ax."

Jane's eyes went wide.

"*What?*" Sawyer asked, blinking at his friend. He couldn't believe it. They had fought that thing off with fireplace tools when they could have been swinging a hatchet.

Ryan threw his hands up in surrender. "I forgot about it," he confessed. "It slipped my fucking mind."

"Are you kidding me?" Sawyer shook his head, backing away from the cadaver on the kitchen floor. "Are you sure that snowplow I asked you about doesn't exist?"

Ryan scoffed. "You got me. It's there. So is the helicopter that'll whisk us to safety. I'll grab the keys."

"We could have been killed," Sawyer insisted. "That thing nearly took off my shoulder. I mean, really?"

"What do you want me to say?" Ryan asked. "I couldn't take inventory of the garage that doesn't belong to me because I was busy *shitting my pants.*"

"What if it had gone after Jane?" Sawyer shot back, aggression tingeing his tone.

"Jesus, seriously?"

"How would you have felt if it had got her and *then* you remembered the ax, Ryan?"

"Hey, guys?" Jane rose from her seat.

"I would have been thrilled," Ryan said. "Really happy. I'd have thrown a goddamn party."

"Yeah?" Sawyer challenged. "And I bet if she was outside you would have gone out there to find her, right? No matter how big of a risk."

Ryan's expression wavered from defensive to guilt ridden. He looked away, and Sawyer immediately regretted going there. He knew Ryan was doing the best he could. He was trying to protect them, trying to keep his shit together despite watching Lauren get torn apart, trying to be the voice of reason while Sawyer swung from cautious to utterly reckless, ready to stomp into the snow like some kamikaze with nothing left to lose.

"Sorry," Sawyer said quietly.

Ryan didn't respond. He marched down the hallway, a flashlight beam illuminating his path.

Sawyer and Jane were left to stare at each other. She tried to look confident, but it was obvious that she was questioning her own plan.

"You think this will work?" Sawyer asked, if only to breach the silence, to keep himself from looking back down at the thing between them.

"I think so," she said after a moment, but she didn't sound sure of herself. He supposed that was just as well. How could they be sure of anything with a nightmare lying at their feet?

"It's a good idea," he said after a moment, watching her vacillate between going through with it or calling the whole thing off. "You're right; we can use its scent to disguise ourselves. If it was just me and Ryan, we'd spend all night kicking the shit out of it or something."

The flashlight beam bounced at the end of the hallway before Jane could reply. Ryan was returning from the garage.

"Hold this," Ryan said, handing Jane the flashlight. She pointed it at the creature's head, and without so much as a warning, Ryan reeled back and brought the blade down on the dead thing's neck.

CHAPTER TWELVE

Ryan took out his anguish on the corpse at his feet. Every ax swing was for Lauren. *Whack.* That was for never seeing her face again. *Whack.* For the sound of her laughter. Her smell. The taste of her lips—a taste he'd never know. He felt nothing but grief as he chopped off that toothy bastard's apelike arms, didn't even flinch when he buried the ax blade in its chest and cracked open its ribs.

He threw down the ax and drew his sleeve across his face, then looked over his shoulder at his sister. To his surprise, her eyes were locked on the bloody mess that he'd created. The girl who couldn't handle a bit of gore on television without covering her eyes was now mesmerized by the copious amounts of foul-smelling blood. That was what the stink had been—rotten eggs and the sharp scent of iron—and the fact that he had split open some sort of organ hadn't helped matters. Ryan waited for her to look up at him, hoping to God she wasn't going into shock. When she finally lifted her chin, he nodded at her as if to tell her that everything was fine.

"Check on Oona?" he asked her. That dog was smart. She hadn't set foot in the kitchen to see what they were doing, remaining in the warmth of a dying fire, the embers giving the living room a haunting glow. Jane slithered out of her seat and carefully stepped around the gore that the tarp failed to contain. Ryan knew there was going to be blood, but he had no idea how much. It seemed like an impossible amount, as though the size of the body couldn't have contained all that fluid. Yet there it was, oozing across blue plastic, creeping across the hardwood floor.

"Are you ready?" he asked.

Sawyer swallowed, then reluctantly nodded, snapping a latex glove onto his left hand before pulling another one on top of that, doubling up for good measure. "We're going to have to be quick," Ryan warned. "I don't want to be in the middle of doing this when another one of these motherfuckers decides to make an appearance."

"Or gets curious," Sawyer said, giving a firmer nod of the head this time.

"God," Ryan groaned, a bloodied glove grabbing hold of the doorknob. "This thing reeks." He jerked the door open and stepped back to the carcass, plunging his hands into its body cavity before hurling the offal into the snow.

Jane stared at the mess at her feet, the contents of the refrigerator unsalvageable, the food that would have sustained them for at least a week completely destroyed. She began to pick up the mess, tossing crushed containers and broken glass into a trash bag, wondering what the hell they were going to do. The snow just beyond the kitchen door was now strewn with body parts and entrails. Despite the moon's dim shine, she didn't need the light to see the dark streaks—black in the moonlight but red in reality—decorating a once pristine white surface like abstract art. She didn't know whether the smell of one of their own would repel the others or attract them, but this was the only way to find out. They'd either avoid the area entirely, repulsed by the scent of the dead, or fall onto it like carrion birds, hungrily picking it apart until there was nothing left.

Not even sure why she was bothering to clean the mess, she left the trash bag beside the fridge and stepped around the island, the two people she loved most in this life squatting around the remains of a monstrous body. Ryan was decorated with a spray of blood, a smear of red streaking his cheek like a brushstroke. Sawyer had gotten gore onto his arms, that beloved T-shirt completely ruined, offering no protection against whatever disease may have been lingering in that creature's fluids. Both of them turned to look at her when she stepped into view, their gazes strange in their expectancy, as if waiting for the schoolteacher to tell them what was next.

"I think we need to leave," she told them. "Today, when the sun comes up."

She watched their faces mirror each other in emotion, shifting from anticipation to a worried sort of surprise. Ryan rose from his crouch next to the tarp, his arms at his sides, rubber gloves slick with blood.

"I thought we were supposed to wait to see what happens," he said. "Wasn't that the plan?"

"Yes, but the longer we stay here, the more opportunity they have to attack too." No matter how much they planned and waited, there really was no guarantee of safety. No matter what they chose to do, it was going to be dangerous.

"You know that if we do that," he said, his voice strangely dry, as though he'd just woken up from an eternity of sleep, "there's no turning back. Once we leave here, we can't come back."

Sawyer stood motionless next to the kitchen door, his eyes fixed on the floor, his arms hanging limp at his sides. Jane looked away from him, knowing that his thoughts were with April. But Sawyer eventually spoke, though he never lifted his gaze.

"I thought we were doing this so we could stay."

Jane's heart twisted. "We don't have anything to eat," she reminded him.

"I doubt they like the smell," Ryan said. "Though God only knows why. It's so fucking pleasant. We can mask our own scent, maybe get to the highway…"

"But what if she comes back?" The hope that flashed across Sawyer's face was too much to bear. She looked away, her jaw clenching tight.

"Did you see the way it stopped?" Ryan asked, steering the topic away from April. Sawyer's quiet desperation was getting to him as well. She could see it in the way Ryan tensed every time April's name came up. "It was scared."

But the fire was almost gone, not having been tended for too long. It was little more than a few licking flames, glowing embers at their base.

Ryan made a sudden move, stepping around the island to the stove, grabbing an empty soup pot that had been left on a burner. Jane had intended to use it to make their next meal, but that was before Ryan had burst through the door and shoved them into the pantry; that was before monsters were real. He set the pot down on the floor, then looked to Sawyer in expectation.

"Help me," he said, crouching to catch the tarp between his rubber-coated fingers.

Sawyer hesitated but did what he was told, carefully pulling the tarp upward to pool the remaining blood into the center of the plastic. Stepping forward, Jane caught the end of the tarp and helped aim it into the pot. The foul-smelling blood splashed against stainless steel.

Jane understood in a horrifying flash of realization: Ryan was serious. If they were going to leave that cabin, they'd do it covered in blood.

It wasn't that Sawyer wanted to stay. He knew they had to get out of there, knew that it was their only chance if they wanted to live. But he couldn't shake a lingering thought—the idea that somehow, by some miracle, April was still alive, and that she was making her way back up the drive through the blizzard; that she would arrive only to miss them by a window of a few minutes, and that in the realization of her being completely alone, she would die not of the cold, not of the beasts outside, but of a broken heart.

His logical mind tried to convince him that it was impossible: anyone who had been outside, even for a few hours, would have first succumbed to frostbite, and then to freezing to death. If those monsters were climbing onto the cabin's deck and peering through the windows, they had either exhausted their food supply out in the wild or were tired of looking when there was a guaranteed source here. April had become part of the wilderness over twelve hours before. He didn't want to believe it, but Ryan was right. She didn't stand a chance. Not out there. Not alone.

The dry crack of wood drew Sawyer out of his thoughts and into the present. Ryan had flipped the coffee table over and was kicking at its leg. There was a wall of firewood stacked along the outside of the cabin just beneath the deck, but despite its closeness it was too far away. They needed fire, and they were now resorting to apocalyptic means.

"The Realtor will be happy," Sawyer said.

"The Realtor won't care. The new owner will be happy," Ryan corrected. "They'll show up, ready for a relaxing weekend in their brand-new, fully furnished cabin…"

"New owner?" Jane asked, the bloodied ax in her hands. She was trying to chop a chair into pieces, but there was no power behind her swing. Sawyer forced himself away from the window and took the hatchet from her, splitting one of the chair legs in half with a single swing. "What do you mean 'new owner'?" she asked. "This place is still for sale." She blinked at Ryan when he failed to respond. "Right?"

Ryan cleared his throat and continued to kick at the table leg.

Jane looked up at the ceiling, as though suddenly overwhelmed by her brother's lack of response. "You've got to be kidding me," she said.

"Nobody told us," Ryan said, defending his decision to crash the place.

"And yet you knew."

"I looked it up."

"Jesus, Ryan."

"What?" he asked with a shrug. "Nobody called us for the keys. It was an innocent mistake." Ryan stopped what he was doing, a look of sudden realization crossing his face. "Oh my god," he said. "I just figured it out. Pops sold the place to those gray alien assholes. *That's* why they're so pissed." He leveled his gaze on his sister when she failed to be amused. "Who cares?" he asked her. "Like anyone should ever come up here again."

"And how will they know that?"

"I don't know," he said. "Maybe by the body parts on the deck?"

Sawyer slid onto the ottoman in front of an overstuffed armchair, picturing an unsuspecting hiker stumbling onto April's body after the first thaw. He pressed his hands against his face, his elbows kissing his knees.

Both Jane and Ryan went quiet, though Ryan kept working. He grabbed the ax Sawyer had abandoned and brought it down against the coffee table's top with a crack. Sawyer winced at the noise, trying to figure out why he had brought April up here at all. Sure, they had had their issues, but what the hell did he expect to happen with Jane being here? Why couldn't he have loved what he had rather than wanting what he had lost? It was pathetic. *He* was pathetic.

Jane slid onto the ottoman next to him.

"Are you okay?" she asked. He felt her hand on his back but couldn't handle the contact. Standing, he left her there, her arm floating in the air. Ryan stopped chopping, and Sawyer watched him give his sister a questioning look while his back was turned, the reflection in the window giving the twins away.

"Hey," Ryan said after a moment. "What's up?"

"What do you mean, what's up?" Sawyer asked, his hands shoved into the pockets of his jeans.

"I told you, you have to stop thinking about it," Ryan said. "I know that's an impossible request, but we have to focus here. You feel guilty.. So do I."

"I don't feel *guilty*," Sawyer's tone was barbed with disdain, but that was exactly it. He had yelled at her. That was why April had taken off into the snow. He had made her feel as though she hadn't mattered to him as much as his friends did, and she had run away. The ax hit the floor next to Ryan's feet with a heavy thump. Out of the corner of his eye, Sawyer saw Jane coil her arms around herself.

"Listen, this isn't exactly what you'd call a normal situation," Ryan said. "This whole thing is fucked up, but right now you have to let it go."

"Let it go," Sawyer echoed, turning to face his best friend. "You know what's going to happen if we get out of here? You're going to go back to your fancy apartment and three weeks from now you'll be on a plane flying out to the Swiss Alps, because the show must go on. The world will go back to normal for you, because that's what you've set it up to do. And I congratulate you on that; I really do. Shit, I'm *jealous* that after all of this is said and done, you can write it off as some terrible nightmare; you can tell this story at parties and impress girls you have no genuine interest in."

Ryan's jaw went rigid.

Jane squeezed her eyes shut, her nails digging into the upholstery beneath her.

"But you know what I get to do? I get to go back to my shitty apartment only a few hundred miles away—so close that I'll be able to smell this place for the rest of my life. And when I get there, I'll unlock my door, I'll walk into my room, and I'll see all of April's stuff strewn everywhere, because she always sucked at housekeeping. Her clothes, her jewelry, her books all over the place; and when I look away in an attempt to find a patch of wall that doesn't have her written all over it, I'll see a crib...a fucking *crib*, still in the box, waiting to be put together for a baby that will never be born."

Ryan's gaze snapped to Jane, but all she did was nod faintly—the slightest gesture to let him know that she knew.

"I can't just let it go," Sawyer croaked. "This isn't just about me anymore. I was supposed to have a family." He felt his throat constrict around those words. "I was supposed to be a dad," he whispered, his face flaring red-hot as his tears threatened to spill over. "I'm so sorry." He turned his attention to a statue-still Jane. "So sorry it turned out this way."

Jane closed the distance and wrapped her arms around him in a tight hug just as a sob tore its way out of his throat. Ryan looked away, battling his own inner turmoil a few feet away. And for the first time Sawyer saw that Ryan's grief matched his own. Sawyer was wrong. He wasn't the only one who had lost someone on this trip. Lauren was gone too, and from the way Ryan had turned away to hide his pain, she wasn't just another girl. Ryan had finally found a girl who mattered, and just like that, she had been stolen away.

Ryan stopped by the pantry on his way to the living room. Save for a bite of chocolate cake, it had been nearly twenty-four hours since he'd eaten, and his stomach was starting to petrify. He grabbed a box of stale graham crackers, tore open the lid, pulled out a square, and stuffed the cracker in his mouth before walking into the kitchen. As he sidestepped the bloody tarp that had been left next to the door, his gaze snagged on the pot of blood in the sink.

The snow had finally slowed. An occasional flake tumbled from the sky, but the latecomers were rare. The clouds were starting to thin, the deep lavender of morning peeking through the gray. With the storm at a pause, now would be their best shot to run. Staring out the window, Ryan couldn't help but replay the events of the night before. It was hard to imagine that only a few hours ago, one of those creatures had stepped into the kitchen like it owned the place. The moment he saw that thing slink inside the cabin, he had been struck by an overwhelming assurance that they were all dead.

He blinked at a swaying tree just beyond the deck, snow falling from its branches as though something were shaking the pine by its base. He couldn't see the bottom of the tree from inside the house—it was blocked by the lip of the deck—but the movement was impossible to miss in a sea of stillness.

Ryan shot a look toward the living room. Sawyer was still brooding, but he was keeping himself busy by sharpening the ends of pool cues with a knife. Jane sat next to the fire with Oona, organizing their gear, trying to consolidate to keep their exit swift. It was good that she was keeping herself busy. When she had nothing to do, she'd fall into a haunting, unnerving silence.

Ryan held his breath when the silhouette of one of those savages came into view, climbing the shuddering pine like a jungle cat. The tree shook beneath its weight, powder falling to the ground in a miniature storm. He nearly yelled for the others to come see what he was seeing when the thing leaped from one tree to another. It was trying to get a look at the deck without coming too close—a sign that Jane's plan was working. It could smell the foul stink of its fallen comrade, and it disappeared as quickly as it had come.

The fact that the damn thing could leap from tree to tree was alarming, but as long as they stuck to the road, there would be no way for the creatures to corner the group from above. They were going to survive this thing. They just needed to get the hell out of that cabin and down to the highway. It was a good five miles, but he was sure they could make it.

About to walk back into the living room and announce that it was time to go, he paused, reached out, and rubbed the fabric of his mother's drapes between his fingers. She had ordered them out of a catalog more than twenty years before, spending an entire Labor Day weekend meticulously measuring each window before placing her order. When her curtains had finally come in, she had admired them for weeks while waiting for their next trip to the cabin. Ryan remembered her stepping back to appreciate her handiwork after she had hung the last one—she had gazed at the very window he was standing at now. Holding that fabric in his hand, he reminded himself of the good times they all had had in that cabin; the delicious meals that they had eaten in that kitchen—Christmases and Thanksgivings, the meals perfect down to the last detail. His mother was somewhere in Phoenix at that very moment, probably sipping tea and watching made-for-TV movies while a maid buzzed around her, paid for by alimony.

And then, as if to solidify that those good times were over, he coiled his fingers into the drapes and pulled.

Jane tore her mother's curtains into long strips before wrapping them around the end of broken coffee table legs. The torches were crude, but they'd do. Ryan returned from his scavenger hunt upstairs, having tossed all their luggage down the stairs like bags of trash. They would salvage what they could. Armed with the large wicker basket from the master bathroom, he tossed it onto the couch. It would hold weapons rather than fashion magazines and luxury car brochures.

"I need to go outside," Ryan said.

His words tingled inside Jane's chest.

"What? No," she protested, but he held up a hand to stop her, the expression on his face confirming that it wasn't up for debate.

"First of all, we need the snowboards. I left them strapped to the top of the car, and Sawyer's is halfway down the road. We're strapping this"—he motioned to the basket—"to one of them. We can't carry all this shit by hand. Second, we need fuel for the torches, and there's no gas in the garage. I checked."

"Ryan…" Jane hesitated. She was scared, not wanting him to go. Crouching next to her and a silent Oona, Ryan offered a faint smile.

"I'm going to need one of those fancy torches," he told her.

"Can we at least *try* the car?" she asked. "Please?"

Ryan frowned, squeezing the bridge of his nose before exhaling a sigh. "You know that isn't going to work. The snow is even deeper than it was yesterday."

"There has to be a way," she insisted. "Walking out there…" She shook her head, not wanting to think about it. It had been her idea in the first place, but now that they were actually going to go through with it, she was sure this plan was crazy. Even with the fire and the blood and the spears, those things were ruthless. "And what about Oona? She can't possibly make it through the snow on her own."

"We're going to make her a sled."

"And you think she'll actually stay on it? Ryan, I—"

He caught her hands in his, leveling his gaze on her. "Hey," he told her. "Trust me, okay? Ten minutes tops. They won't bother me if I have fire."

Jane's stomach churned with nerves, but she nodded anyway. There was no way around it. They were all eventually going to end up outside in the cold with those things stalking them in the shadows. It was either that or stay here forever, where they would eventually grow so weak with hunger those creatures would simply walk in and take them without a fight. She swallowed against the lump in her throat, hoping that maybe, by some miracle, they'd be saved. Maybe a ranger would show up, making sure people were okay after all that snow, or a lineman would appear, since the electricity was out; perhaps the new owners would arrive, ready to indulge in their brand-new home; or maybe, as if being drawn down from the sky by the hand of God himself, their father would come, responding to a bad feeling he couldn't shake, a cosmic connection with his kids, knowing that something was wrong.

Ryan stood up, grabbed a torch, and turned to step out of the room.

"Wait," Sawyer said, dropping what he was doing. The two locked eyes, Ryan looking defiant. Ryan hadn't said a word about it, but Jane knew he had been hurt by Sawyer's outburst, suggesting that Lauren hadn't been important, that she had been some weekend thrill, when he had finally made a connection with someone. Whether Sawyer had meant what he had said, or whether he had been rambling his way through a breakdown, it was undeniable that Ryan was struggling to forgive and forget.

"I'll go," he said. "You stay here with Jane."

Ryan furrowed his eyebrows at the offer. Jane's heart rattled in her chest. She desperately wanted Ryan to stay, but she knew it wasn't his nature. Once Ryan had a plan of action mapped out inside his head, he was the one who had to execute it. It had been that way their entire lives, one of their father's lessons that had been ingrained in him despite Ryan's animosity toward him—*if you want something done right, you have to do it yourself.* That advice had gotten Ryan further than anyone had ever expected; the business, the traveling, following his passion.

Ryan shook his head in refusal.

"Then I'll come with you," Sawyer told him. "What are you going to do, hold a flaming torch while siphoning gas?"

Sawyer had a point, and it was apparent that he was confident in his reasoning by the way he sprang into action. He left Ryan standing there as he moved through the kitchen, heading to the hallway where most of their things were piled up. Suddenly, Jane realized something she hadn't thought of until then. A sweeping numbness slithered over her insides.

"Hey, Ry?" she said softly. "He can't go with you." The backs of her eyes went hot. She felt the flare of tears burn the delicate tissue of her sinus cavity.

Ryan looked away from the kitchen, frowning when he saw the look on her face.

"Sawyer's clothes," she told him. "They're in the Jeep." Sawyer wouldn't last ten minutes in jeans and a T-shirt before the painful itch of frostbite would start in on his toes. Jane and Ryan had their gear, but Sawyer's things were halfway down the road.

Ryan pressed his hand to his forehead, shoved his fingers through his hair. "Fuck," he murmured before stepping away, about to give Sawyer the bad news.

Ryan was biting back a laugh while Jane hid her mouth behind a hand, but her eyes gave her away as she watched Sawyer pull on her boarding pants. She was just as amused as her brother. Her pink-trimmed pants weren't really Sawyer's style.

"Maybe I should have taken my chances," Sawyer mused, pulling the zipper up on a jacket that was nearly too small to close in the front. There was no way around it: he looked ridiculous, like Alice in Wonderland after she'd eaten the side of the mushroom that made her grow larger, except the clothes hadn't grown with him.

"You look good," Jane said. "Stylish."

Ryan nudged Sawyer's shoulder. "Maybe rather than attacking us, those things will just die laughing."

Sawyer rolled his eyes. The jacket was biting into his armpits and the pants were riding up his crotch. And her boots were an impossibility unless he broke all his toes. He wasn't sure whether to view the black galoshes Ryan had located in the garage as a blessing or a curse.

"You think this is really going to work?" Sawyer asked, pulling two pairs of thick socks over his original pair. He could hardly shove his feet into the galoshes with all that padding, but it was either that or lose his toes.

"It should," Ryan shrugged. "At least for the time being. I sure as hell wouldn't want to walk five miles like that."

Pulling his woven beanie over his ears—the one that matched April's scarf—Sawyer mumbled and let his hands fall to his sides.

"This too," Jane said, offering him the jacket he'd stormed back inside the cabin in. It was the only piece of clothing, other than what he was wearing, that had made it back up to the house after his blowup with April. Sawyer stuffed his arms into his coat, zipped it up to his chin, and exhaled a humiliated sigh.

"Okay," he said. "I'm ready."

"You sure are," Ryan told him.

Jane grinned as Sawyer stepped past her, waddling like a duck, unable to bend his knees because the pants were too tight.

"Let's get this over with," he said, stopping a few feet from the kitchen door. Ryan pulled his backpack on, the ax handle jutting out of the top of the pack like a flagless pole. He looped the plastic tubing he had pulled off the back of the washing machine around his shoulder. They could only hope it would work for siphoning gas out of the Nissan.

Sawyer gripped one of the sharpened pool cues in a gloved hand as Jane detoured into the living room, then stepped back into the kitchen with two torches in tow, one lit, the other not. The strips of drapery she'd wrapped around the tops made them look like giant Q-tips, but they wouldn't last long. They had no fuel to soak the fabric in, which meant it would burn fast. Without fire, they would have no protection against what was out there.

"Don't light this one until you put some gas on it," she warned, handing Ryan the unlit torch while the lit one smoldered above Sawyer's head, filling the kitchen with smoke. Ryan patted the front pocket of his jacket, and the outline of the revolver should have made Sawyer feel better, but it did little to soothe his nerves. All it would take was one slipup, one second of letting their guard down. And then there was the question of whether those things really were afraid of fire. Sure, the one that had wandered into the house appeared to have been, but what if they had fears as unique as humans did? What if the fear of fire wasn't universal? Sawyer squeezed his eyes shut, trying to put all of the what-ifs out of his mind. Ryan stepped around him to get to the door.

"Wait," Sawyer said. "Wait, wait, wait. What about the blood?" The pot of blood was still in the sink, at the ready. But Ryan shook his head.

"We need to save it."

"Save it for what? A better time? Are you kidding?"

"Five miles is a long way. We're taking it with us."

Again, Sawyer wanted to protest. There was no better time than the present. They were potentially walking into the snapping jaws of death. But before he could argue, the kitchen door swung open and the oppressive chill of the air hit Sawyer head-on, biting at his face.

The snow crunched beneath their feet and Sawyer's gaze darted to the torch blazing above him; he was scared that as soon as they were out in the open, it would blow out in the wind. But it stayed lit as they both maneuvered around the disembodied carcass and strewn innards on the deck. Jane shut the door behind them, sliding the dead bolt into place. She stared out at them, her palms pressed to the glass, the helpless look on her face rousing a wave of foreboding in the pit of Sawyer's stomach. He took a moment to stare back at her, considering the fact that this might be the last time he'd see her, hating that if it was, he couldn't see her smile instead.

Eventually turning away, he followed Ryan around the side of the cabin, his boots feeling impossibly tight. They descended the stairs and immediately sank up to their knees in powder. Despite all the layers of clothing, the cold still managed to make Sawyer's bones ache.

They waddled around the Nissan, which was buried past its fenders. Sawyer searched the tree line behind them, his breaths coming in gasps now, steam puffing out of his chest like a locomotive. Ryan pulled open the hatch and grabbed a red gasoline container from the back before moving around to the driver's side, fumbling with the little door that allowed access to the fuel cap.

Sawyer saw movement. His heart hitched in his throat.

"I see them," he said. "Oh fuck, man, they're here."

Ryan's face registered alarm but he kept focused, snaking the tube he'd torn away from the washer into the tank as fast as he could. He put the opposite end in his mouth while Sawyer's heart rattled inside his chest. A second later he was spitting onto the ground, exhaling a moan of disgust while the liquid hit the bottom of the gas can.

"Sawyer." Ryan motioned to the torch in Sawyer's hand. "Give me that. Get the boards."

Sawyer gave up possession of the one thing that made him feel safe—who knew if a bullet would do a damn thing to those monsters, and for all they knew the pool cues would be useless as well. He pulled himself onto the Xterra's running board, then unsnapped the clamps that held three boards on top of the car. He tossed them off the roof end first, and they stabbed into the frozen terrain like toothpicks, pointing up toward the sky.

Ryan handed the torch back before shoving the unlit one between his legs, carefully pouring gasoline onto the rags twisted around the tip. Lifting it up, he touched it to Sawyer's burning end. It burst into flames, the fire momentarily warming them.

"Put that out," Ryan told him, motioning to the torch Jane had lit. "Stick it in the snow."

Sawyer plunged the burning end into the powder, only to have Ryan pull it out a moment later, pouring gas onto the charred fabric, then relighting it with his own. He pulled the hose out of the gas tank, secured the cap over the plastic canister, and wrapped the leash that was attached to Jane's board around his wrist. They weren't even half done, and those things were getting curious. They were hovering just behind the trees, watching, waiting to lunge.

Ryan felt like he was having a heart attack. His pulse rate was through the roof, whooshing in his ears like a drum. They had to get down to the Jeep for Sawyer's clothes and back up to the cabin before the fire went out, and these demon fucks weren't about to give them a running start if they ended up on the bad side of luck.

"Maybe she's in the Jeep," Sawyer said after a moment of silence. Ryan said nothing as they moved down the slope. He didn't dare look down as they crossed the exact place Lauren had died, didn't dare mention that she'd been sprinting down the hill after she saw April's scarf rolling across the driveway. Ryan tasted blood at the back of his tongue. His chest heaved. He was sure April was dead. There was no possible way she could have survived this long. But he couldn't bring himself to solidify Sawyer's loss. To shatter Sawyer's already dwindling hope. He'd shut down, and then Ryan and Jane would lose him too.

Reaching Sawyer's car, they piled two backpacks and a duffel bag onto the top of Jane's board, winding the straps and handles around the boot bindings to keep them in place. Sawyer grabbed his snowboard off the roof rack and secured the leash to his wrist.

"Okay, let's go," Ryan said. There was nothing else they could salvage that was of use to them.

"Wait." Sawyer leaned into his car and grabbed at a small voodoo doll that hung from his rearview mirror. Its lasso snapped with a firm tug. Ryan didn't ask, but he assumed it was a memento, a token of lost love.

But Sawyer wasn't given the opportunity to succumb to his emotions. A distinct, guttural rumble sounded from behind the nearby trees. It was followed by a bizarre cry, a whooping bark that was unmistakably some sort of signal. They stared at each other for a moment, frozen in place, before they pivoted and began to run as fast as the snow would allow.

That was when they saw it: one of those things had emerged from the trees, and it was blocking their way back to the cabin, watching them with that sick curiosity. Ryan's entire body felt like one giant, throbbing heart. This may have been the exact creature that tore Lauren apart, back for more. But he couldn't allow himself to think about that now, couldn't allow himself to simply stand there and stare.

"Keep walking," he said into the cold. "Don't be afraid. We'll burn this fucker down if he doesn't move."

The creature watched them for a long while, but its posture changed when Ryan and Sawyer continued toward it, refusing to back down. Ryan watched it hesitate, taking a few steps backward as it growled deep within its throat, those beady black eyes flashing with uncertainty. Ryan swung the torch in front of himself, jutting the flame outward to breach the distance between man and beast. The demon reeled back, then opened its giant mouth in a hiss, saliva sliding down its protruding teeth.

"Get the fuck back," Ryan warned, waving the torch at it while the rest of the creature's family watched from behind the trees. He was waiting for them all to spring into action at any moment, to fall on him all at once, leaving him without a shred of a chance. But they didn't move from the shadows. They were cowards, seeing whether their prey was aggressive, whether it would attack in return. They were scared of people—that was why the one Lauren had screamed at had bounded away—but their hunger was forcing them to face their fears. They were all in the same situation, man and monster, left with no other choice.

Ryan's eyes narrowed as he pushed forward, more determined than ever, his legs burning with effort. And then he lunged forward, jabbing the torch as far ahead of him as he could. He felt it connect, and the moment it did the thing bolted backward with a screech.

"Jesus!" Sawyer yelled from behind. "Are you *trying* to piss them off?"

But they didn't all lunge out into the open. Ryan could see them slither backward as their wounded comrade fumbled up the hill before leaping into the trees.

"Did you see that?" Ryan asked, looking back at Sawyer with a victorious grin. "I burned a hole right into that asshole's chest!" But Ryan's smile faded as soon as his eyes found Sawyer's torch. It had gone out, and his victory fell flat when he spotted one of those creatures lurking just a few yards shy of his friend. In their effort to scale the drive, Sawyer had fallen behind. It wasn't far—just a dozen feet or so—but it was enough, and before Ryan could react he watched a gray-skinned demon leap out into the open behind his friend, lift an overly long arm over its head, and draw its wide, clawed hand through the air.

Ryan couldn't breathe.

He couldn't scream.

He couldn't move.

Sawyer stared at his best friend, wide-eyed, before sinking to his knees, collapsing into the snow that was now up to his waist. The torch he held disappeared beneath the blanket of white as bright red bloomed behind him.

The world went silent.

The creature lunged forward, challenging Ryan to fight, but all fight and logic had left him. He could do nothing but stumble backward, inadvertently pulling Jane's board along with him. Had it not been attached to his wrist, it would have been long gone, skittering down the slope of the hill, taking all hope of escape with it.

Sawyer's mouth opened and closed as he gasped for air. Other than the crimson stain behind his friend, Ryan couldn't see an injury—but he could only imagine what was going on beneath the padding of Jane's jacket, beneath Sawyer's Sisters of Mercy T. The color drained from Sawyer's face as his blood spilled onto the frozen ground behind him.

The creature continued to advance while Ryan tore the glove off his hand and pulled out his father's gun—one hand holding the torch ahead of him, the other pointing the pistol at the monster that continued to approach. The creature hesitated, but the scent of warm blood was too much for it to resist.

Ryan pulled the trigger, nearly dropping it when it snapped his wrist back on the recoil.

The monster froze in place at the blast, startled by the noise. But Ryan had missed. His hand was shaking so badly he could hardly aim at all.

The creature crouched down, its sinewy muscles coiling beneath a thin sheath of skin.

Ryan shot again, grazing its shoulder.

The thing screamed, enraged. It bounded forward, its jaws wide open.

Ryan yelled into the cold and pulled the trigger for the third time.

The creature's midair leap was cut short. It fell to the ground like a stone, clawing at the side of its face, the hollow point having torn half of it away. The familiar stink of rotten eggs wafted up into the wind. It reeled away, wounded, trying to run across the road and into the trees. But it stumbled, sinking into the snow, and eventually stopped moving entirely.

Ryan veered around to stare at his best friend. Sawyer's face was ashen. He trembled in the cold. Ryan bolted for him, sinking to his knees in front of his friend.

"Sawyer," he said, breathless. "You're going to be okay, man. Come on." Sliding an arm beneath him, his now gloveless right hand felt the warmth of blood pouring from Sawyer's back. He tried to pull Sawyer to his feet without letting go of his torch, but Sawyer was resisting the help.

"You're a lousy shot," Sawyer whispered, his face twisted in pain. "You used all the bullets."

Ryan dug through the snow, anger giving way to panic. He picked up Sawyer's torch, relighting it with his own. "Here," he said, grabbing Sawyer's arm, forcing the torch into his hand.

Ryan watched him close his eyes, his breaths shallow with anguish. His freshly lit torch fell to the ground for a second time, the faint scent of smoke and gasoline rising from its resting place. He snatched up the torch again, shoving it back into Sawyer's hand.

"Fucking *hold* that. We're going to walk."

Trying to heft him up again, he nearly had Sawyer on his feet when his own foot slipped on the slick surface of the ground. Both of them sank back into the cold, Sawyer's torch extinguishing yet again.

There were eyes on them. Ryan could feel them watching. A sickening, communal purr resonated from the pines—a buzz that almost sounded like pleasure, like those goddamn things were getting a kick out of watching them struggle and panic.

"Goddamnit, *why are you doing this*?!" Ryan yelled, his right hand burning now, his fingertips numb, exposed to the air. "Get up!"

Sawyer managed a ghost of a smile.

"What are you smiling at?" Ryan demanded. "Get up! We have to get ready to go, okay? Sawyer? We have to get ready to go. We're going to make it." He swiped at his cheeks, wiping away the cold sting of tears. The arm looped across his shoulders went limp. Ryan's eyes went wide as Sawyer slid away, and he was left to stare at his friend, the sleeve of his jacket coated in Sawyer's blood, Ryan's breath hitching in his throat. He wanted to blame it on his panic, wanted to not understand what he was seeing, wanted to pretend that the scene unfolding before him looked a lot worse than it was because he couldn't think straight, couldn't comprehend. But the look on Sawyer's face confirmed what was occurring; Sawyer was dying, and he was doing it right in front of Ryan's eyes.

"Sawyer?" He watched his friend raise his eyes to him, listening.

Curiosity got the best of another one of those things. It cautiously slunk out of the trees on all fours, its posture apelike as it made a strangely slow approach. Ryan spun around, the flame of his torch cutting through the air.

"Get away!" he screamed.

The creature pitched backward at the yell, its hands leaving the snow as it put its weight on its hind legs.

Ryan was suddenly overwhelmed, not with fear but with utter contempt. He grabbed the sharpened pool cue that Sawyer had dropped in the snow, baring his teeth at the monstrosity that was watching him a little too intently, as though it were learning. And while it teetered there, Ryan lunged, burying the end of the cue deep between its ribs.

The thing stumbled backward as if in surprise. Its arms flailed around the stick jutting out of its chest, trying to grab at it with its large, cumbersome claws. Ryan took its distraction as an opportunity. He took another step forward, jabbing his torch into the thing's face, purposefully aiming for one of its eyes. The monster emitted an ear-piercing scream as it stumbled backward, falling into the snow. It blindly groped at the ground, trying to regain its bearings with only one eye, but its depth perception was off. Shuffling through a few uneasy steps, it pitched forward against the slope of the road, and the pool cue that was still stuck between its ribs burst through its back, releasing a geyser of blood that arced across the sky.

Ryan turned back to Sawyer, grabbing the board attached to Sawyer's wrist and pulling it forward. "Get on," he demanded, helping his friend to roll onto the board. As soon as Sawyer was lying on top of it—the bindings jabbing into his chest and hips—Ryan began to pull as hard as he could.

And as he dragged his bleeding best friend up the driveway while those creatures were distracted by the death of one of their own, he heard Sawyer speak above the deafening thud of his own pulse.

"You're a badass," Sawyer wheezed. "Holy shit, dude. Holy shit."

CHAPTER THIRTEEN

Jane had jumped at the sound of the gunshot, her eyes wide as she ran from window to window, trying to see through the trees that blocked her view. When two more reports echoed through the hills, she bounded up the stairs, a muted scream stuck in her throat. She took a hard right into the master bedroom, dashing to the picture window that offered a bird's-eye view. Pressing her palms to the glass, she spotted movement behind the trees, but she couldn't see the road. Even from this vantage point, there was no way to get a clear view.

She bolted into the hall with Oona at her heels, stopping at the bay window in its center, trying to get a look, but it was no use. Her hands hit the door at the end of the hall as she entered the room Sawyer and April had occupied. Dashing to the window there, she fumbled with the string of the blinds. She gave it a hard pull, and they went up at a skewed angle. Ryan came into view, one snowboard piled full of supplies behind him, a torch throwing black smoke above his head. She felt a stab of panic when she saw that he was alone, only to see Sawyer being pulled along behind him a second later. But the relief she expected failed to come. Watching her brother stumble, frantic as he moved up the driveway directly beneath her, blood trailed behind a wounded Sawyer. Clinging to a second board, he was too still for comfort.

He looked dead.

A sob began to bubble upward until it was cut off by utter panic. She was supposed to stay in the kitchen. The door Ryan was heading for was locked.

She sprinted toward the stairs as fast as she could, leaped down them two at a time. She met Ryan around the side of the house, and before she could freak out about the blood, he was shoving the leash of the supply board into her hand.

"Take this," he commanded, leaning down to help Sawyer up. But Jane couldn't move. She stood motionless, her eyes wide at how pale Sawyer's face was, how obviously the pain washed across his face when Ryan tried to move him. "*Jane.*" Ryan snapped, thrusting the leash at her impatiently.

Jane grabbed the gas can in one hand, shoving it onto one of the steps before hefting the board up and sliding it onto the porch. She nearly lost her footing as she bolted for the open kitchen door, thrusting the board into the house, almost dropping the gas can just inside the door before veering around and dashing back to her brother. She looped an arm beneath Sawyer's shoulder and helped Ryan pull him up the stairs, slamming the door shut as soon as they were inside.

Snow sprayed off Sawyer's clothes and onto the floor and bloodied blue tarp. He was terrifyingly pale.

"Oh my god," Jane exclaimed. "What happened?"

"His back," Ryan told her, rolling Sawyer onto a clean stretch of floor. Sawyer gave a muffled cry when he was moved, and Jane gasped at the three long gashes in his coat. They needed to get Sawyer's coat and the one beneath it off him as fast as possible. "Get some towels," Ryan said, but Jane was on autopilot.

She bolted across the kitchen to the living room, grabbing the kitchen shears out of a pile of knives before skidding back in place. She grabbed the bottom of Sawyer's coat, shoving the scissors into place. Ryan grabbed her wrist.

"What the hell are you doing?"

"We need to get these off." She began to cut, but he shoved her hand away, grabbing the shears and sliding them across the floor.

"How do you expect to get out of here?" Ryan demanded. "He's wearing your coat."

Jane blanched at the realization, at the huge mistake she had almost made.

"Get some towels," he told her again. "Hurry up."

She sprinted down the hall and careened into the guest bathroom. Snatching all the towels she could find—all of them embroidered with an elegant *A*, she dashed back into the kitchen.

Sawyer was sitting up as Ryan peeled the coats from his back. He was teetering at the edge of unconsciousness. Jane dropped to her knees in front of him, caught his face in her hands.

"Tom," she said. "Hey, come on." She patted his cheeks, trying to wake him up.

"Your brother," Sawyer said weakly.

"Don't talk," she insisted. "It's going to be okay." But the look on Ryan's face wasn't at all reassuring. She watched his expression go ashen when the second coat hit the floor, and she knew it was bad—worse than Ryan had expected.

"He, like"—Sawyer wheezed—"he *Kill Bill*ed the shit out of..."

She couldn't help it. Jane slid around to where Ryan was, only to release an involuntary cry at what faced her. Sawyer's back was sliced into thirds, his ribs peeking through layers of skin, fat, and flesh.

Ryan looked at her, trying to keep himself in check, but there was panic in his eyes. Jane didn't know what to do either, but they had to stop the bleeding. "Lay him down. Put pressure on that. We need sheets," she said, then scrambled to her feet.

Running up the stairs, she tore the sheets off the beds in the master bedroom. When she returned to the kitchen a few minutes later, Ryan had stripped Sawyer down to his pants. Sawyer lay on his stomach in the kitchen, and her heart lurched when she realized his eyes were closed. He was dead. He had to be—but she saw his shoulders lift just enough to assure her that he was still breathing.

Ryan shook his head at her. "That isn't going to work," he said, nodding to the bedding piled in her arms. "We need to stop the bleeding *now.*"

She said nothing as he slowly stood, leaving Sawyer where he lay. And she felt her legs go weak when Ryan stepped into the living room and thrust the small iron shovel into the flames of the fire.

With the smell of burning flesh filling his nostrils, Sawyer found enough breath to scream.

Ryan tore through the bags he'd brought back from Sawyer's Jeep, seeing what could be used and what could be left behind. In April's bag he found a can of aerosol hair spray. In Sawyer's he found a cheap gas station lighter tucked into a half-smoked pack of cigs. He paused, listening to Jane comfort Sawyer in the kitchen, before exhaling a breath. He would never admit it, but he was terrified. If they had a hope of getting out of the cabin alive, Sawyer's injury had just cut those chances down. But if there was ever a time to leave, it was now. If they didn't, Sawyer was dead, and Sawyer couldn't be dead. Ryan wouldn't allow it.

Pulling on every last stitch of gear he had, he stepped into the kitchen. He looked like an abominable snowman, wearing twenty pounds of clothing, his torch burning next to him, freshly lit by the fire in the living room. Jane opened her mouth to speak from where she sat on the floor, her arms around Sawyer, Sawyer fading in and out of consciousness, a bedsheet securing the Saran wrap they had wrapped around his torso; but she didn't get a chance to speak. Ryan stepped through the kitchen to the door, unlocked it without a word of warning, and ducked into the snow. Moving back into view with Jane's board sliding behind him, he stuck the burning end of the torch into the snow just beyond the door, extinguishing it, and stepped inside.

She watched him in silence as he crouched in the hallway, removing the board bindings with a multitool he had stashed in his backpack. Then he lashed both boards together with a menagerie of power cords the five of them had brought with them; cords for computers and iPods, cell phones and cameras. Perhaps their love of the digital age would save them in the end.

"You can start securing that basket to your board," he told her, tossing her a cable. "Just make sure it's tight. We can't lose it."

Jane caught the wicker basket by its handle and jabbed the end of the cord between the wicker weaving.

"What are we going to do?" she asked meekly. Her tone gave her away. She knew their chances were slim to none now, but Ryan wasn't about to acknowledge her suspicion.

"What we were always going to do. We're leaving in ten minutes."

Jane felt her face flush as she worked, clumsily tangling the cord around the front binding before triple knotting the end, trying not to cry.

"He could die," Ryan said under his breath, hoping that that sobering reminder would snap her out of her fear. This was no longer about should they or shouldn't they. This was now all down to a simple question of when, and when had to be now.

Ryan didn't wait for her reaction. He climbed the stairs to the center landing and plucked a picture off the wall. Their mother had bought it on a whim in an antique shop in Durango when they were kids—an artist's rendition of the teddy bears' picnic, except the bears weren't stuffed animals—they were real bears, some of them looking bizarrely vicious as they danced, hand in hand, around a campfire with their kin. There was something malign about that picture, like a serial killer painting clowns or twisting balloon animals at a kid's birthday party. Bringing the painting down into the hall, Ryan lashed it on top of both boards.

He stood, examining their handiwork, and nodded in satisfaction.

"Let's gather up the stuff," he said, motioning for her to follow him into the living room. There, they picked up the two remaining table leg torches that had yet to be lit, the collection of knives, and the pool cues Sawyer had sharpened to a point. The ax was in Ryan's backpack, ready to go.

"We're going to need to walk Sawyer down into the garage," he explained. "We'll put him on this." He motioned to the make-shift gurney he'd fashioned out of two boards and their mother's weird art. He had no idea whether it would work, if the snow would even hold Sawyer's weight or if they'd end up getting stuck, but it didn't matter anymore.

"What about Oona?" Jane asked.

"She'll have to ride with him."

Jane looked startled by his answer. It was an insane plan.

"We're out of options," he told her. "I'll get all this stuff down there. You dress him in everything we've got. Grab a spare blanket to wrap him in and then dress yourself."

She nodded, trying to look brave, but her bottom lip quaked with emotion.

"Hey." He caught her by the shoulders, giving her a steady look. "I need you, okay? I can't do this alone."

She nodded again, then turned to do what he'd asked of her, and Ryan was left staring at the teddy bears' picnic, wondering whether the artist had been trying to say something through his sinister art, like the fact that there was something in the woods, something that should have been a fantasy but was dangerously real.

Jane swallowed against the lump in her throat. She had forgotten all about the pot of blood until Ryan grabbed it from the sink and walked it out into the garage.

"Are you sure this is absolutely necessary?" she asked, her voice echoing against the cold cinderblock walls, but it had been her idea in the first place—an idea that had worked.

"It's absolutely necessary," he told her, blocking Oona from scrambling back up the stairs. Sawyer sat against the wall, bundled up from head to toe, wrapped in the thick quilt Jane had found in the armoire upstairs. He looked terrible, but at least he was awake.

She squeezed her eyes shut as tightly as she could, steadying her nerves. "Fucking fuck," she whispered, anticipating what was to come.

Peering into the pot at her feet, she reeled back at the smell. Her throat started to tighten—the sensation of inevitable sickness.

Ryan braced himself as he held on to Oona's collar. "Just do it."

She grabbed the handles of the pot, hefted it up to her waist, and tipped it over Oona's clean black-and-white fur. As soon as the thick liquid hit her back, Oona let out a loud whine and curved her back downward, trying to get away from the stuff that was slithering down her coat. Ryan gagged, but he held his hand steadfast beneath the stream of blood, ladling it onto her head, rubbing it into her snout. Oona sneezed once, twice, then wriggled out of Ryan's grip. A second later she was shaking out, spraying the garage with a putrid red mist.

Jane turned away, sure she was about to puke. The stench was intense, permeating her nostrils, crawling to the back of her throat. She whimpered when Ryan pulled her back by the wrist. She sank to her knees and covered her face, her eyes watering from the stink. When she felt the liquid hit her shoulders, her stomach clenched. She tried to sit there as long as she could, but it only allotted Ryan a few seconds before she was up on her feet, vomiting onto the concrete floor.

Ryan braced himself when it was his turn. Had they been in any other situation she would have laughed at the intensity in his face. But she was too sick and too disgusted to even smile at his expression. She backed away from him when he shot up to his feet, and Ryan rubbed the foul-smelling stuff into his jacket and pants despite his obvious revulsion. They looked like a pair of serial killers fresh from a sloppy kill, and they smelled as good as they looked. Oona was having a sneezing fit, rubbing her face against the floor, desperately trying to get the stuff off her skin.

Ryan grabbed the half-empty pot of blood with bright red hands and walked it over to Sawyer. "Your turn, man," he said.

"Oh," Sawyer said weakly. "Fantastic."

"Just pretend you're Dracula." Ryan tried for humor, but Sawyer only released a weak breath and covered his face with the quilt that was draped around his shoulders. He hardly made a peep when Ryan rubbed gore into his hair.

With the four of them drenched, he put the pot in their basket of gear. It was for later. They would remain covered in this stuff until they hit the highway, and then—*Oh god*, she thought, *imagine seeing three bloody hitchhikers walking down the road. Nobody will stop.* Nobody in their right mind would ever slow down.

Jane whimpered softly as she stood there, wet and sticky, not wanting to move, but there was no time for disgust.

"Hold her," Ryan said, motioning for Jane to grab Oona. Picking up the gas can from the basket, he doused the ends of three torches in gasoline. "You have to keep an eye on this. You can't let it go out. I burned one of them when Sawyer and I were out there and they freaked. They know it can hurt them."

"What if it starts snowing again?" she asked. It was a distinct possibility. The clouds were still thick. "Or if the wind picks up and blows the fire out?"

Ryan thrust the torch into her gloved hand, giving her a look. She knew it was stupid to question it, knew it was a waste of time to think of all the things that could go wrong, because a million things could. If they operated on what-ifs, they'd never go through with it; they had to save Sawyer.

"They're afraid of it," he told her again. "If you see one come close, hold the fire out in front of you."

"Okay," she said, her voice fading to nothing.

Ryan looped an arm around Sawyer and helped him across the garage, and for a moment she was frozen in place, refusing to believe their situation was so dire, that the pain that flashed across Sawyer's face was real. But she wasn't given time to dwell on those emotions. Ryan looked over at her and she immediately fell into step, limping across the concrete floor to help get Sawyer situated on his makeshift gurney. She didn't want to think about what they'd do if the wires they had used to tie the thing together came apart, or if Sawyer lost consciousness again and they couldn't manage to keep him on that crude sled, or if Oona leaped off Sawyer's lap and was buried chest-deep in the snow.

Wrapped in the quilt their mother had sewn when they were kids, Sawyer tried to give them both a courageous smile through his pain before coiling his arms around Oona, holding her in place.

Ryan paused as if thinking the whole thing over, then shook his head and tied the leash of the supply board around one of his belt loops. "You're going to lead. We'll keep Sawyer and Oona between us."

"But—" She didn't *want* to lead, but bringing up the rear seemed like an even more precarious position.

"Janey." Ryan looked at her steadily. "This is how it's got to be. Let's go."

Before she could say another word, Ryan rolled up the garage door and the cold swallowed them whole.

Jane's eyes watered against the wind. She pulled her scarf over her mouth and nose, hiding from the gale, breathing through her mouth so that her breath warmed the yarn closest to her lips. Reaching the driveway that would take them down the slope and away from that cabin forever, Sawyer and Oona sat on their makeshift sled like blood-soaked royalty. Ryan motioned for Jane to move ahead of him, and despite her trepidation she did, torch held out ahead of her.

They trekked past Sawyer's Jeep without incident. The trees were still, and no matter how hard she looked, Jane didn't spot any shifting shadows behind the pines. But she knew they were there, waiting for the perfect moment to strike. When Oona whined in Sawyer's arms, Jane's eyes went wide with panic. She shot a look behind her at Ryan, but Ryan didn't see anything either. He shook his head at her, his expression anxious but mercifully put together. All it would take was for Ryan to lose his cool for the entire expedition to fall apart. Jane knew that if that happened, her own resolve would crumble beneath the weight of her fear.

"Where?" she asked, shoving her scarf down to her chin. "I don't see anything. Where are they? Do you see them?" She waved the torch to and fro, spinning around, knowing that facing one direction for too long would render her vulnerable to an attack.

As though having heard Jane's question, one of them showed itself. It stood a few yards down the slope as if planning on boxing them in. The moment Jane spotted it every nerve in her body stood on end, crackling with terror. She veered around, staring wildly at her brother.

"Face forward!" he demanded. He grabbed the leash of the supply basket and jerked it up the slope toward himself, grabbing April's hair spray out of their arsenal. Oona bared her teeth and snarled, but Sawyer held her tight. His expression was unnerving, almost blank, as though his brain refused to register any more fear, as though it had shut down all his senses, overwhelmed by physical pain.

"I thought they were scared," Jane screeched. "You told me they were scared!"

"They *are* scared," he told her, trying to sound calm. He took a few steps down the slope toward the thing, and the creature crouched down, everything about its posture setting Jane's teeth on edge. What if it lunged? What if it got him? What did he expect her to do if she was left alone out here with Sawyer and Oona? She couldn't possibly pull them on her own.

Lowering his torch, Ryan pointed the spray can in the creature's direction and pressed down on the trigger. A blast of heat hit Jane's face as the snow lit up in a dazzling display of glittering ice crystals, fire shooting toward the monster that had decided to try its hand at derailing their escape. Ryan was too far away for the flame to reach the thing, but the explosion of fire had obtained the desired effect. The beast jumped back, startled, and ran away.

Jane found it almost disconcerting how easy it was to scare them. Was that all it took? A little fire and they were powerless? On one hand, she hoped to God that was all they needed to survive; on the other, it made her queasy to think that if it was that easy to make them scatter, all five of them could have been walking out of there instead of only three.

While Jane and Ryan slogged through the snow, Sawyer tried to stay alert. He felt strangely removed from the situation as he watched them struggle. Other than hanging on to Oona, there was nothing he could do. The pain that encompassed his back was indescribable—a kind of agony he'd never felt before. Jane had fed him a handful of Tylenol, but it hadn't done anything to alleviate a sensation that teetered between hellfire and numbness. Sawyer was almost positive that the numbness wasn't his back at all—it was him slithering in and out of responsiveness, balancing on the knife's edge of consciousness and catatonia. The nausea that roiled in the pit of his stomach was unbearable, but the cold that whipped across his face helped ease the discomfort.

At least until a haunting wail echoed off the trees around them.

It sounded almost human, like a valley of people moaning before death. Sawyer connected with something in that mournful chorus. At that very moment, it became undeniably clear—whatever these creatures were, they were in pain, more than likely racked with starvation, forced into a slow and bitter end. Somehow, on some primal level, he could relate to their plight. He swallowed against the lump in his throat, every breath harder than the last, his guilt over April subsiding enough to let a wave of calm drift over him. He had been so sure that he had lost her, but he'd been wrong.

He hadn't lost anything. They'd be together soon.

The creatures were mercifully keeping their distance—a blessing, since the group had to stop every few minutes to catch their breath, pausing every hour for an even longer break. Maybe those things had been spooked enough to search for alternative prey. Maybe it was the blood that had frozen to their faces like war paint, stained their clothes, and clumped and matted in their hair. Ryan didn't know exactly why they were being given this opportunity to make headway, but he also couldn't be bothered to care. Both he and Jane were exhausted. Sawyer didn't look good, hardly able to keep his eyes open for longer than a few minutes at a time. They were losing daylight with each pause, and all Ryan could hope for was that they'd hit the highway before nightfall. If they didn't, they'd have to make camp, and he wasn't convinced any of them would survive the night. Their stash of food was meager, their energy was low, and despite the lack of snowfall, the wind was relentless, biting at any exposed bit of skin. The chill would only grow more bitter with the onset of darkness. The windchill alone would be enough to end them.

But after hours of trudging forward at a snail's pace, there was no denying that they weren't going to make it in a single day. The five miles from the driveway to the highway suddenly seemed like five hundred. They were drained, and if they pushed themselves too hard, they wouldn't have the energy to defend themselves if they were attacked.

Ryan shot a look over his shoulder at the tree line a hundred yards away. They were there, lurking in the shadows, watching their kill move farther and farther away as they moaned and growled within their throats; what Ryan had expected to be welcome distance made his nerves buzz with trepidation. Perhaps he had been wrong. Maybe they weren't afraid. Perhaps they were simply waiting for the light of day to burn away before making their final move. He shoved his sleeve upward with his glove, exposing the watch that was wrapped around his wrist. It was a few minutes shy of four in the afternoon. The sun would be gone in an hour. If they were going to make camp, they had to start now.

"We should stop here," he announced. Jane's expression immediately shifted from pained to anxious.

"What? Why? I thought we were going to the highway."

"We are. But we're only about halfway."

Jane shook her head in disbelief. "That's impossible," she insisted. "We've been out here for hours."

"Believe it," Ryan told her. "We've gone two miles, three if we're lucky. Sunset is in an hour. If we keep going, we'll get a quarter of a mile farther. We need to set up camp or we'll freeze."

Jane's gaze flitted to Sawyer, her face twisting with dread. Ryan knew what she was thinking—they didn't have much time. Sawyer was weak, and without moving around like they were, he would be cold. If he didn't make it through the night, the blame would be on Ryan. But he had expected this. He knew the trek was going to be hard and, with Sawyer incapacitated, even longer than it would have been if the three of them were able-bodied. They could continue through the night, but there was no doubt in his mind they'd collapse only hours after nightfall—spent, freezing. Sawyer wouldn't survive it. But there was a possibility he'd survive the night tucked into a snow shelter away from the wind.

"I knew this would take longer than a day," he confessed, hoping that his admission would somehow soothe her nerves. He had kept it from her on purpose, knowing that if he had mentioned it earlier, she would have demanded to stay in the cabin rather than fight to survive.

Jane's expression flitted between fear and anger. But without saying anything, she silently turned away from him, unstrapped the leash supply board she had taken over from her belt loop, and grabbed the lead to Sawyer's gurney from Ryan's hand, beginning her indignant march away from the group. She lumbered along for a few feet, the black smoke of her torch spiraling into the gray clouds overhead, releasing a frustrated cry of exertion as she tried to pull Sawyer and Oona along. But they hardly budged. Oona whined from Sawyer's lap as she watched Jane struggle back in the direction from which they had come.

"Jane." Ryan sighed. "Come on, stop it."

"I'm going back!" She continued to push through the snow, stumbling once before regaining her footing, Sawyer's sled sliding ever so slowly behind her.

"Why?" he asked. "We're halfway there. Go forward if you're going to go anywhere."

Jane stopped where she was, as though considering it. Then she whipped around and began to trek forward, deciding that the highway was a better option. But by the time she reached her brother again, she was too winded to go any farther.

"Will you please calm down?" he asked her. "We're going to make a shelter, okay?" Ryan leaned down and swiped the supply board's leash up in his hand, holding it out for Jane to reattach. Then he looked around, evaluating their position, took a few steps away from Sawyer and Oona, dropped to his knees, and started to dig.

Jane turned her face up to the darkening sky, shook her head after a moment, and whispered, "Goddamnit," before dropping to her knees next to him, burying her gloves in the snow.

CHAPTER FOURTEEN

Thirty minutes before sundown, they completed digging and packing their shelter in the snow. With the tarp secured over it, Ryan could only hope it would be enough to shelter them from the cold. He'd watched enough survival shows to know how to navigate down a snowy mountain, and he knew the best way to live through an avalanche, but he'd be damned if he could recall an episode that taught him how to fend off man-eating hellions in knee-deep powder.

Those things continued to prowl just beyond the tree line, their shadows seemingly more active as the daylight bled dark. It made him nervous, because in this worst-case scenario, there couldn't be anything more disastrous than those creatures sneaking up on them after dark. The possibility of an ambush made his hair follicles tingle.

Jane sat on top of a tightly packed lump of snow she had created for herself—a lookout, of sorts. Sawyer and Oona were next to her, Sawyer not having spoken in the past few hours. Jane tried to get Sawyer to drink some Diet Coke from their inadequate stash of food. She fumbled with a cellophane pack of stale saltines, trying to tear them open with her teeth without pulling off her gloves. Eventually getting the packaging open, she fed Sawyer a cracker while he remained bundled and motionless under the quilt.

With the sky a pale purple, Ryan unloaded a good amount of gear from the wicker basket atop Jane's board, dumping spare pool cues and torches into their shelter before turning his attention to his sister and best friend. It was time to move Sawyer into the den.

Ryan pulled Sawyer as close as possible to the snow shelter before both he and Jane hefted him up, their shoulders beneath his arms. Sawyer tried to brave the movement without a sound, but he couldn't help crying out when they lowered him into the hole in the hard-packed snow. Oona and Jane followed him inside a moment later.

"Stay here with him," Ryan told her, tying the leash of the supply board around his belt loop. If they were going to make it through the night, they needed fire.

"Where are you going?" As soon as she saw him preparing for another trek, Jane instinctively crawled out of the shelter and back into the snow. It crunched beneath her. The sun, however slight, had melted it enough so that it refroze into a brittle glittering crust. Ryan motioned toward the trees as he plucked up his torch.

"Wood," he said. "Stay in there." He nodded at their makeshift shelter. "The more people inside, the warmer it'll be."

"But what about you?" she asked. "You can't go out there alone. What if they come back?"

What if they had *learned*? The idea of it made his mouth taste acrid, his fear breeding a sharp, metallic taste. But he refused to let those kinds of thoughts dictate his movements. They were out of options, and showing weakness now would send Jane over the edge.

"I've fought them off before," Ryan said, emptying most of their supplies onto the snow. He'd need room for firewood and Jane would need weapons in case she and Sawyer were the ones attacked. But Jane wasn't satisfied with his answer. She shook her head, resolute.

"Oona will warm the place up. I'm coming with you."

"No, you aren't."

"Why not?" she demanded. "This is insane. It's like splitting up in the movies. Nobody comes back alive after splitting up; you *know* that."

"Jane." He gave her a steady look. "I'm just going to be over there." He pointed to the trees in the distance. He knew they were farther away than they looked, but he didn't mention it. "You can watch me if you want to, but I need you to stay with Sawyer, okay? We can't leave him alone. Try to get him to eat some more crackers. He needs to keep his strength up."

Jane gave in, nodding with a frown. "Fine," she told him. "Just be careful."

Ryan began to slog through the snow. The closer he got to the wall of pine, the more nervous he felt. The trees they had left in their wake were the closest to their camp, but those were the trees where Ryan had seen the shadows shift. There was another thicket to the north, close enough to walk to in five or ten minutes on a warm summer afternoon, but trying for them now would eat up the last dregs of daylight.

With only a few yards left between him and the pines, he couldn't help but think that maybe he was wrong. Maybe those things weren't waiting for nightfall after all, but for this exact moment; for Jane and Ryan to split up, for one of them to come close enough to the forest to be pulled into the branches. He swallowed against the thudding in his throat, forcing himself to continue forward with a torch held over his head, the ax handle sticking out of his backpack, the wicker basket skidding across the top of the snow behind him. Finally reaching a tree on the outermost rim of the woods, he slid his backpack from his shoulders and grabbed the hatchet. But there was no way he could chop at the tree one-handed. Daylight was dwindling. He had to be quick. Chewing on his bottom lip, he scanned the trunks and branches ahead of him, waiting for one of those creatures to launch itself at him before he could think to defend himself.

It was deathly silent.

He didn't hear any throaty growls or mournful moans.

Only the wail of the wind.

Slowly leaning down, he stabbed his torch into the snow a few feet away from where he stood, hoping like hell that he'd have enough time to retrieve it if he needed to.

The ax in both hands now, he took a swing at the low-hanging branch of a sickly looking tree. He didn't know whether live wood would burn, so he went for the conifer that looked the least healthy, hoping that the inside of its branches would be dry enough to catch a spark. The tree shuddered beneath the hit, and snow fell to the ground not just from that limb, but from the branches over-head as well. He swung again. After two more attempts, the bough released its grip on the trunk and fell to the ground. As he pulled it to the basket, it left a delicate brushstroke across the snow.

He went for a bigger branch next. There were smaller ones he could have worked on first, but he had to get back to Sawyer and Jane. Deep indigo was bleeding into the lavender sky. The shifting color of the clouds was making Ryan nervous. The sun was setting faster than he had anticipated. The second branch came down after five solid swings, then joined its brother on the board. Tackling the third branch—this one even larger than the second—he told himself this would be the last. As soon as he cut it down, he would turn tail and book it back to the shelter. The tree shuddered as he tried to lop the bough loose, shaking snow onto the ground from a good eight feet up. It began to sag beneath its own weight, the spot where the ax blade struck exposing virgin wood. His final swing brought a thud of snow-fall onto his head. He stumbled backward as ice flakes bit into the back of his neck, swiping at the collar of his jacket, trying to dust away as much of it as he could before it melted down his back. And then he grabbed the end of the large branch he'd just conquered, turned to pull it toward the supply board, only to stop short.

The snow hadn't just gotten the back of his neck.

It had gotten his torch as well.

Jane tried to feed Sawyer another cracker, but he shook his head faintly and ducked farther beneath his blanket. "I just want to sleep," he croaked dryly. Eventually, she let him rest, turning her back to him to peek her head out from beneath the tarp and watch her brother from a distance.

The white landscape had settled into a cold, pale blue—the only spots of brightness the torch that burned next to her, and the torch that burned three hundred feet away. She coiled her arms around herself and listened to the whap of metal against wood, each strike echoing around them like the gunshots she'd heard that very morning. She never understood why snow seemed to make the world go silent. It was haunting, the way all sound seemed to be erased from the world.

Jane imagined Lauren sitting next to her right then, assuring her that things were going to be all right, that they would be *more* than all right, because after they made it out of this they'd get millions for their story. They'd be on TV. They'd write a book. And then, of course, there would be a movie. Both she and Jane would attend the premiere wearing gowns worth more than Lauren's car while mingling with the likes of Brad Pitt and George Clooney—Lauren's two favorite actors. "George Clooney," she had once said. "Now there's a man whose money I wouldn't mind spending." Jane smiled to herself as Lauren planned her phantom future inside her head. Lauren always had a way of looking at the positive side of things, always had a way of reaching out and grabbing life by the horns. She had been full of life and passion; funny and gorgeous and smart, so much that she had caught Ryan's attention. His laughter had been a little freer around her, his smile a little more soulful.

Rocked by the memory of her best friend—a face she'd never see again—Jane pressed her gloved hand onto the scarf that was covering her mouth and nose, trying to stifle the sob that inevitably tore itself from her chest. *This can't get worse*, she thought. With Lauren and April gone and Sawyer injured, things couldn't possibly get more grim. She attempted to squelch her tears, reminding herself that Ryan needed her to keep it together. Wiping at her eyes, she looked up just as Ryan took his final swing.

And then the snow fell.

Ryan's torch went out.

She saw a shadow shift, and suddenly she couldn't swallow or breathe.

She clawed the scarf away from her face, opening her mouth to scream, scrambling out of the snow shelter before stumbling toward him. Despite their distance, she saw the very moment realization dawned on him. He caught sight of her and stared. She blinked when she realized that in her panic, she had left *her* source of fire behind with Sawyer. Her torch burned just beyond the bloodied blue tarp, stabbed into the snow.

"Go back!" he screamed, tossing the ax into the basket before snatching his torch up off the ground. He had left the gas can with Jane, but he had April's hair spray somewhere beneath those boughs. Tearing his right glove off with his teeth, he shoved his hand into his pocket, his fingers curling around Sawyer's old lighter. His eyes darted to the tree line as he jammed his arm elbow-deep into the sappy needles atop Jane's snowboard, feeling around the basket's bottom for the can he knew was there.

Jane screamed.

He whirled around, his head throbbing with the whoosh of his own pulse. He was sure he was about to see his worst nightmare come to fruition, that Jane's scream was attached to a scene that he'd never forget—whether he lived fifty years or fifty seconds—but when he spotted her in the distance, he blinked in bewilderment. *Thank god*, he thought, because she was safe in the clearing. Nothing was coming at her, nothing was about to cut her down. But she continued to scream anyway, her words indiscernible, her arms waving every which way. Ryan veered around to look ahead.

The beast towered over him, standing on its hind legs, its impossibly wide jaws pulled back in what looked like a nefarious smile. To Ryan's horror, he found himself staring at an oozing lesion just above those massive teeth, one of its eyes all but burned away.

Ryan jammed his arm into the basket again, desperately groping for the aerosol can. His gloveless hand tried to spark a flame from Sawyer's lighter as he continued his frantic search, but the demon had learned its lesson. Rather than giving Ryan time to arm himself, it crouched low in the snow and sprang forward within a blink. Ryan hit the ground, feeling like he'd just been punched in the chest. Behind him, Jane continued to scream. The creature emitted a gut-wrenching squeal, as if trying to speak, trying to tell him, "An eye for an eye." Ryan scrambled to his feet, but his right hand came up empty.

The lighter was gone, somewhere under the snow, knocked out of his grasp.

At that precise moment, Ryan was a boy again. He stood in those very hills, the snow having melted away. A young Jane and Sawyer laughed next to him, the three of them running through a prairie of dandelions and wild grass. The peaks of distant Colorado mountains stood out against a bright blue sky, still capped with snow despite the sun that warmed their skin. Jane took both of their hands between her own, swinging them back and forth as she skipped across the prairie, her laugh like the tinkle of tiny silver bells. She turned to look at him, her eyes full of childhood wonder, but her expression eroded right before his eyes—shifted from joy to utter horror as her smile twisted into an O. Her eyes went saucer round as she drifted away from him, pulled back by an invisible hand. The bright green of spring browned and turned to ash. To ice. To snow. And in the distance, she screamed. And screamed. And screamed.

The creature lunged again, its gangly arms swinging ahead of it, its claws slashing through the air. Ryan felt a surge of heat light up his shoulder as he threw himself at Jane's board, grabbing the first thing that fell into his hand. He swung the cloth-wrapped table leg at his aggressor, connecting with the savage's stomach. The thing scrambled backward, trying to regain its bearings.

It was Ryan's turn to not give it a chance.

Flipping the torch so that the padded end was in his grasp, Ryan charged forward, holding the table leg out in front of him like a battering ram. It connected with the creature's ribs. The thing gave an ear-piercing screech in response, its teeth snapping wildly, and again Ryan moved, jamming the end of his torch into the parasite's jaws as hard as he could.

The monster flailed its arms about its head, trying to wrap its talons around the thing in its mouth. Ryan twisted in the snow while it struggled, his shoulder throbbing beneath the padding of his coat, a sweater, a couple of shirts. He yanked the glove off his left hand, tossing it in the basket with its mate, before grabbing the ax from a bed of pine. The creature threw itself onto the ground, thrashing as it choked on the broken piece of furniture rammed down its throat. It tossed its head from side to side, the torch whizzing through the air like some broken, unhinged metronome. With the hatchet's blade balanced above his shoulder, Ryan tried to time his attack just right. The fiend threw its head to the side, its black eyes locking on Ryan as he approached. He sprang forward, jamming his foot on top of the torch that was still jammed between the monster's teeth, putting all his weight into holding it and the creature's head firmly in place. And then he reeled back and swung.

The ax blade sank into the beast's neck, a crimson spray arching upward, atomizing foul-scented blood across an otherwise flawless expanse of white. Ryan shot a glance behind him, his chest heaving, his shoulder burning beneath his coat. Jane was bounding toward him, choking on her sobs as she exerted herself, her torch blazing over her head like a beacon of hope. She slowed. Her eyes went wide. Ryan knew exactly what he'd find when he looked up again—more of them—but there was no time for fear.

"Come on, come on," he told her, waving her forward. Despite the terror drawn across her face, Jane pushed ahead. Ryan grabbed the branches he'd cut, tossed them aside, and exposed the aerosol can he hadn't been able to find. Dropping the ax into the basket, he held out his arm, trying to breach the remaining dozen feet between them as Jane struggled on.

"Throw it!" he yelled, and Jane did as she was told. They both watched their lifeline sail through the dusk, the weight of the burning end of Jane's torch angling the flame toward the snow.

Ryan's heart skipped a beat as their source of fire spiraled toward the ground. He bounded forward, catching it just before it hit the snow, the flame licking his exposed fingers as he readjusted his grip. And then he veered around, facing the three hissing, moaning creatures that he hadn't bothered to look at but knew were there.

Ryan pointed the burning torch toward them and sprayed April's hair spray in a graceful swoop. Jane yelped as a wall of flame went up around them. The savages reeled back and scrambled away.

"Oh my god," Jane gasped, and he was whirling around again, searching for another parasite to toast. "Ryan, you're bleeding." She reached out to touch his shoulder but pulled her hand away just shy of contact. "Oh my god," she repeated, on the verge of a breakdown. "Not you too," she cried. "I can't...*not you too.*"

"I lost the lighter," he told her, not giving her concern a second thought—he couldn't afford to. First aid had been the one thing he hadn't thought to bring, and Sawyer was in far worse shape than he was. Handing her the torch, he approached the dead demon in the snow, secured a boot against the thing's massive head, and yanked the table leg from its jaws. He held it up to Jane's fire, waiting for it to catch. When it did, he turned back to the carcass in front of him, sprayed the thing with aerosol, and lit up the dead.

Ryan jerked awake with such a start he made both Jane and Oona jump. Jane stared at her brother as he patted himself down, his expression a strange mix of fascination and disbelief. She had worried that he would lose too much blood throughout the night, that he'd slip away from her when she succumbed to exhaustion, but he had insisted whatever damage had been done to his shoulder wasn't that big a deal. Compared to Sawyer's injury, it was little more than a scratch. Before she could ask him what was wrong, he was scrambling out of their shelter, shoving a corner of the tarp aside. Jane shielded her eyes against the glare of the sun, the snow sparkling around her like diamond dust. Ryan's plan had worked—the small bonfires he'd built around the opening to their shelter had kept those things at bay. They had survived the night.

Oona scrambled out after him, immediately up to her haunches in the drift. Jane moved only when she heard Ryan laughing. Crawling into the sun, she squinted up at him.

"Look!" he said, presenting a breathtaking wonderland of white as though it was hers for the taking. "It's the fucking *sky*." And so it was, blue and enormous with a few fluffy clouds drifting across. She grinned as Ryan laughed up at it like a lunatic. They weren't home free yet, but the feeling was mutual: it was hope. The clouds had burned away. The wind was gone. It was a perfect day.

"Thank you!" he screamed up at the sun, spinning around to look at her a moment later. The expression on his face was enough to assure her that they had made it. It was over. Just as abruptly as the nightmare had started, it was gone.

"Tom, look!" Jane twisted around to face Sawyer, unable to keep Ryan's joyous laughter from creeping into her tone. Sawyer was huddled beneath his quilt, his head bowed, nothing but the top of his hat visible.

She blinked when he didn't move. Her smile faded. Her heart squeezed itself into a fist.

"Tom?"

Nothing.

Her breath hitched in her throat. Her face went hot.

Ryan was singing something as Oona barked, but for Jane, all sound was muffled. They sounded like they were underwater as she slowly sank down next to Sawyer, her hands trembling as she reached out toward her mother's old quilt. The tips of her gloves brushed across the blanket, pulling back as soon as a corner fell away, unwrapping the man huddled inside.

A sob tore from her chest when Sawyer didn't move, but rather slowly tipped to the side, filling the space where she had tried to sleep throughout the night—she and Ryan on either side of him—in an attempt to keep him warm.

Ryan blotted out the sun when he filled the entry of their shelter. At first his expression was nothing but confused, but as soon as Jane turned away from Sawyer, choking on her tears, his bewilderment was replaced with realization.

Sawyer was gone.

Ryan silently packed their gear as Jane sobbed next to him, her cries muffled by her gloves. He had re-covered the shelter with the blue tarp, stabbing one of their torches directly in front of it to keep those creatures away. He didn't want to think that it would go out within a matter of hours, that by nightfall, Sawyer's body would more than likely be gone, claimed by the things that had taken Lauren, that had most certainly taken April.

"We have to go," he murmured, placing a hand on Jane's shoulder. He couldn't let the emotions overtake his logic, couldn't allow the sorrow to keep them from their goal. They needed to get to the highway. They needed to walk.

It took Jane a few minutes, but eventually she rose to her feet and began to walk. She didn't look at him. Didn't speak.

They followed the protocol of the day before—an hour of trekking, then a break, stopping every few minutes when Oona would jump off Sawyer's gurney and into the snow. The throb of Ryan's shoulder had dulled to a nagging ache, and he had to constantly roll it to loosen the wounded muscles that had cramped beneath his coat. But he couldn't help himself when he spotted something in the distance—hope filled his chest, dulled by sorrow but still burning hot. He grabbed Jane's hand and pulled her along, motivated by his curiosity to discover whether what he was seeing was real or a mirage.

He shook his head, almost brought to tears by what unspooled before them; a beautiful black ribbon of glistening tarmac. It was the highway. They had made it.

"I can't believe it," Ryan marveled, staring at the miracle before him. But rather than sharing in his fascination, Jane lifted her gloved hands to her face and cried.

"We were so close," she sobbed. "Just a few more hours...just a few more and he would have been okay."

He pulled her into a tight embrace, letting her weep into his jacket until she went quiet. He couldn't allow himself to break. Not yet. They still had the challenge of spotting a car in the middle of nowhere, let alone getting that car to stop for a pair of blood-covered pedestrians. Inhaling a shaky breath, Jane pulled on the leash of their supply board and started to walk once more.

"I'm never seeing snow again." She sniffed, wiping her nose with her glove. "I'm done with mountains and boarding, okay?"

Ryan nodded faintly, his legs suddenly feeling heavier than ever as they sank into the snow. His grief was starting to poison his bloodstream. He struggled against the burn of tears against the back of his eyes, squeezing his eyes shut as they continued to march. *Fucking Sawyer*, he thought. *Just a few more hours.* A few more hours and they would have made it. They would have survived this thing.

The road ahead of them was so close, yet so far away. Every step was torture. He yearned for that clear asphalt, for the ability to stomp his feet against the ground without powder sucking him down.

"We're almost there," he said, baiting both of them to keep going.

And after a grueling half hour, they finally made it to the embankment, snow piled high where the plow had pushed it to the side of the road.

It was the most beautiful thing he'd ever seen: a rich black ribbon twisting through a white landscape. The double yellow line that followed its contour reminded him that there was color in the world, assured him that with each step they were getting closer to something he hadn't been sure would ever come. When they finally climbed over the embankment, he stood staring at it as though it were an absolute miracle. The tarmac was a line drawn in the snow, a line that despite all logic, he was sure those creatures couldn't cross.

Jane sank to the ground. It was as good a place to stop as any. The nearest town was more than twenty miles down the road and they had no chance of making it on foot. But that didn't matter, because that hadn't been the plan. This was where they'd wait until a car showed up, and when it did, Ryan would be damned if he'd let it pass them by. He'd jump in front of it if he had to. All he knew was that the next car going in either direction was their ride, whether the driver liked it or not.

Forty-five minutes later, Ryan's elation had dwindled to disbelief. Not a single vehicle had passed by, and he couldn't help but wonder if despite the road having been cleared, somewhere down the line the transportation department had shut the damn thing down anyway. But that didn't make sense. People lived up here. This was the only access road to a majority of the houses in the area, and while he was sure most of them were empty, there had to be at least someone up here for skiing. The resort had been packed.

Unless the residents out here had all been attacked just as they had been.

Unless all those people were dead.

Jane's teeth chattered as she pulled into herself for warmth. They had kept warm by walking, but now that they had nowhere to go, the chill bit through the layers of their clothing. And the fact that the sun had shifted in the sky hadn't helped. The trees on either side of the highway cast a cold shadow over the tarmac. This part of the road had always been treacherous after a snowstorm. It caught sun early in the morning but spent the rest of the day in the shade. Ryan had watched cars fishtail on this stretch of highway a half dozen times, actually witnessing an accident a few years back when a little hatchback had caught some black ice and veered off the road.

"I don't think anyone is coming," Jane said through chattering teeth.

"Someone will come," he told her, despite not being sure himself.

"What if they don't?"

"They will," he insisted. "They have to."

"Why do they have to?" Jane asked weakly, looking up at him from where she sat.

He stared at her for a long moment, not sure how to answer. And then he shook his head and tried for a brave smile. "Because we're here," he assured her. "Because we've made it this far."

Jane couldn't see him anymore, but she knew he was close. Ryan had wanted to keep walking, but she was exhausted. Her legs felt like they were on fire. The cold had cut through her boots; she couldn't feel her toes. Ryan had relented, pacing up and down that stretch of highway, waiting for a car to come. Jane remained where she was, holding on to Oona.

She was starting to doubt the reality of that highway entirely, wondering whether it was just a figment of their imagination. It seemed altogether possible that after a day of walking and a night in the snow, after losing April and Lauren and finally Sawyer, they'd both lost their minds, and now they were standing in the middle of a snow-covered field, waiting for a car to come when there was no road at all. She leaned forward enough to press her gloved hand to the frozen asphalt, making sure it was actually there. When she was satisfied she wasn't dreaming, she sighed and leaned back against the embankment, trying to imagine herself somewhere else.

If they got out of here, she was pulling all of her savings out of her account and going to the Maldives. She'd buy herself a tiny bikini—the kind that made everyone do a double take—and rent a little hut out over clear turquoise water so transparent that she could watch tropical fish of all colors of the rainbow lazily drift beneath her feet. She'd get Ryan to go with her, convince him to forget the Alps and move to the tropics. He'd give up snowboarding and take up surfing instead, and neither one of them would see snow ever again.

Just then Oona raised her head, her ears perking. Jane glanced toward the road, listening for the rumble of an engine. She didn't hear anything, but Oona was insistent. She tried to pull away from Jane's grasp, but Jane refused to let go of her collar.

"Stop," she said, tugging the dog backward as she got to her feet. Her heart thudded in her chest when she saw Ryan bolt into view.

"Get the torches," he yelled at her. As soon as his demand set in, Jane's body went numb. It couldn't be. This was supposed to be over. She stood frozen in place as Ryan bounded toward her, skidding to a stop with a look of disbelief. She couldn't decide whether he was surprised by what was happening, or flabbergasted by her lack of movement. Jane yelped when Oona gave her arm another jerk. The husky took off, but rather than heading for the open road, she ran for the pines just shy of where they had come from instead.

Jane's throat went dry. Frustrated tears sprang to her eyes. She looked to Ryan, but he was in another world; his expression had blanched, as though coming to a final, irrefutable conclusion. With the sun shining brightly overhead, they had felt safe. Those things had only come out in the gray of the storm and under the cover of night. Jane and Ryan had never actually discussed it, but she was sure they both assumed those creatures couldn't come out into the sun—like vampires, trapped in the shadows forever. It had been an assumption made against all logic, without a shred of solid evidence; it had been something to cling to when the sun had finally come out to warm their skin. In their elation of finally reaching the highway and sun warming the frozen ground, they had let the torches burn out, forgetting one tiny detail: Sawyer's lighter had been lost.

A sob stifled her breathing. How could they have been so stupid? They had been so careful this entire time, only to let their guard down, only to rob themselves of the one thing they were sure those things were afraid of.

Oona snarled at something unseen as Ryan grabbed the ax. She could see it in his eyes—he was ready to come apart, unable to believe they were worse off than before, that he had made such a damning mistake.

"Fuck!" he screamed.

Jane swallowed hard as Oona continued to bark in the distance—the kind of bark that held a warning: Stay back.

That now all-too-familiar guttural purr sounded from the shadows. But this time it was different. This time it sounded like there were dozens of them, as though they had gathered up the troops for a final assault.

Both she and Ryan exchanged a terrified look. Her heart pounded so hard against her ribs it nearly rocked her where she stood. She opened her mouth to speak, to tell him she loved him, to tell him that they'd be okay—they had to be. They hadn't dealt with so much and come this far just to die. But before she could find the words, one of those emaciated creatures launched itself out of a tree and onto the highway. Jane gripped Ryan's arm as the thing bared its grisly teeth at Oona.

"Oh my god," Jane whispered, and then she turned around and ran back to their basket of supplies.

It was beautiful, the way the sun danced through the clouds, catching the bright blue of the sky before glinting off the snow. It was as if God were performing a light show—a silent sound track to the last moments of Ryan's life. This was why he loved winter, the mountains. This very view was why he had fallen in love with the slopes.

Looking over his shoulder, he watched Jane run back toward the unplowed road that had brought them here, the sun shining bright against the snow. He wished that she would keep running, that she'd forget him and save herself somehow—though how, he wouldn't have been able to say.

He took a few forward steps, his hands tightening against the ax handle. He was too far away to make it to Oona before that hellion decided on a course of action. So rather than crossing the distance himself, he'd have that predator come to him. Ryan puckered his chapped lips and gave a shrill whistle. Oona reflexively turned, bolting away from the creature and toward her owner. The demon squatted low, its muscles coiling beneath its waxy skin, and fell into a four-limbed run. Jane screamed as Oona bounded past her owner, breaching the chill of the shadows that had swallowed Ryan and most of the road. He reeled around, expecting to see his sister being torn apart, but she simply stood in the sunshine, a sharpened pool cue in her hands, her tears shining like diamonds upon her cheeks.

Ryan looked back to the beast that had its sights on his dog, but the once rampaging creature was now standing at a dead stop just a few yards away. It toed the line between the sunlight and the shade, its nostrils flaring as it tried to breach the perimeter, only to emit a pained hiss, shaking its head as though it had been stung. It was their eyes; whether Ryan had been right and those creatures had come out of a cave, or whether they were simply so used to the shade that was forever present among the trees, they couldn't handle the intensity of the sun.

He turned to look at his sister. She was seeing it too. For a moment he wanted to laugh, wanted to fall to his knees and kiss the sunlit ground. But that promise of salvation was short-lived. The shadows were growing longer by the minute. Eventually the sun would set, and they'd be left out there with nothing. No light. No fire. Just the dreaded anticipation of the inevitable.

Ryan tightened his grip on the hatchet, trying to formulate a plan. He pivoted on the soles of his boots and ran back to his sister, his breath puffing ahead of him.

"We're going to be okay," he told her. She shook her head at him as if stunned by his statement, her expression asking him *how?* How could they possibly be okay? They were boxed in, shadow on either side of them. Their little patch of sunlight was dwindling fast and that wet rumble was getting louder, more incessant, hungrier by the minute. It was over. They were both dead.

"Janey, I need your help," he told her, grabbing a couple of pool cues from their supply basket. "We're going to go over there." He motioned to the thing still trying to brave the glare of the sun.

"And do what?"

Ryan weighed the heft of the ax in his hand. "What do you think?" he asked her. "We're going to kill it."

Jane stared at Ryan with wide eyes, his image rippling through her tears. He turned away from her before she began to cry, and she followed him toward the edge of sun and shade, trembling beneath her layers of clothes. He handed her the ax when they were only a few yards from the sneering, slavering hellion, readjusted his grip on the makeshift spear in his hand, and got a running start as he bolted toward the monster.

Jane wanted to look away, numb with panic, the wind biting at the tracks of her tears, but she knew she couldn't. She was going to have to move soon, regardless of her fear.

Ryan impaled the thing, and before the creature had the chance to scramble backward, he switched directions and pushed the pool cue to the side, forcing it into the sunlight. The screech was deafening as Jane lunged at it. It didn't see her coming, too stunned by the attack, blinded by the sun. She brought the ax blade down against its back, its fetid blood splashing across her face and coat. She tried to pull the hatchet free, but the thing was flailing so frantically she let the handle go with a yelp and backed away.

Ryan wasn't so careful.

He stepped up to it and jerked the pool cue out of its gut, the creature's blood spraying out onto the road in a fan of gore. After a few seconds of thrashing, it fell to the ground, the ax still firmly embedded in its flesh. Ryan stepped around the thing so that he was standing directly over its head; he angled the cue downward.

His face twisted with vengeance as he sprang up and stabbed the creature through its eye, the pool cue clacking against the asphalt, piercing the thing clean through its skull.

Jane stared at him, speechless as Ryan pressed his boot against the monster's head and pulled the spear free. Rolling it over with a groan, he retrieved the ax from its back and handed the bloody thing back to her. Reluctantly, she took it, blinking at her silent sibling, unsure exactly what he expected her to do with that weapon, until she looked up from the carcass between them and to the shade it had come from.

There, on the road, were three of the thing's brothers, their teeth clacking together, their arms gangly and thin, all of them ready for their turn at the prey.

Ryan shot a look at his sister, wordlessly asking her if she was ready. Jane pulled in a breath and nodded. Ryan started to run again, aiming himself at the monster closest to the edge of sunlight.

He stabbed it, swung it around, and Jane embedded the ax in its spine. But this one took a different trajectory after Ryan pulled the spear out of its gut. Rather than falling to the ground next to its dead kin, it stumbled back into the shade. Jane gasped when she realized where it was going, bolting after it with her arms outstretched. But it was too late. The creature crumpled to the ground and seized before going still, well within the boundary of shadow, the ax still in its back.

There were seven of them now. The others had come out after Ryan had managed to take down one more of those bastards with the pool cue alone, stabbing it repeatedly after it had fallen to the ground, stabbing it so violently that the cue snapped in half, leaving Ryan weaponless. He sat with his sister in their dwindling slice of sunlight, their weapons down to a single spear. Ryan was convinced they knew—the sun would be gone in less than an hour, leaving their prey defenseless. They were waiting. And it wouldn't take long.

Jane had checked out, trembling beside him as she stared at the ground. He supposed it was for the better. There was no way out of this. He only hoped that she could forgive him before it was over. He only hoped she knew that he loved her, that he had loved Sawyer, that he had wanted a chance to love Lauren, that if he had known, he would have sacrificed everything—Switzerland, his company, his life—to take back the last four days.

With less than thirty feet of sun, Ryan exhaled a slow breath and touched his sister's hand. He knew it was over. They had maybe an hour left, maybe less. There was no way he could fight those things by himself, but that also meant that he couldn't protect Jane from them either. But he couldn't just sit there, couldn't allow them to inch closer until they were on top of him, tearing out his throat. He owed Lauren more than that. She had jumped in front of one of those creatures to protect him and had died because of it. The least he could do was do the same for his sister, his other half, the one girl who had stood beside him through thick and thin. Maybe if they had him they'd retreat—let her live.

"Janey," he said, but she didn't respond. She shivered, her teeth chattering behind her wind-chapped lips. "Jane," he whispered. "I'm going to go, okay?"

Whether she understood or not, she didn't say a word. Ryan squeezed his eyes shut, swallowed against the lump in his throat, and pressed a gloved hand to his face. He couldn't let it end this way, not without a final fight. He owed it to her, owed it to everyone. This trip had been his idea, his demand. He had wanted them back together for one last time, a farewell to Colorado, if only for the memories. Pressing a kiss to Jane's forehead, he held her close for a moment before backing away. He turned to the supply basket, slowly lifted the pot with the last remaining pint of blood, and shook his head. He knew it was pointless, but it would make him feel better—and so he tipped it over his sister's head, pouring the last of it onto her hat and the shoulders of her jacket. And then he took the final pool cue and turned away from her, staring ahead at the creatures who waited.

The landscape blurred around him as he cursed himself for what he'd done. He would have bled himself dry for his father's pistol, would have sold his soul to the devil for two rounds, for the smell of gun powder and the taste of metal in his mouth. He closed his eyes, the backs of his eyelids glowing orange in the sunshine, remembering the summers he and Jane had spent up here, exploring the forest without a shred of fear. He remembered when they were kids, when they had wandered too far away from the cabin, had gotten turned around only to realize they couldn't remember which way was which. Jane had sat on a fallen tree trunk, crying into her hands, her yellow dress glowing in the sunlight like a beacon of hope. Back then he had promised her the same thing: that they'd be okay, that they'd find their way home. Except that time they had. Hand in hand, he had led her through the trees, not knowing where he was going, blind faith pulling him forward, until he caught a glimpse of the cabin and knew they were safe. It was what he had hoped for this time as well. There had been holes in his plan, but he had to believe. He had wanted to save his sister the way he had saved her before— because that was what he *had* to do; that was why there were two of them: to protect each other, to never let each other down.

Jane finally managed to look up from where she was sitting, her expression dazed. He watched her, waited for her to come to the bitter realization that they had reached the end, yearned for her to tumble headlong into another bout of hysterics. But instead of dread and panic, a haunting smile drifted across her blood-soaked face. She was somewhere else, far away from that highway, and Ryan was glad...because he wasn't ready for that final good-bye.

The creatures lingered in the shadow of the trees, that ghostly, guttural groan filling the silence. They snapped their teeth and prepared themselves to pounce if Ryan dared breach the perimeter of darkness and light. But despite those monsters salivating over their next meal, the breeze that drifted across Ryan's face eased him into an eerie calm. In the otherwise still outdoor air, it drifted around him like a phantom, and for the slightest moment he didn't feel as alone as he knew he was. Drawing his hand across his eyes, he began to walk away, leaving Jane behind. Oona quietly trotted beside him, her barking silenced by what he could only assume was her own realization: there was nothing left to do. They were both at fate's doorstep, and there was no other decision left to make.

He stepped toward the shadow that was slowly growing wider, that would eventually overtake the hill. He looked up at the sky, the sun still shining bright. Oona whined as she looked up at her owner, and Ryan recognized understanding in her eyes. She knew. Of course she knew. She was a fighter, and so was he.

He looked ahead, those creatures watching him with interest.

His fingers tightened around his weapon.

His weight shifted to his toes.

And then he ran.

———

The stereo was turned up loud enough to rattle the windows of the Land Cruiser, but that was the way they liked it—loud and fast as the trees whipped past the car, each icy turn taken just a little too fast, each mile of highway rolling beneath them with reckless abandon. Troy sucked in a lungful of smoke while his right arm jutted out the rolled-down passenger window, his hand skating along the cold current just beyond the car. Carla and Allison sat in the backseat, singing along with the music between bouts of drunken laughter, the bottle of Jack they'd cracked open three hours prior nearly half gone. Sid was the only sober one of the bunch, but he intended on remedying that as soon as they reached their destination.

"Do you see this?" he asked, dipping his head to bring his chin level with the top of the steering wheel, gazing up at a mountain covered in fresh snow. "It's incredible," he said. "I haven't seen snow like this in years, man. This is going to be off the hook."

Troy rolled his head to the side, offering his friend a lazy grin. "Gonna tear it up," he mused. "Gonna tear. It. Up."

The Land Cruiser took another curve, fishtailing when it caught a spot of black ice beneath a back tire. The group tensed, holding their breath in unison as the music kept on, the thud of bass shaking the door panels. Sid eased his foot off the gas, taking the needle of the speedometer down from sixty to forty-five.

"Goddamn," he grumbled, turning the music down a notch, ready to complain about how whoever had salted the road had done a shitty job. But he didn't get the chance. The SUV took another mountain curve and Sid slammed on the brakes, the girls flying forward, both of them crashing into the seats ahead of them with a squeal.

"What the *fuck*, Sidney!" Allison screamed.

"Great," Carla snapped, holding the bottle of Jack at arm's length, the front of her shirt and pants soaked in alcohol.

But the boys didn't respond. They were too busy staring at the girl huddled along the side of the road, shivering, covered in blood.

"Holy shit," Troy said, his cigarette clinging precariously to the swell of his bottom lip.

Sid slowly rolled the Toyota forward, road grit crunching beneath the tires.

"We're stopping?" Allison asked.

"Jesus, Allison." Troy craned his neck back. "You want to leave an injured human being along the side of the fucking road?"

"What if it's a trick?" Carla asked, sounding tense. "What if she's a decoy and some psychopath is waiting for a car full of suckers to stop and help, only to slash our throats?"

"Ridiculous," Sid said beneath his breath, easing the car along the side of the road. "You guys are drunk."

"I bet she's one of those wild people, the kind that live in the woods all their lives. I bet she has rabies," Carla said, searching for something to dry herself off with. "Which you deserve to get after that little stunt, Sid." She dropped her voice an octave. "Fucking asshole."

Sid pulled the e-brake and both boys immediately popped their doors open while the girls watched them, Allison's face twisting with concern, Carla rolling her eyes at the whole thing.

Troy was unsteady on his feet, the Jack making him sway. He immediately fell behind, but Sid's steps were balanced, slowly closing the distance between himself and the girl along the side of the road. He shot Troy a look, holding out a hand to tell his friend to stay back before crouching a safe distance away.

She was sitting in the last slice of sunlight as if to warm herself—the wedge of sun not more than a few feet wide.

"Hello?" Sid said, nervously catching his lip between his teeth. "Miss? Can you hear me?"

But the girl didn't respond; she only trembled, mute. Sid cast his gaze down the road ahead. There was blood—lots of it. There must have been some sort of accident, but where were the cars? Where were the bodies?

Sid narrowed his eyes, inching closer to the girl, his nose wrinkling as soon as he got a whiff of whatever covered her. "Hey, there," he said, unsure of himself. "Are you okay? Were you in an accident? Are you hurt?"

Just as Sid was sure the girl wasn't going to reply again, he was startled by the weak whimper that bubbled up from her throat.

"Troy!" Sid searched for his friend. "Help me!"

"Dude." Troy wavered in the shadow of the road, holding up what looked to be a broken pool cue in his right hand. "What the fuck is this?"

Sid shook his head, rising to his feet. "This isn't right," he decided. "We need to call somebody. She needs help."

Troy threw the pool cue into the trees, craned his neck back toward the Land Rover, and yelled, "Call somebody!"

A moment later Carla yelled back. "No reception, genius. Who would have thought?"

"We can't leave her here," Sid said, looking back to the girl. "We need to take her into town, to the police station or the clinic or something."

"The cabin is closer," Allison called out. "My parents have a landline. We can call from there."

"She smells like crap," Troy whispered. "You really want to put her in your car?"

Sid scowled at his friend. "Are you kidding?"

Troy held his hands up in surrender. "It's your car," he muttered. "Hey, man, whatever."

"Miss?" Sid crouched down again, extending a hand to the girl the way someone would to a dog. "We're going to help you up, okay? We're going to take you with us where it's safe and warm." He slowly touched her sleeve, and when she didn't jump back or scream or try to claw him, he closed the distance, sliding his arm around her to help her up. Troy was reluctant, but he eventually fell into step, helping Sid lead the stranger to their car.

Carla and Allison nearly sat on top of each other in the backseat, trying to give the feral-looking girl the most room possible, both of them shielding their mouths and noses from the stench. The smell was bad enough to make Sid's eyes water, but he kept the windows rolled up and blasted the heater, if only to get their passenger warm.

After a few minutes of silence, there was a murmur from the backseat.

"Where are we going?" the girl asked, her words hardly above a whisper, her bloodied hair hanging in front of her face.

After a beat of silence, Allison finally replied. "To my parents' cabin."

"In town?" the girl asked, slowly looking up at Allison and Carla.

"No," Allison said. "Town is almost twenty-five miles away. The cabin is just up the road by the lake."

"The lake…" the girl echoed weakly.

"Yeah, the lake in the woods."

Suddenly the girl began to panic. She pulled at the door handle, as if ready to jump out of the car, but it remained shut, keeping her locked inside. She slammed her hands against the window, leaving bloody handprints against the glass as Allison and Carla gasped.

"Hey, hey, hey." Troy twisted in his seat, reaching back to try to soothe their passenger. "It's cool, man, we're going to get you some help, okay? Just sit tight. We're almost there."

But the girl was thrashing. She spun around in the seat and pounded the back window with her fists, sobbing to be let out of the car.

"Jesus, hurry up, Sid!" Carla yelled from the back as Sidney eased the car off the highway and onto the road that would take them to Allison's parents' place.

"What the hell did you just sign us up for?" Troy asked Sid beneath his breath. "I thought we were going boarding, man. I thought we were going to carve the slopes, not play search and fucking rescue."

"It's going to be fine," Sid insisted. "We're going to call for help, someone will pick her up. First thing tomorrow we'll be on the mountain."

"Better be, man." Troy sulked. "I'm not letting another season go by without putting my ass in a chair li—" His words tapered off as he furrowed his eyebrows, leaning forward to peer through the windshield.

"What?" Sid asked, but he saw what Troy was looking at before Troy had the chance to reply. A tall pine was swaying in the distance while its brothers stood perfectly still, rocking as though someone was shaking it by its base. "Elk," Sid concluded. "They rub their antlers against the tree trunks."

It was only after Troy leaned back in his seat that Sid realized the silence had returned. He craned his neck, shooting a look toward the backseat and the strange girl they'd picked up. She was pressed up against the door, so close to the window her nose was almost touching the glass.

"It's just elk," he repeated, trying to soothe her. "Or someone cutting down a tree for firewood or something. Happens all the time."

But she continued to stare at the shuddering pine in the distance.

Her eyes wide.

So impossibly wide.

ACKNOWLEDGMENTS

Once again, endless thanks go out to my friends and family, my husband, Will, and all of the incredible people I've been given the honor to work with. Terry, David, Tiffany, and all of the folks at 47North and Amazon Publishing, you guys are amazing.

But most important, my gratitude belongs to my readers. Without you, this book wouldn't exist. Thank you all.

ABOUT THE AUTHOR

Born in Ciechanów, Poland, Ania Ahlborn is also the author of the supernatural thrillers *Seed* and *The Neighbors*. She earned a bachelor's degree in English from the University of New Mexico, enjoys gourmet cooking, baking, drawing, traveling, movies, and exploring the darkest depths of the human (and sometimes inhuman) condition. She lives in Albuquerque, New Mexico, with her husband and two dogs.